The Cipher Garden

a&b

The Cipher Garden

MARTIN EDWARDS

First published in Great Britain in 2005 by
Allison & Busby Limited
Bon Marché Centre
241-251 Ferndale Road
London SW9 8BJ
http://www.allisonandbusby.com

10 9 8 7 6 5 4 3 2 1

ISBN 0 7490 8286 0

Printed and bound in Wales by
Creative Print and Design, Ebbw Vale

MARTIN EDWARDS was born in Cheshire. He read law at Oxford and then trained as a solicitor. He is married with two children, and is currently a partner at Mace & Jones law firm, based in Liverpool and Manchester. The author of the acclaimed series of legal mysteries featuring Harry Devlin, he is also a critic and has edited various short story collections.

Dedicated to
Stephen

'I thought you were dead.'

Warren Howe hadn't seen the hooded figure approaching, hadn't heard a footfall. He was digging in the rain and his work consumed him. Only when he put down his spade did he realise that he was not alone. Someone in a waterproof jacket stood on the ridge above the trench, someone he recognised. How long had he been watched? He didn't care, nothing and nobody could rattle him. His jeering words were chosen to wound.

'Sorry to disappoint you.'

Warren spat on the ground. 'You might as well be dead, as far as I'm concerned.'

'It's time for us to talk.'

'Nothing to talk about.'

'You're wrong.'

Warren clambered out of the trench and lifted his spade in the air, a gladiator wielding a trident. The hooded figure took a step backwards, bumping into the low trailer that held the garden tools.

'Nobody tells me I'm wrong.'

The intruder edged down the path. The rain was slackening to a drizzle, but the stone flags were as sleek as a ski run. How easy to slip and pitch head over heels into the trench or down the uneven ground towards the silent cottage.

'You hate it that I'm here, don't you?'

'I couldn't care less.'

'What do you care about?'

Warren stabbed the sodden earth with his spade. He'd never believed in explaining himself and he wouldn't start now. He was what he was. A plantsman, and proud of it. Plants didn't make demands the way people did, they didn't nag or whine or sob. Even if they shrivelled and died, it was so easy to start again. He liked heathers, sedges and rushes as well as shade-loving field roses with purple stems. Tender buds, voluptuous blooms, seductive perfumes, all were to his taste. And there was something else. Once you understood how plants behaved, you could bend them to your will.

The hooded figure inched forward, as if along a tightrope, flicking nervous glances up the fell-side. But they were alone, even the ravens had fled from the trees.

'We need to talk.'

'For Christ's sake.'

'You can't have what you want. It's impossible. You owe it to…'

'Listen.' Warren took a long stride forward, felt his visitor's breath on his cheek. 'Watch my lips, I don't owe anyone anything.'

The hooded figure grasped Warren's wrist. 'You can't do this.'

Warren pulled his arm away in an easy, powerful movement. 'Go before you get hurt.'

The hooded figure reached into the trailer and yanked out the scythe. Warren's oldest gardening tool, a favourite since he was eighteen. He'd cared for it as others might look after a much-loved pet. He'd taken pains to keep the blade clean and sharp.

'If you could only see yourself,' Warren scoffed. 'In that hood and holding a scythe. Fancy yourself as the Grim Reaper?'

The scythe rose in the air, blade grinning like a Cheshire Cat. Warren folded muscular arms, showing his tattoos. Two dragons, belching fire. He stood his ground.

The scythe wavered and Warren took a pace forward, arm outstretched. His boots skidded on the greasy stone and his legs gave way under him. As he sank to the ground, he saw the blade – his lovely blade – glint in a sudden shaft of sunlight.

For so many years, to hold the scythe in his hand had made him feel strong. Powerful. The blade could not betray him now. Yet it had such a wicked edge.

The sun blinded him. He could no longer make out the face beneath the hood. His heart was thudding, his forehead moist with sweat and yet he knew he must be strong. Without strength, he was nothing.

'You'll never do it.' It might have been a prayer, but he made it sound like a dare.

The blade fell and for a split second he understood his mistake. When the metal sliced against his flesh and pain bit into him, he screamed.

Part One

Chapter One

Welcome to Paradise.

Daniel Kind shaded his eyes against the sun as it streaked the surface of the reed-fringed tarn with gold. He'd taken refuge from the heat and hard labour. The garden bench stood in an arbour formed by the stooping branches of an old copper beech. The breeze ruffled leaves of a fragrant lavender bush, an orange-billed oystercatcher emerged from a tree stump, then vanished from sight.

Even Paradise offered no escape from nettles or scratches by bramble thorns. His hands were stinging and blood smeared his forearm. Sweat glued his shirt to his skin. Hours spent digging out tree roots had left his body pleading for mercy. His spine yearned for the soft recesses of his battered leather armchair at Oxford, but the stone bench was cold, as if carved by a Puritan intent on deterring indolence. As he rubbed the stings with a dock leaf, his gaze travelled up the steep rise of Tarn Fell towards the straggle of fell-walkers on Priest Ridge. Heedless of pagan folklore, a young couple and their children were clambering on to a dour grey anvil outlined against the sky. The Sacrifice Stone.

If he didn't start moving, his vertebrae might seize up. Bones creaking, he crunched over the gravel path that looped around the water's edge. Fronds of an ostrich fern brushed his face, red admirals skittered around the michaelmas daisies. The path curved around a rhododendron bush before coming to an abrupt halt in front of a cracked and ancient mirror nailed to a trellis on which ivy and flowering jasmine intertwined. The glass created the illusion of an arch festooned by climbers, beyond which the path continued past the tarn towards the damson wood. Even now the mirror had the knack of deceiving him.

His tanned reflection returned a wry smile, as if wondering whatever happened to the pale-faced academic who had downshifted to the Lakes and made this his home. He still couldn't trust his luck. Last night in his dreams, he'd become a tourist whose fantasies of escape dissolved when duty dragged him back to college to teach Victorian history.

Turning back, he headed back past a mass of purple foxgloves. He loved this garden, but it mystified him. The serpentine byways and dead ends made no sense. There was something unnatural about them, a sense of something fashioned with a purpose. Three months after moving here, he still hadn't fathomed that purpose.

Conundrums entranced him. He had this need to know. In the days when he'd read *The Times*, he'd never been able to abandon the crossword until the last cryptic clue was solved. He was his father's son. Ben Kind had been a career detective; after the divorce, he'd come up here to the Lake District and the two of them never met again. The old man was dead now, leaving his son to nag away at the mystery of the garden. There must be a reason for it, a secret waiting to be uncovered.

Clouds sneaked into the sky as he checked his watch.

Does a chief inspector do lunch? I could call Hannah Scarlett, pass the time of day. Where's the harm?

As he scraped soil off his spade, he surveyed the patch of ground that he'd cleared. Before he'd moved to the countryside, blackberries conjured images of sweet-tasting fruit pie and verdant hedgerows. Bramble was another name for the same plant, but more ominous. Brambles were sinister, the gardener's foe. The first time he'd cut back their green foliage, they'd fooled him. It wasn't enough to snap brambles off at ground level. If the crown was left, the stems grew a couple of inches each day, making the thicket ever more impenetrable. Today he'd taken care to extract the whole of the roots, tracing each stem back to the end to remove any runners that had anchored themselves. *Solving crimes must be like this, all about taking infinite pains.*

The shrilling phone shattered the peace. *Hannah?*

They hadn't spoken for weeks, but he couldn't scrub her out of his mind. A couple of days ago, he'd rung her mobile and left a message on her voicemail. She hadn't called back. Of course, he didn't want anything to happen between them, any more than she did. They both had partners, it was out of the question. But she'd worked with his father, they could talk about the old man over coffee, maybe a glass of wine.

He ploughed through foliage, his aching back forgotten. Following the paths was too roundabout a route. Seconds before he reached the phone, the answering machine started up.

Miranda's soft voice knocked the breath out of him. She never rang when she was on her way back from London. He felt a twinge in his stomach. Disappointment? Couldn't be. Miranda was the one he loved.

The train's stuck in Crewe station, would you credit it? The guard says we may be stuck for a couple of hours, God knows why. I'm waiting for the excuses. Wrong kind of sunshine, something like that. Hope you're OK. Why aren't you answering? Don't tell me you're working in the garden. I bet it's pouring down, I never knew a place like Brackdale for rain.

He wanted to protest, but when he glanced through the window he saw squiggles of damp spreading over the paving stones.

Not quite Paradise after all, then.

'You want the good news or the bad news?' Hannah Scarlett asked.

Nick Lowther went through a pantomime of deliberation as he stirred the coffee in its recycled paper cup. Not a bad actor, Hannah thought. A useful talent in a detective sergeant.

'You know how I feel about the power of positive thinking,' he announced. 'Go on, then. Give me the bad news.'

The police canteen was filling up and so were the members of Cumbria Constabulary. In a campaign to prevent their officers' arteries furring, the senior management team had insisted that the catering franchisee should wipe the Big All Day Breakfast off the menu during summer. The main difference was that the air was thick not with the smell of Cumberland sausages but the aroma of giant pickled onions from Hungry Ploughman's Platters.

Hannah scowled at the briefing notes on her clipboard. 'Half the general public doesn't have confidence in the police. Which may be connected to the fact that we spend half our time on paperwork in the office instead of tedious frontline duties like catching criminals.'

'Only half the time? Feels like more. And the good news?'

'Cumbria Constabulary has clawed its way to the top of the Home Office's performance league table.'

Nick pretended to choke on his chocolate muffin. The campaign to promote organic eating options had passed him by. He still preferred calorie-laden junk food that resembled an exhibit in a long ago poisoning case. Infuriating that he never seemed to carry a surplus pound.

'You forget, I'm a Carlisle United supporter. So naturally I have a deep distrust of league tables.'

She slid a sheet of paper across the table. The diagram looked like the work of a statistician on an acid trip. A red-edged, irregular hexagon with a blue shaded area inside and black arrows flying around in wild confusion.

'Don't just take my word. Here's the official spidergram to prove it. Only those Celtic super-sleuths in Dyfed-Powys performed better, if the police standards unit are to be believed.'

'So Lauren's cracking open the champagne?'

'When she called us in to announce the glad tidings, she actually said that we mustn't be triumphalist when we brief our teams.'

'That's like being told to stand up straight by the Hunchback of Notre Dame.' He swallowed a mouthful of coffee and pulled a face. 'Thought I'd try the new Guatemalan roast. Give me Tesco's own brand any day.'

Hannah stifled a yawn. Not through boredom, for Nick never bored her, although she'd needed to fight to keep her eyes open during Lauren's spiel. Maybe she should have risked a black coffee before seeing the Assistant Chief Constable. The bitter taste on your tongue was enough to make you retch, but it kept you alert. Another poor night's sleep was taking a toll. At four a.m. she'd been lying in bed, trying to shut her ears to the boom of Marc's snoring.

'Yeah, our performance in the exotic hot drinks table was a big disappointment to Lauren.'

Nick grinned. The ACC was engaged in a passionate long-term love affair with official statistics. Data in bar charts and seminars on monitoring, these were a few of Lauren's favourite things. Who needed handcuffs or DNA samples when they had key performance indicators? Once upon a time, the powers-that-be liked to boast that they were tough on crime, tough on the causes of crime. These days they preferred to drive up standards through quality assessments and eye-catching initiatives. Lauren was a relentless moderniser, an evangelist for joined-up thinking and institutionalised number-crunching. In today's police service, everyone was encouraged to remain permanently upbeat. Figures offered crumbs for the morale of hapless underachievers. Things could only get better. If detection rates fell, citizen focus might swing upwards. Solving fewer crimes could be explained away as a statistical quirk or due to more rigorous selection of cases for prosecution.

'So the Cold Case Review Team lives to fight another day?'

'She's negotiating an extended stream of funding. As you know, what the ACC wants, the ACC gets.'

Nick leaned over the table, voice barely audible above the raucous banter between a couple of vice cops queuing at the counter and the cheeky girls behind it. 'If my legendary powers of deduction aren't waning, you're not overwhelmed with gratitude.'

Hannah shrugged. 'Would I lie to you? This project's a backwater, we all realise that. Somewhere convenient to park me ever since I messed up the Rao trial. Out of harm's way.'

'Relax. You're too hard on yourself. Heading up the unit will look good on your CV.'

'You're confusing me with Lauren.' To her dismay, her face was hot with blushing. 'I couldn't care less about my CV.'

'You all right?'

'Yeah, I'm fine. Knackered, but fine. Sorry.'

'Only…if you aren't fine, you can tell me. OK?'

'Thanks for the offer,' she said. 'Not that I expect to take you up on it. A good night's rest is all I need. I shouldn't moan. We have some good people in the team and we've had a couple of results. I don't deny it, it can be fascinating to exhume the past.'

'But?'

'But it's not forever. I want time off for good behaviour.'

The canteen door swung open and Lindsey Waller loped in. She was skilled at making an entrance and for a moment the aisle between the tables became a catwalk. Everyone's eyes followed her swinging hips, especially the vice cops'. Accustomed to admiration, she took no notice. She'd have been unbearable, if she hadn't been so down to earth and such good company.

'Ma'am, you'll want to see this.' She was clutching a sheet in a protective plastic wallet. 'We've had a tip-off about a murder that was never solved. Ever heard of a man called Warren Howe?'

Nick sat up. 'Warren Howe was a landscape gardener, lived out by Esthwaite Water. I worked on the investigation. What sort of tip-off?'

Linz waved the sheet as if signalling by semaphore. 'Someone's given us the name of a suspect.'

'Who?' Nick demanded.

Hannah stared at him, struck by his uncharacteristic intensity. 'His wife.'

'Tina?'

'Yes, Tina Howe.'

He leaned back in his chair, the metal legs scraping on the floor tiles with a screech that set Hannah's teeth on edge. She watched as he weighed up the news.

Is it my imagination, or is he relieved it isn't someone else?

As Daniel parked outside Tarn Cottage, Miranda flicked a stray blonde hair out of her eye and asked, 'So where are the builders?'

He took a breath. Now for the tricky bit. Driving her back from the station, he hadn't got round to breaking the news. Downshifting to a dream cottage in the Lakes was one thing. Rendering the house and outbuildings habitable was quite another. For weeks the air had been thick with dust and dirt. As well as varied and ingenious excuses for the slow rate of progress.

'Eddie's off sick. Asthma attack, allegedly. The other lad and his brother decided to go back-packing around the Philippines and didn't give any notice.'

'Jesus, so they haven't made a start on the bothy?'

The renovated bothy was to be her sanctuary. She'd planned it out before they moved in. A studio flooded by light, a chart of acupuncture centres on the pine-clad wall, the décor in natural colours, oaten and wheatmeal, a massage bed in the centre, dominating the room. She'd written articles on the importance of de-cluttering your life. Less is more.

Daniel shook his head. 'A week on Monday if we're lucky.'

'Get on to Stan Mustoe, tell him it isn't acceptable.'

'This is the best he can do, he claims we're getting preferential treatment. Same with the plumber. The latest bulletin from Casualty is that he broke an arm playing cricket. Trying to fend off a bouncer when he should have ducked. We won't be seeing him for a fortnight. You want to hear about the electrician?'

She put up her hands in surrender. 'Taken hostage by terrorists? What's wrong with these people?'

'Can't get the staff, Stan Mustoe's very words. He mourns the old apprenticeships.' Daniel put on cod local accent. '"All the kids keep boogering off to university, that's the trouble. Lads have got fancy ideas these days, they're poncing around on courses about media studies and such-like. What's wrong with plumbing and plastering, that's what I want to know?"'

'Just as well I have a bit of good news, then.'

On the way home, he'd decided she was building up to something. Something he wouldn't like, so she needed to pick her moment. They'd chatted about London and she kept saying how much of a buzz there was in the city. Suki, who edited the magazine she wrote for, had taken her out clubbing. Not that she really liked clubbing, she added quickly, but it made a change. And Suki was fun.

'What news might that be?'

'Suki's introduced me to her old boss, Ethan Tiatto. He likes my work. Next month he starts publishing a new magazine and he'd like me to contribute lifestyle features.'

'Perfect.' He kissed her cheek. 'Congratulations.'

She drew back. 'There's just one snag. I'll have to spend more time in London. Ethan wants me to attend the editorial conference every fortnight.'

'You could go to Kendal or Lancaster or somewhere, talk to them by videolink.'

'Sorry. It's part of the deal, I have to be there in the flesh. Ethan sets a lot of store by brainstorming ideas. Remote discussions won't do. But it isn't so bad. I'll need to stay overnight, though he did say he'd pay for me to fly from Manchester.'

'They must be keen.'

She gave him a mock bow. 'Of course they are.'

She loved writing, it was one of the things that had drawn them together in the early days of love's madness. She saw her journalism in mystical terms, the way she talked about it was exhilarating. Once, after they'd shared a bottle of Merlot, she'd confided that although she wasn't sure about having kids, every piece she wrote was like a child of her imagination.

Suitcase in hand, he led the way up the front path. 'That's great. I'm pleased.'

'I thought you might be cross with me,' she said when they'd settled in the living room. She was lying on the sofa and he was cradling her head in his arms.

'Why?'

'Well...this was my idea, wasn't it? The rural idyll.'

'It was a wonderful idea. I'm a convert to this way of life. Dangerous as it is out there. See the scratches on my arm?'

She laughed. 'I never realised you'd go native.'

'So you said in your last column for Suki.'

'You don't think I wanted to buy the cottage simply because I was looking for copy?' Her voice rose. 'I mean, nothing could have been further from my mind. I adore this place. It's so peaceful, so – away from it all. It's just that...well, I like London too. That's why I don't want to sell my flat. It's a bolt-hole.'

'Why do you need one?'

'Hey, you don't understand. I want a foot in both camps. I need to keep writing.' A line of counter-attack struck her. 'And we could use the cash. The money you made on your place in Oxford won't last forever. Not at the rate we're spending on these vanishing builders. Your TV royalties are down to a trickle. I want to live the dream too, but we can't live on fresh air.'

'At least here it is fresh.'

She feigned a coughing fit. 'Am I imagining this dust?'

'You know what I mean.'

When they'd met she'd been miserable and unfulfilled. He'd sacrificed his career to move here with her – his choice, no regrets. Yet he hadn't managed to give her peace of mind. Not that she was a pessimist. She believed that happiness was just around the corner. Her life revolved around her latest passion, until a few months later, she was ready to move on. In dark moments, he wondered if one day her passion for him would burn out too.

He bent down and they kissed long and hard while he started unfastening her silk shirt. Soon they were making love on the rug by the hearth. Afterwards, she propped herself up on one elbow and smiled at him.

'Trust me, Daniel, we can do it. You and me, we can get the best of all possible worlds.'

Before he could answer, the phone rang.

Chapter Two

Tina Howe was jealous of her husband Warren, so she murdered him.

'Whatever happened to the finest traditions of anonymous mail?' Linz tutted as she laid the message flat on the circular table for Hannah and Nick to see. 'Me, I yearn for the good old days. The golden age of the poison pen. Letters cut out of a newspaper and glued on to paper. They always seem so spookily romantic and mysterious, don't you think, Sarge?'

'Too right. Brown capitals in broad felt tip? Hopeless. Totally lacking in character, let alone charm.' Nick ran a hand through his eternally untidy hair. 'Even if this note is in freehand, our correspondent might just as well have used a stencil. How bloody inconsiderate.'

'Would handwriting analysis be a waste of time?'

'Try it, we need to tick all the boxes. But if you ask me, we'd get better information from an ouija board.'

Linz giggled. She often giggled in Nick's company. For an idle moment Hannah wondered whether there was something going on between her sergeant and DC Waller. Surely he wasn't the type. Though in her head sounded the voice of experience. It belonged to Terri, her oldest friend and a woman so jaundiced about the opposite sex that she claimed she could scarcely bear to bank her exes' maintenance payments.

All of them are that type, Hannah. Trust me. Men I know about, OK?

Terri had trotted down the aisle three times before she was thirty, and each time her wedding dress was cut lower and her heels were higher, but did that prove how much she knew about men or how little? Hannah had never seen Nick flirting with Linz. She always felt safe with him; in weak moments, she'd even found herself fretting that her own charms were fading. Terri must be wrong. Nick had never given Hannah any reason to doubt that he was a happily married man. The odds were that Linz saw him as a challenge. Which was fine by Hannah, as long as her attempts to curry favour with him didn't mess up morale on the team.

'What do you reckon, ma'am?'

'The perfect tip-off. Clear, concise, no sitting on the fence. Only trouble is, there may not be a shred of truth in it.'

'No signature, ma'am, no contact details. Obviously we have to view a message like this with a huge amount of suspicion.'

Linz shook her mane, initial enthusiasm fading fast. She always took her cue from senior officers. Hannah wanted her to risk backing her own judgement more often, but Linz must have studied the methods that had taken Lauren Self to the giddy heights of ACC. Play the percentages. Never go out on a limb.

'Chances are, it's the work of someone with a grudge against this Tina Howe and it won't take us anywhere in detecting the crime. But that doesn't mean we should discount it. Especially since the ACC wants the Cold Case Review Project to keep on rolling.'

'Cool!'

Linz showed a lot of white, hungry teeth. No hint of irony. Hannah felt a spasm of guilt for her own mixed feelings. She had a good team, loyal and cohesive. Not too clannish or inward-looking, like some police units, not too many monster egos. Nick worked tirelessly at keeping colleagues enthused. A natural gift; he'd never read a motivational handbook in his life. Perhaps that was his secret.

'So in cases where we don't have anything more than an anonymous tip-off, you might consider a detailed inquiry?' Nick asked.

'If it seems justified and we have the capacity to take it on.'

'We can't investigate every lead on every case from the past twenty years.'

'We have to prioritise, but if this message takes us along an interesting road, let's not turn back at the first bend. When did the message arrive, Linz?'

'In the morning post, ma'am. The envelope's on my desk. Same style of writing, addressed to the Cold Case Review Team. Local postmark, no fingerprints. Presumably whoever sent the message wore latex gloves. Should I arrange for the old files to be brought out of archive?'

'Please. If we decide to investigate in-depth, we can have a full team briefing when everyone's around. In the meantime, let's go back to my office for ten minutes. DS Lowther can give us a quick overview of the case from his own recollection.' She turned to Nick. 'Did the original inquiry ever put anyone in the frame?'

His face might have been sculpted from the stone of Scafell. 'One thing stands out in my mind about the murder. When we looked for whoever wanted Warren Howe dead, we only had one problem. We were spoiled for choice.'

'Daniel, this is Louise.'

'Louise?'

She'd caught him off guard, otherwise he wouldn't have repeated her name into the handset in that baffled way, as if uttering a mysterious foreign term for the first time. Of course, being Louise, she allowed a pause long enough for the realisation of his stupidity to sink in. A familiar feeling, as if he were eleven years old again. His shoulders tensed. Never mind garden nettles; the sting of her sarcasm couldn't be rubbed away with a dock leaf.

'Yes, Louise. For Heaven's sake, don't tell me you've forgotten who I am?'

'Sorry.' He could hardly say: I've been hoping for a call from someone else. Especially not with Miranda draped over the rug a yard away. The moment she heard Louise's name, she spread herself out in a pastiche of a Modiglani model, mischievously hoping to distract him into a further gaffe. She'd never met his sister, but from what he'd said about her, she guessed the two of them would never be soul-mates. He dragged his eyes away from her and tried to focus on appeasement. 'Louise, long time no speak. How are things?'

'All right.' She didn't sound it. 'And you? Settled into your leafy idyll?'

'We can finally move from room to room without choking on dust or gagging at the smell of paint. I love walking the Brackdale Horseshoe and I've never felt fitter. At least I hadn't until I started trying to civilise the garden. I'm not sure my back will ever forgive me.'

'I would never have thought it of you.'

'You sound like a priest scolding a choirboy for nicking the silver collection.'

Louise sighed, a low gust of disappointment echoing down the line. In her teens, she'd specialised in sighs the way impressionists specialise in funny voices. Tragic sighs, frustrated sighs, patronising sighs; her stock was inexhaustible. 'You know perfectly well what I mean. Ever since you were a child, you always had your nose buried in a book. You were so desperate to make it to Oxford. I never imagined that you'd leave of your own free will.'

'Things change, Louise. Run their course.'

'True.' She spoke so softly that Daniel wasn't sure he'd heard correctly. Louise agreeing with him? Amazing. She'd be voting in favour of closer European integration next. 'Mind you, I'm glad that Mum isn't alive to hear you say that. Honestly, Daniel, I bet she's turning in her grave. She was so proud when you started publishing. Let alone when you signed up with the BBC. She insisted on recording all your television programmes, you know.'

Daniel held his tongue. When Louise talked about their mother, it was usually the prelude to a dig about their father. She'd never forgiven the old man after he'd abandoned them for a blonde floosie. Their mother had made them promise never to speak to him again and Louise had kept her word, although many years later Daniel had talked to him on the phone. Like his sister, he'd been hurt by the betrayal, but he didn't want to be soured by bitterness. He'd been sure his father loved them and he'd yearned to know Ben Kind's side of the story. But he'd never heard it.

'Are you still there?'

'Uh-huh.'

Miranda continued to distract him. She'd become bored with giving him a show and was hunting around for the bra that she'd dropped somewhere three quarters of an hour ago.

'I suppose you're wondering why I've called like this. Out of the blue.'

He groaned inwardly. Surely I remembered your birthday? What else can I have done wrong?

'It's good to hear from you.' As soon as he said the words he realised, almost to his surprise, that he meant them. 'We ought to keep in closer touch now I'm up here in Brackdale. The Lake District's much nearer to Cheshire than Oxford. Straight up the M6, you could be here in no time.'

Miranda paused in the act of slipping on her thong as she heard him extend the invitation. She raised her eyebrows and mouthed: *is that such a good idea?*

'Kind of you,' Louise said.

She sniffed loudly. For a moment Daniel thought she might have a cold before realising to his horror that she must be trying to suppress tears.

'Are you OK?'

'Yes, yes, I am. Well…no, not really.'

'What's the matter?'

'No, it's nothing. I feel so pathetic. Me, a grown woman, behaving like a soppy teenager.'

One thing about Louise, she'd never been a soppy teenager. After their father's disappearance, she'd grown up fast. Mum had leaned on her and she never had the time for self-indulgence.

'Rodney and I have split up.'

He had to restrain himself from punching the air. Rodney was an up-and-coming associate in a large firm of solicitors, a specialist in mergers and acquisitions, aiming to make partner in the next couple of years. Louise was a lecturer in law and they'd met at a seminar, proving that romance can blossom even over a chat about minority shareholders' rights. Rodney had acquired Louise, it seemed to Daniel, in much the same spirit as he'd picked up the P.G. Wodehouse first editions that he kept in a display cabinet. He didn't do a lot of reading, he didn't have the time, and frankly he didn't have much of a sense of humour. But a client had told him that Wodehouse was a sound investment.

'Louise…'

'He's met someone else. She's a junior lawyer in the corporate department. Name of Felicity, they call her Fliss, can you imagine? Sometimes they work through the night together, working on big deals. She's set her sights on him from day one, if you ask me. And he's fallen for it. Formed a merger all of his own.'

Better give her the chance to let all the poison out. He recalled one night in Manchester when, over a glass of Glenfiddich, Rodney expounded his business credo. His cheeks were pink, his breath had a touch of halitosis, and his pupils dilated as he described how much he admired his most aggressive clients. Actually, Daniel old chum, there's no such thing as a merger. There are only takeovers.

'You know what he said? He told me he'd been striving to fight temptation! Pity he didn't fight a bit harder. Anyway, he says he wants to spend the rest of his life with her. No reflection on me, blah, blah, blah. He's moved into her place in Didsbury. We'll have to sell the flat, of course. The mortgage is crucifying.'

He could hear her crying and wanted to fling his arms around her. But she was far away and all he could do was scrape around for words.

'I'm so sorry.'

'Thanks,' she said in a muffled tone. 'Are you sure you wouldn't mind if I came to stay? The new term doesn't start for ages. I have a few things to sort out here, but I could be with you on Friday.'

Miranda was checking her hair in the mirror for split ends. He covered the phone with his hand as he consulted her.

She shrugged. 'If you're sure you won't be at each other's throats.'

He said into the phone, 'Louise? Yes, that's fine. We'd love to see you.'

'Warren Howe.'

Nick let the name hang in the air, for Hannah and Linz to absorb. Warren Howe, Warren Howe, Warren Howe. In murder cases, names of the dead echoed in your brain.

'He was a gardener. Partner in a landscaping business with a man called Peter Flint. Tina Howe was Warren's wife. They had two teenage children, Sam and Kirsty. They all lived in Old Sawrey, a stone's throw from Esthwaite Water.'

'Old Sawrey, isn't that where Beatrix Potter lived?' Linz asked. 'So Warren Howe was a latter day Mr Macgregor?'

'Warren didn't chase rabbits. He preferred going after the ladies and by all accounts he usually caught up with them. As for the Potter house, it's at Hill Top, a mile away in Near Sawrey. Old Sawrey is at the end of a lane that wanders around Claife Heights. There's a restaurant and bar as well as a handful of houses.'

They were sitting around the small circular table in Hannah's office. A whiff of peppermint came from the packet of sweets she kept in her top drawer. The icons on her computer screen were lined up in neat rows, Stone's, Blackstone's and the PACE manuals stood to attention on the single shelf. A pair of graceful palms arched over matching pots on the window sill. Nick said the room suited her craving for order, it was her refuge from the untidiness of the world outside.

'How did he die?' she asked.

'The Grim Reaper called early. Warren was murdered with his own scythe.'

Linz wrinkled her nose, a favourite mannerism. 'In his own back yard?'

'No, he was working in a client's garden, in between the Sawreys and Hawkshead, looking out over the lake. Lovely setting, Wordsworth probably wrote a poem about it, but the crime scene was a mess. Scythes may be old-fashioned, but they can do plenty of damage to soft human flesh. Trust me.'

Nick paused, letting their imaginations roam. In his twenties he'd acted in a local drama group. *Charley's Aunt* and period thrillers like *Gaslight*, the occasional Oscar Wilde or Francis Durbridge. He'd given up because police work and marriage were incompatible with committing to weeks of rehearsals, but he hadn't lost the knack of drawing an audience into his world.

He opened his mouth to speak again, but Linz beat him to it. 'Who was he, the client?'

Obvious question, but Nick snapped, 'She was Roz Gleave. Before anyone dreams up an exciting theory about her, let me tell you that she had a cast-iron alibi.'

Linz's eyebrows zoomed up. Far enough to irritate Nick.

'She ran a small press from home, literally a cottage industry. The day Warren was murdered, she was in Lytham St Annes, giving a presentation to a business that supplied books to libraries.'

Hannah said, 'Did she live alone?'

'Chris Gleave, her husband, wasn't around at the time.' Nick hesitated. 'He'd disappeared from home a while before the murder and didn't show up again until weeks after it. It turned out that he'd had a sort of breakdown and went off to London until he got himself straightened out.'

'So. A woman on her own has given work to an inveterate womaniser. Perhaps he thought his luck was in.'

'Warren Howe thought his luck was in every time any woman with a pulse exchanged a pleasant word with him. Single or not. Roz's best friend, Bel Jenner, for instance, he'd always carried a torch for her. She ran the restaurant and had recently been widowed. But Warren didn't get far with her. Bel had her eye on the young chef. Warren had more joy with his partner's wife, Gail Flint. Gail admitted they'd had a fling, but claimed it was all over between them.'

'Did she have the opportunity to commit the crime?'

'We couldn't prove it. She was laid up in bed at the time with a badly sprained ankle. No witnesses – and no evidence she was lying, either. The injury was genuine, but whether it was as serious as she cracked on was anybody's guess.'

'Would a woman have had the strength to kill him?' Linz asked.

Nick nodded. 'It looked as though he'd fallen or maybe been pushed, and attacked when he was on the floor. The scythe belonged to Warren, it wasn't brought to the scene. The blade was a brute, you wouldn't have needed to be Schwarzenegger to slash someone to pieces with it. The corpse wasn't a pretty sight.'

'An opportunistic crime, then?' Linz asked. 'The killer didn't come equipped with a murder weapon. Presumably they quarrelled and the crime was committed on impulse?'

'Not necessarily. Warren had used the same scythe for years, it was a prize possession. Roz Gleave's garden was a jungle. Anyone who knew him might have expected he'd have it close at hand.'

'Anyone seen in the vicinity around the time of the murder?'

'The house is at the end of a track. We interviewed walkers, as well as the locals, but they gave us nothing to work with. The forecast that morning was bad enough to deter any faint-hearts and the all-weather fanatics kept their heads down, making sure they didn't lose their footing in the wet. No reliable sightings of suspicious cars or vans around the crucial couple of hours.'

'Any problems in the gardening business?'

'Not if you don't count Warren shagging his partner's missus.'

Linz giggled. 'Were they making money?'

'Plenty. Flint was a studious type, a creative thinker, he specialised in garden design. Warren Howe provided the muscle and the green fingers. They were polar opposites, but the combination worked. If Flint knew Gail was sleeping with Warren, he didn't open his heart to us. To listen to him, Warren Howe was the perfect foil.'

'Tell us about Tina,' Hannah said.

'Some of the lads on the team reckoned she looked like a horse, nicknamed her Black Bess. But she was sexy. Strong, too. Had to be, to cope with Warren. My guess is that he could respect someone who stood up to him. If anyone was weak, he steam-rollered them. Tina knew what he was like, none better, but she coped. If his affairs bothered her, she didn't let it show.'

'Did she get her own back?'

'During the inquiry, she played the loyal wife. I actually heard her saying that life with him had its compensations. Such as their kids. Kirsty was sixteen, Sam eighteen. And they looked after her. Both of them confirmed her alibi.'

'Which was?'

'Tina was a keen amateur photographer. The day of the murder, she took the SUV and drove over the Hardknott Pass towards Wasdale, looking for fresh scenes to snap. The kids came along with her for company. At the time her husband was killed, they were all up by the old Roman fort. No independent witnesses that we could trace, but she did show us the pictures she'd taken.'

'Suppose the son drove and the daughter took the pictures?'

'Quite a conspiracy.'

'Stranger things have happened.'

'You're right. They could have been lying, but we couldn't break their stories.'

'Were the children suspects?'

'We ruled nobody in and nobody out. Warren wasn't exactly a caring father. But if there'd been sexual abuse, incest, whatever, nobody was admitting it. Kirsty constantly broke down in tears, but she was a kid and her dad had been murdered, so it wasn't a surprise. We never got much sense out of her. When Sam was interviewed, he answered in sullen monosyllables. Chip off the old block. He'd felt the back of Warren's hand more than once, even though he'd left school and was as big as his father. I could picture him retaliating with a punch or a kicking. But murder? We had nothing to pin on him.'

'All the data tells us that patricide is rare,' Linz said.

'Sad epitaph for the tombstone,' Hannah said. 'Everyone wanted me dead.'

'One more thing. Whoever killed Warren Howe pushed him into the trench he'd excavated and threw a bit of sacking and a few rose petals over him.'

A picture formed in Hannah's mind, as dark as if painted by Cézanne in his bleakest mood. The torn and blood-soaked corpse, dumped in the damp ground.

'To my mind,' Nick said, 'that was Warren Howe's epitaph. *He dug his own grave.*'

Chapter Three

The gathering dusk had become a favourite time for Daniel. He wandered outside the cottage and savoured the scent of old roses, and the colours mingling on the fell, tints of blue and indigo deepening as the sky grew dark. The slopes looked so rich and sensuous that if he could only brush them with his fingertips, it would be like touching velvet.

The evening air was chill after the heat of the day, but he stoked the cast-iron chiminea and smelled the logs as they burned. A fox on the prowl rustled in the bracken, a trio of brown-breasted mallards squealed and flapped as they rose from the tarn and fled over the trees. But whatever the tourist brochures said, Brackdale wasn't a wholly peaceful place. Years back, a young man who lived at Tarn Cottage, Barrie Gilpin, had been suspected of killing a woman whose body was laid out on the Sacrifice Stone.

Thank God, that was done with. Sitting down on an upturned crate between the potted lavenders, he shut his eyes. It awed him that the bedrock of the Lake District was as old as any in the world. The constancy of the lakes and mountains satisfied a need within him. Ever since his father had torn their family apart, he'd burned with desire to belong, to feel complete. At last he'd found a place he wanted to become part of.

He would love Louise to see the Lakes as he saw them. Splitting up with Rodney might be the making of her. Like a modern counterpart of a tightly-corseted Victorian, she needed to unbutton herself, learn the art of relaxation. The last time they'd spoken, she'd made it clear that for Daniel to downshift to the Lakes at the precise moment his career was taking off was madness.

But he'd needed to escape. For as long as he could remember – certainly since his father abandoned the family – Daniel had worked. And worked and worked. After school studies, academic research. Each year he set new goals, more demanding than the last. He didn't care about the money, although he earned a lot of it. What mattered was to break new ground. Soon everyone wanted a piece of him. Success made him a minor celebrity, people he didn't know envied him and he'd overheard someone in the Senior Common Room referring to him as The Lucky Kind. Always another project, always another offer he could not refuse. No time to think, no time to relax, but that didn't matter because he was doing so well and you had to make the most of every opportunity and, and, and, and…

And he'd been away when his father died and he'd missed the funeral, and then Aimee, his lover, had embarked on another suicide attempt and he'd been too late to save her from throwing herself from the top of a tower.

Miranda came into the sitting room, wrapped in a yellow bath towel. She loved aromatherapy and there was a glow of contentment about her. He could smell rosemary and juniper.

'Any luck at the church?'

'I asked the rector if I could see the parish records, but all he could do was refer me to the County Records Office, and I didn't find anything useful there. But I had a look around the graveyard and found where the Quillers were laid to rest.'

Their cottage had been built over a century ago, by a cousin of the man who owned Brack Hall. His name was Jacob Quiller and after he and his wife died the place had changed hands several times before the Gilpins arrived.

She feigned a yawn. 'Am I right in thinking you won't rest till you've made sense of that crazy garden?'

He glanced through the window. Outside, darkness had fallen. A lamp cast a pool of brightness over the path leading to the tarn, but the effect was to make the dark shapes of the trees beyond reach of the beam all the more mysterious. He caught sight of a movement in the plants by the side of the path. The fox was getting bolder. At night-time the garden became a different place, the kingdom of unseen creatures. The patterns that men imposed on the landscape were only skin deep.

'I must admit I'm intrigued.'

'Another crusade, huh?' She wasn't into the past; the present was all that mattered to her. Already she was preoccupied with unbuckling his belt. 'Come and join me on the rug. Better make the most of our freedom before your sister arrives.'

He was glad she'd changed the subject. Too easy for him to develop a fresh obsession with the mystery of the garden. It had scarcely been touched for many years and he suspected that the underlying design dated back as far as the Quillers' time. Their grave was situated under the leaves of a spreading oak in the churchyard. Its marble headstone was large, but lacked the grandeur of the vaults dedicated to the squires of Brack Hall and their families. No twee verses, no doleful epitaphs.

Three people were buried there. And here was an oddity: Quiller and his wife Alice had died on the same day, the first anniversary of the date given for the death of their son. He was named as Major John Quiller of 1st Northumberland Fusiliers and he'd died on 5 April 1902. The tail end of the Boer War, though there was no indication that he'd been killed in action. Beneath his parents' names were four words.

Died of broken hearts.

Warren Howe's face leered at Hannah out of the glossy file print, as if he were about to proposition her. Hannah contemplated the dead man, wondered how to climb inside his mind. Murder victims forfeited their privacy. Human rights? Forget them, they were an indulgence for the living. She stared into his eyes, searching for a clue to what he'd done to earn such a savage fate.

He wasn't bad-looking in a louche kind of way. Unruly dark hair and old-fashioned sideburns, full lips, a wide fleshy face. Teeth marred by a chipped front incisor that accentuated a small gap. The deep-set eyes were his best feature, startling and blue. One ear had a discreet ring. A strong face, with a touch of devil-may-care. Easy to understand why some women fell for him, despite knowing he was a serial seducer.

The picture featured in a brochure extolling Flint Howe Garden Design and a dog-eared copy had been kept in the file. A footnote credited the photographer, Tina Howe. She'd also been responsible for the shot of her husband's partner. Bespectacled, with a fuzz of greying hair, high forehead and long nose, Peter

Flint looked as though he'd be more at home in a college library than getting his hands dirty in the great outdoors.

Family snaps spilled out of a buff folder. The Howes, parents and children, lifting celebratory glasses at a table in a restaurant. 'In happier times', as the gossip columns might say. A painting of a crimson sunset above shadowy heights hung behind them; Hannah guessed at nightfall over the Langdale Pikes. A card propped up next to an empty bottle of Bollinger depicted popping corks and proclaimed Have a Wonderful Anniversary!

Tina Howe's equine appearance lived up to its advance billing, but her bone structure had a subtle elegance. Hannah understood why Nick had seen past the horsy jaw and tombstone teeth, and discerned a formidable spirit. Plenty of men would be attracted to such a woman, and not merely because her black top displayed a dramatic cleavage. Few would be a match for her.

Sam was a more obviously handsome version of his father. His sister had laid a hand on his arm, as though trying to protect him from committing some faux pas. A mass of auburn hair tumbled on to her shoulders, her features were unmistakably those of a Howe. She must have been about sixteen and her demure cocktail dress hinted at a figure that might one day rival her mother's, but Hannah thought the smile was misleading. Everyone else was enjoying themselves, but Kirsty Howe had anxious eyes.

Nick came in and glanced at the file. 'Taken at the restaurant in the village, a couple of weeks before the murder. Warren and Tina's china wedding anniversary.'

'China?'

'Twentieth.'

'You know everything.'

'I wish. Finished the file yet?'

'Half way through. Seems the team never got near to making an arrest.'

'Spotted the name of the SIO?'

'Clueless Charlie deceased? Yeah, explains a lot. The criminals of Cumbria were heartbroken when he suffered that coronary.'

'It wasn't brought on by overwork. He could have scuppered

the force's spidergram single-handed if he was still around. Charlie certainly lived up to his nick-name during the Howe case. The inquiry was all over the place, we seemed to do nothing but thrash around in the dark. One thing about Charlie, he gave good PR, and the Press loved him for it. Did you ever work with him?'

'No, but I gather I missed a treat.'

'He was a throwback to the fifties, Fabian of the Yard plus handlebar moustache. Rumours swirled that he might even dust off his old trilby for the cameras. Anything to divert attention from lack of progress to report. Before it came to that, the trail got cold and the media lost interest. So did Charlie. One more unsolved crime. You and I owe him a vote of thanks. For cold case work, he was a one-man job creation scheme.'

Hannah laughed. 'So he never came close to an arrest?'

'I actually once heard him say *cherchez la femme*. At least I think that's what he said. With a Geordie accent that strong, it's not easy to tell. He liked women almost as much as food, did Charlie, but the female psyche baffled him in a way shepherd's pie and chips never did. When Roz Gleave confounded him with her alibi, he turned his attention to her mate Bel Jenner. Personally, I suspected it was an excuse to ogle her while sampling three courses of home cooking in her restaurant.'

'And did you fancy Bel Jenner?'

'A beautiful woman,' Nick said carefully, 'none the worse for being a wealthy widow still on the right side of forty. Her husband was much older and he'd died a couple of months earlier and the new young chef was drooling over her. For all we knew, they'd been having an affair while the husband was on his deathbed. Oliver, the chef's name was, Oliver Cox. The little boy who kept coming back for more, Charlie called him.'

'Oh yeah? Tell me about the husband's death.'

'Don't get too excited, it was natural causes. Brain tumour. As far as Bel Jenner was concerned, Charlie was pissing in the wind. She had no motive, and it was the same with Roz. Suppose Warren Howe tried it on with one of them, so what? Bel and Roz had grown up with him, they were ex-girlfriends with no illusions about the great charmer. If they were in the market for a quick shag, fine, but they'd have known there wasn't any more to it than that. You ask me, he was content to stay married to Tina.'

'Why did she put up with him?'

'Why do so many women put up with unsatisfactory men?' Hannah shrugged. Good question.

'Christ knows how long the marriage would have lasted once their children left home. Why resort to murder? Charlie wondered about Kirsty Howe, before he decided that his prime suspect wasn't female at all, but her brother Sam. As far as most of us were concerned, that as good as ruled the boy out of contention. Poor old Charlie, he had a reverse Midas touch.'

Legend had it that Clueless Charlie's final promotion to the heady rank of Detective Superintendent was intended to keep him out of harm's way, far from the sharp end of detective work carried out by the humble foot-soldiers. By a bitter irony, he hadn't been smart enough to draw the fat pension earned by dint of fabled incompetence. He'd made the ultimate bad career move in succumbing to the charms of a voluptuous civilian worker from police HQ. Her voracious sexual demands had taxed his portly frame once too often. Result: a massive coronary and a funeral where his widow wept for more than one reason.

'How about Sam as a father-killer?'

'If every kid who ever had a set-to with his dad turned to murder, the world would soon be an empty place. In any case, I told you that Sam's sister and mother alibied him. That trip up the Hardknott was convenient for all three of them.'

'Too convenient?'

'I was reluctant to believe it. Sam was supposed to have been helping his father in Roz Gleave's garden, but he cried off at the last minute. Our difficulty was, they had their story and they stuck to it. Word perfect.'

'Suspicious in itself, then.'

'Yes, but who was covering up for whom?' The careful grammar struck Hannah as a clue to Nick's character. His instinct was always to obey the rules. 'Tina may have been guilty, but we never found any buttons to press that would have prompted

Kirsty or Sam to grass up their mum. To lose one parent is a misfortune, as Lady Bracknell said, to lose two…'

'You know what statistics tell us. Most murder victims know their killers.'

'And most of the killers are lovers or partners, past or present. But that didn't narrow the field of suspects much in this particular case.'

'So we're wasting our time if we follow up the tip-off?'

'You're the boss.'

'I'm asking your opinion.'

'You said yourself, the likelihood is that someone's trying to settle a score with Tina. This note doesn't offer any corroborative evidence. Not a sliver.'

Hannah glanced again at the photograph of Warren Howe, taken by the woman accused of slashing him to pieces. Despite the smile, his blue eyes were watchful and she saw a challenge in the bared teeth. He was daring her to solve the mystery of his death.

'Once I've read through the file, I might drive out to Old Sawrey, get the feel of the place. I've never been further than Hill Top.'

Nick took a breath. 'If we start turning over stones, who knows what we'll find? Plenty of worms, but maybe nothing to do with the crimes we're investigating.'

'Such is life.'

'That's the danger, don't you see? It's a risk with all the cases in our too-difficult file. If we don't solve the crime, we can cause more harm than good. Hurt people who don't deserve it. Didn't someone once call it ordeal by innocence?'

Hannah had never visited Old Sawrey before. The Lake District was full of tucked-away spots known by dedicated walkers to the last blade of grass, but ignored by most of Cumbria's natives. You never check out what's on your own doorstep.

Should she commit resources to reopening the Warren Howe inquiry or go along with Nick and let this particular sleeping murder lie? Before deciding, she wanted to get a feel for the area where Warren lived and died. Reading a file without visiting the scene was like hiring a DVD of a concert instead of watching it live. You needed to soak up the atmosphere. No matter how scrupulous the original investigation (and scrupulous wasn't a description anyone ever associated with Charlie), the paperwork could never tell you everything. Most of the suspects lived in and around Old Sawrey. Had done all their lives, probably still did. She wanted a picture of the place in her mind, as well as a picture of the dead man.

One Lake District village was, in Hannah's opinion, very much not like another. Each had its own unique identity. How could you compare Troutbeck, Cartmel, Watendlath? Even the tiniest settlements were distinctive. She'd once gone on the statutory day trip to Near Sawrey, to take a timed ticket courtesy of the National Trust and traipse round Beatrix Potter's old home, accompanied by a coachload of Peter Rabbit fans who'd made a special journey from Osaka. Across the hay fields, Far Sawrey boasted its own church, shop and part-time post office. Old Sawrey must be the poor relation, skulking among the oak trees up a lane that petered out into a path winding up Claife Heights.

The sun blazed as she threaded through the narrow byways to the west of Windermere. On days like these, she loved driving. She had the roof open, breathing the hot air, letting Bill Withers' 'Lovely Day' wash over her. A month earlier, she'd taken delivery of a gleaming two-litre Lexus and she was still relishing her new toy. She qualified for an essential user car loan and on impulse had dug into her own pocket as well and gone for something livelier than a boring old Mondeo or Vectra. Motorway driving was tedious, too many roadworks, but the gentle pace of the lanes was fine, at least until she encountered a minibus full of tourists coming in the opposite direction and had to reverse all the way back to the nearest passing place.

After a couple of wrong turnings, she found the 'no through road' sign she'd been seeking and squeezed her car between steep grassy banks. To her right she caught glimpses of a strip of water through a cluster of rowan trees. Beyond a farm gate, the lane became a rutted track, climbing through woodland. On a post beside a wooden gate, she saw a green slate nameplate marked Keepsake Cottage. The Gleave house, scene of the crime.

She pulled up at the end of the lane. Neat and whitewashed, the cottage was elevated so that even ground floor rooms commanded a view of Esthwaite Water over the tops of the trees. Scarcely 10 Rillington Place or 24 Cromwell Street, yet this was where Warren Howe had been butchered.

His body had been discovered in the back garden. So close to civilisation and yet a murderer had been able to scythe down Warren Howe in the open air with little fear of being observed. Nobody walking the path up the incline would have had a clear sight of the grounds of Keepsake Cottage; the woodland was too dense.

On impulse, she walked up the driveway, the urge to explore overpowering caution. If someone came out of the cottage and demanded to know what she was up to, she would produce her ID. It almost always did the trick; most people wanted to keep on the right side of the law.

Suddenly a bark broke the stillness and a sleepy-eyed mongrel, a canine Robert Mitchum, moseyed down the path. It looked in the mood to bite the hand that fed it identification. She swore and beat a retreat to the Ford. The dog followed her to the bottom of the drive and gave an uncompromising yelp as it watched her leave. As she executed a three-point turn, she took a hand off the wheel and pretended to shoot the pooch, but it gave her a sidelong glance packed with Mitchum-esque scorn.

Soon she was on the lower slopes of Claife Heights, driving past a large green board with yellow lettering outside the entrance to an old farmhouse set back from the road. FLINT HOWE GARDEN DESIGN. So even after all these years, Peter Flint had kept the memory of his partner alive in the name of the business. She wasn't naïve enough to write off suspects on the basis of knee-jerk amateur psychology, but it didn't seem like the act of a man with murder on his conscience.

The lane forked and she followed the sign marked OLD SAWREY ONLY. As she climbed the hill, she passed a scattering of houses before seeing a building perched on the brow, overlooking the lake and forest and fells beyond. The Heights looked like a small and ancient village pub with a conservatory extension tacked on at the front to enable diners to make the most of the view. Tubs overflowing with yellow and purple pansies bordered a pathway connecting the restaurant to a large detached house, set further along the slope. The grounds of house and restaurant were divided by willow screening. The car park was almost deserted and Hannah reversed into a space between a purple Citroen and a board outside the canopied entrance displaying times of opening. The restaurant was shut to customers for another couple of hours. Above the door a notice confirmed that Isobel Marie Jenner and Oliver Cox were licensed to sell intoxicating beverages. So the widow and the chef were still together after all these years.

As Hannah switched off the ignition, the restaurant door opened and a solidly-built young woman in a white T-shirt and denim jeans hurried out. She reached the Citroen and fumbled in a battered bag for the key. Her face was blotchy and her eyes full of tears. With a start, Hannah recognised her. The red hair was shorter than in the photograph she'd studied earlier in the day, but the blue eyes and jutting jaw were unmistakable.

The woman in distress was Kirsty Howe.

Chapter Four

The giant hog bared its teeth at Kirsty Howe. She halted on the pathway between the trees, then took a pace towards the beast. For all her distress, she could not help smiling as she reached out and patted its head.

She loved Ridding Wood. Since childhood, she'd felt safe here, surrounded by the weird creatures carved from wood and iron. For all their fangs and contorted faces, they never hurt you as people did. In her early teens she'd confessed to Sam that she thought of the sculptures as friends, each with a pet name, but he'd taunted her without mercy. Now she knew better than to share secrets with her brother, but to this day, she remembered what she used to call the hog.

'Hello, Boris. How are you today?'

Babyish, Sam would say, but she didn't care. This leafy haven was her second home, a refuge she escaped to when things went wrong. After her father's death, she'd wandered around the by-ways of Grizedale Forest for hours, struggling to reconcile herself with what had happened, and there was scarcely a route that she did not know by heart. She liked to come here for the setting of the sun, when families had returned home and hikers had tramped on. Even on a summer afternoon, with whooping kids on the hunt for wild animals along the sculpture trail, the exercise soothed her, as words of comfort never could. She drank in the soft air and the mossy smells, she swayed to the music echoing through the woodland, as unseen wanderers struck the huge wooden xylophones standing beside the route to the stream. Even today, with the words of the cruel letter burning in her brain, Ridding Wood did not fail to work its magic.

She ran her hands over the hog's back, careless of splinters. She envied artists, people who began with a blank canvas or page or a block of marble and had the talent to create something fresh. Imagine the sense of freedom it must give. Whereas she stayed in Old Sawrey, waiting at table and yearning for something that always seemed tantalisingly out of reach. Wanting it so badly that someone who must hate her had noticed, and was tormenting her because of it.

After blundering out of the restaurant, she'd needed to get away. Driving on auto-pilot, she'd wound up at Grizedale Forest, and parked near the old Hall. Would they miss her if she never showed up again? Oliver, how would he react, would he suffer a pang of regret?

She crossed the high bridge. On the other side of the water, a circle of steel glinted from the branches of a spreading copper beech. Each familiar landmark she passed calmed her, made her feel more secure. Further on, lights powered by the sun flickered in an elaborate beehive hanging high in the trees. From the river, she heard the shouts of paddling children and the conversation of their parents. Somehow she couldn't imagine having kids of her own. Plenty of time, her mother said, but that wasn't the point.

The track emerged from a leafy tunnel into open grassland and she subsided on to a large carved seat, allowing the sight of fields and fells to wash over her.

She glanced at her watch. Oh God, better get going.

Jumping to her feet, she felt her muscles straining. She'd need to get into shape before her next parachute jump. As for Oliver, she would not give in. She would see this through.

'You never said if you fancied anyone as Warren's killer,' Hannah said.

'That's right, I didn't.'

Nick was sitting at his desk in the corner of the CCR team's room. He was entitled to an office of his own and there'd been talk of him sharing with Les Bryant, who had come out of retirement to give the team the benefit of his wisdom on the fine art of murder investigation. Whether Nick's preference for remaining in the thick of things was down to an egalitarian impulse or a wish to escape being holed up with the dourest of Yorkshiremen, Hannah wasn't sure. Right now her sergeant's gaze was fixed on the computer screen. With all the ringing phones and competing conversations, his voice was so quiet that she had to bend over his shoulder to hear his reply. His aftershave had a subtle tang.

'Any particular reason?'

'Nobody believed it was a stranger homicide. Finding evidence to justify an arrest was a different story.'

'You must have had your suspicions.'

He'd been scrolling through his emails, scrapping routine messages. The sight of his still-overcrowded inbox made him sigh. 'Why do people send out so much garbage? Half the stuff I'm copied in on isn't worth a glance. Talk about information overload.'

They often cried on each other's shoulder about the time-wasting bureaucracy of the modern police service. But she could spot a diversionary tactic a mile off.

'Did you have a hunch?'

'Remember the Gospel according to Ben Kind? Theories are for losers.'

A shrewd blow, if below the belt. She hadn't just been the late Ben Kind's sergeant, she'd been his disciple. Ben had taught her more about police work than all the trainers in Hendon put together and, though it had taken her years to admit it, even to herself, her affection for him had teetered on the brink of something more serious. More dangerous. Not long after retiring he'd been killed in an accident, with so many things unspoken between them. She still mourned him, still thought about him now and then. She could still hear the scorn in his voice at team briefings when eager subordinates indulged in fanciful speculation. Like Nick said, theories were for losers.

'OK, you win.'

He stabbed *delete* with his forefinger one last time, then turned to face her. 'It's not about winning. The simple truth is that we never came near to making an arrest. If you ask me, this so-called tip-off won't take us any closer.'

'I'm not long back from Old Sawrey.'

'So that's why you disappeared. Off to catch up on the village gossip?'

She shook her head. 'I just wanted to get a feel of the place before I summoned up the energy to plough through the rest of the files. I see that Bel Jenner and her chef hold the licence of The Heights jointly.'

'Oliver Cox fell on his feet. The previous chef left soon after old man Jenner died and soon Oliver was giving the widow something to smile about. The restaurant may not be full to bursting every evening, but Bel won't lose sleep. Her husband left her with a few quid. The business was more like a hobby. Probably still is.'

'I saw Warren Howe's daughter.'

'Last I heard, she was working there as a waitress.'

'Kept yourself informed about what goes on in the village, then?'

He shrugged. 'Chris Gleave and I were at school together. He was a couple of years older than me, but we got on all right. We haven't spoken for ages but we never lost touch completely.'

'So you knew the man who owned Keepsake Cottage?'

'He and his wife still live there.'

'They own a foul-tempered mongrel.'

'Name of de Quincey.'

'Yes, it gave the impression it was as high as a kite. What's wrong with a nice harmless pet called Tabitha or Tom Kitten?'

Nick laughed. 'Did de Quincey take a piece out of you, by any chance?'

'No, but it looked as though it would love to. Tell me about Chris Gleave.'

Nick's eyes flicked back to his screen. More messages had popped up while they had been speaking. 'Better catch up on the backlog first. Fancy a drink later on?'

'Sure.'

Marc was going to be late home this evening, which made things easier. He seemed jealous of her friendship with Nick. Yet they never as much as exchanged a peck on the cheek. It wasn't that sort of relationship.

'See you in the Shroud, then.'

Half a mile from The Heights, Kirsty stopped at a passing place when she saw a van coming towards her. As it drew near, she recognised it as belonging to Peter Flint. Oh God, there was no escaping him at present. She lowered her head, keeping her eye on the foot pedals, but predictable to a fault, he didn't drive on past. He stopped when his car was level with hers and wound down his window.

'Off to work?'

Silly question. She was tempted to say so, just to wipe the cheerful beam from his face. Their relationship was fraught, but she knew he was making an effort and she always found it difficult to be rude

'That's right.'

'I've just been talking to Bel. She wants help with that little garden at the back of the restaurant. Moles have been playing havoc with the lawn and she'd like the border replanting. Oliver's no gardener, so I said I'd ask that brother of yours to lend a hand.'

'Best of British.' She couldn't think of a reply less sarcastic.

'I know, I know.' Peter's sigh was theatrical. 'Sam doesn't like knuckling down, he doesn't seem to understand, this is a service business. The client is king. Or queen, in Bel's case. But I haven't given up hope. Deep down, he has a genuine feeling for plants. Like Warren, of course.'

Kirsty gave a brusque nod and Peter seemed to realise that it wouldn't be tactful to embark on a conversation about her father.

'Well, must be getting on. Nice to see you. And if you speak to Sam before I catch up with him, you might mention the job for Bel.'

'I'll see if he can fit it in his busy schedule.'

He chuckled to show that he saw the funny side of her brother's idleness and with a wave was gone. Turning into the car park at The Heights, Kirsty spotted Gail Flint's sporty yellow Toyota. As usual, Gail had parked in a space reserved for the disabled, it was the type of thing the old bag did just for the hell of it.

Gritting her teeth, Kirsty walked into reception. No sign yet of either Arthur the barman or the Croatian kitchen girls. Gail and Bel were chattering away on the sofa where, during opening hours, customers waited while their table was prepared. Two expensively dressed forty-somethings, one blonde, one brunette. Everyone always said Bel was stunning (for her age was Kirsty's unspoken qualification) but Kirsty suspected she might be putting on a pound or two around her waist. Wishful thinking, probably, but nobody could deny that her nose was too beaky to be remotely beautiful. So was Oliver's, but somehow it suited him, lent a kind of distinction.

As for Gail, she was fixated on defying the passage of the years. A few weeks ago, Kirsty had overheard her telling Bel that when her divorce finally came through, she'd celebrate by splashing out on more cosmetic surgery. She'd already had a discreet nip and tuck around the jaw-line and kept harping on about a boob job. Poor flat-chested creature, she could do with one. Now the blonde hair had lengthened overnight and Kirsty was positive she'd invested in extensions. Pity she couldn't do anything about that letterbox of a mouth. Over the years, Gail had tried her hand at a variety of small enterprises before becoming a supplier of wine. The Heights was her best client, and she and Bel were friends. Gail was scheduled to make one delivery each week, but dropped in every other day. They spent more time yapping about clothes and television than discussing business.

'Hello, Kirsty, how are things?'

No mistaking the fruity smell on Gail's breath. Her favourite tipple was gin made from damsons harvested in the Lyth valley. Sweet and strong, no wonder she was having to take care not to mix up her words. An empty glass stood in front of her. Bel, always the goody-goody, was sipping fizzy water.

'All right, Mrs Flint, how are you?'

'I told you before, sweetheart, my name's Gail. None of this Mrs Flint nonsense.' Gail's trout-like lips (Kirsty suspected excessive Botox injections) formed a smile. 'I'm fine, but you do look a little flushed, if you don't mind me saying so. You're not working her too hard, Bel?'

As Bel smiled and shook her head, they heard a car pulling up outside. Kirsty caught sight of Oliver through the window, lifting a crate of glasses from the boot of Bel's gleaming BMW. It always gave her a kick to see him without being seen. She adored his elegance of movement, the movement of his shoulder blades under the thin cotton shirt. He didn't bother with the gym, but he had as much feline grace as Bel. Even when peeling potatoes or carrots, he seemed incapable of clumsiness. Tall, dark and blue-eyed, in some ways he reminded her of Sam. But her brother's muscles were running to fat. Too many chip suppers.

Sam had no time for Oliver. He was dead jealous, bound to be, but he loved to wind her up by insisting that Oliver was gay. All chefs were, in his book. Oliver had flowing locks, down almost to his shoulders, high cheekbones and manicured hands; very different from close-cropped, grubby-nailed Sam. But Oliver wasn't gay, she was sure of that.

He came into reception and put the box down. When his eyes met Bel's, the intensity of his gaze made Kirsty shiver with cold despair. It was as if the woman were a hypnotist, as if at a snap of her fingers, he would satisfy her every whim. Kirsty imagined Oliver as wild and passionate. Dangerous, even. Yet Bel had tamed him, made sure he did her bidding. Lucky, lucky woman to have that lithe body wrapped around her in bed every night.

'Where shall I put these glasses?'

Bel reached out and ruffled his hair. 'Let me show you.'

Her tone was flirtatious, her eyes sparkling with promise, like a teenage coquette. She led him by the hand to the kitchen. For a quick grope, presumably, the woman just couldn't keep her hands off him.

Gail leaned forward and whispered, 'Much as I love Bel, I can't help a twinge of jealousy, how about you?'

It was as if she got a kick out of twisting the knife. Kirsty coughed, scouring her brain for an excuse to get away.

'She tells me Oliver's very sensitive to her needs. All he cares about is giving her pleasure. I mean, I'm bound to be jealous, aren't I? The younger men I've known, it's always wham, bam, thank you ma'am.'

Oh God, too much information. 'I'd better be getting on with my work.'

Gail smirked. 'Don't let me keep you, sweetheart.'

Bel and Oliver were coming back already. His hair was messed up and Kirsty yearned to smooth it back into place, it was like a physical ache. But she had to choke her instincts. She dared not touch him.

Time to take refuge in the bar. Oliver didn't even spare her a glance as she scuttled out. Her throat was dry and she poured herself a glass of water, downing it in a couple of gulps.

Through the thin wall, Kirsty heard Gail squawk with laughter. Did she detest Gail more than Bel, or the other way round? And was it because they had both screwed her father? She didn't think so. Roz Gleave was another member of that not very exclusive club, and Kirsty liked her. But Gail was a first class bitch. Tina Howe reckoned that Gail was all fur coat and no knickers, though while Gail was married to Peter Flint, no-one doubted who wore the trousers. Tina said it was a wonder he'd stuck with her so long. Gail loved talking about girl power and making out that she and Kirsty were bosom pals, but if you stripped away the chatter, underneath she was as hard as nails. She was like Dad in one respect; they both thought only of themselves. As for Bel, she'd been a kid when she'd slept with him. According to Sam, Dad had always fancied her, kept pestering her even when she was safely married to a wealthy man, even when that man was dying, even when he was still warm in his grave. In different circumstances, Kirsty might have felt sorry for Bel. But Bel had Oliver in thrall, and that was reason enough to hate her.

Hate, hate, hate. It was a cancer, eating away at her insides. She could feel it spreading through her, insidious and irresistible.

A couple of times lately, she'd even fantasised about catching Bel alone in the restaurant and bashing her on the head until the life seeped out of her. She could pretend the killing took place in the course of a burglary gone wrong. Of course, she'd never do it. It wasn't lack of nerve, the truth was she didn't have a violent bone in her body. But her dreams were becoming desperate. Even on a summer day, they made her cold with fear.

Marc Amos's bookshop flirted with the senses. If the whiff of old books and background Debussy were insufficiently seductive, the casual visitor would be lured from the craft shops in the courtyard by the rich aromas wafting from the cafeteria. It shared the ground floor of the old mill building with a maze of ceiling-to-floor shelves. Leigh Moffat's succulent home-baked desserts had found fame beyond this corner of the South Lakes and as many people gorged on her lemon cake and Death by Chocolate as on the tens of thousands of books in the store.

Amos Books wasn't on Daniel's route to collect his sister from the station, but he calculated he could get away with an hour's diversion. It was an indulgence, and not only of his incurable bibliomania. The last time he'd met Hannah, he'd told her about Aimee's suicide – something he seldom spoke of – but although she'd hinted that she and Marc were having difficulties, she hadn't confided in him about her private life. Impossible not to be curious. He liked Marc as well as Hannah. The complication was that he'd felt a strong stirring of attraction to her, unexpected, unwanted, yet unmistakable. A couple of times it had kept him from sleeping. He and Hannah were both in relationships, and he didn't want to wreck things for either of them. But she'd known his father, been close to him, there was so much that she could explain about him, helping Daniel to fill in the blanks. He couldn't simply forget her. They could still make a friendship work.

'Hello Daniel, long time no see,' Leigh Moffat said as he moved along the counter, ignoring the fudge cake and millionaire's shortbread with an effort of will little short of heroic. 'What can I tempt you with?'

Their last encounter had been a fiasco. She'd visited Tarn Cottage, distressed by his interest in the killing on the Sacrifice Stone, and left infuriated by his refusal to let go of the past. He guessed it was rare for Leigh to lose her poise. This afternoon she looked cool and elegant in her neat uniform, though if she sampled much of her own baking, she must have needed a pact with Beelzebub to preserve that slim figure.

'Thanks, I'll have a double latte. How are you?'

'Fine. Is the cottage renovation progressing?'

They chatted idly before he sat down with his drink at a table near the till. After scanning the ground floor for a couple of minutes he caught sight of Marc Amos, emerging from the office at the back of the building where he dealt with the mail order side of the business. Marc was heading towards the café and he tossed a broad grin at Leigh before spotting Daniel a moment later. Sidling past a couple of backpackers clutching Ordnance Survey maps, he took a seat opposite Daniel and indicated the emptiness of the table to Leigh.

'Couldn't you persuade him to sample the cake?'

'Some people obviously like to take the moral high ground.'

Marc turned back to Daniel. 'I was worrying that you'd forgotten us. Hunting for anything in particular?'

'The history of Brackdale? There's a family, the Quillers, I'm interested in. Jacob Quiller was a cousin of the Skeldings of Brack Hall. He built Tarn Cottage.'

Marc pushed a hand through a thicket of fair hair. Good-looking, Daniel thought. He had a youthful carelessness and energy that lots of women must find attractive.

'The name Quiller doesn't ring a bell, but Brackdale rates a couple of pages in most books about the South Lakes. Let's have a look.'

Daniel finished his drink and clattered after Marc up the rickety stairs to an airy room overlooking the weir at the back of the converted mill. Marc climbed a library stool and plucked a few sunned tomes from a high shelf.

'Doubt if there's much in either of these. Borrow them if you like. No obligation.'

'You'll never get rich that way.'

'If I wanted to get rich, I wouldn't have opened this shop in the first place. Be my guest.'

Through the door Daniel saw the first floor crammed with people of different nationalities, cameras slung around their necks. 'Business is brisk?'

'I like it best when they buy instead of simply admiring the stock,' Marc grinned. 'Hannah and Leigh moan that I devote too much time to acquiring books, not enough to getting rid of them. I'm off to Ravenglass in ten minutes. An executor's looking to flog her uncle's collection. He was an aficionado of detective fiction, there may be a few gems amongst the ex-library dross. I'll email you with details of anything worthwhile. You like a mystery, Hannah told me. The detective thing must run in the family.'

Daniel gave a cautious nod. 'And how is Hannah?'

'Still trawling the cold case files.' Marc glanced skywards. 'It frustrates her, not being in the thick of the action all the time. But I tell her, not everyone can make it to chief constable. And given that the people at the top have to spend all their time toadying to politicians, who would want to be? Your dad was content to stop climbing the greasy pole and I don't blame him.'

'Uh-huh.' Daniel glanced at the books in his hand. 'You're too generous. I'll happily buy these. And – give Hannah my regards.'

'What are we going to do?' Kirsty Howe asked.

At long last she and Oliver were alone in the restaurant. While she finished laying the tables for dinner, he'd made them both a pot of Earl Grey and put on Bel's CD of Andy Williams' greatest hits. Music to soothe girls by. They were sitting next to the window that looked out towards the lake, but neither of them spared it a glance. They had twenty minutes before Bel returned from the shop in Hawkshead, but Arthur and the Croatian girls might show up at any moment.

'Nothing.'

'We can't do nothing!'

She pulled a piece of screwed-up paper out of the waistband of her skirt and laid it on the table and smoothed it out again. Her face was as crumpled as the sheet bearing the stark stencilled words.

Keep your paws off that chef, you dirty little whore.

She stifled a sob. 'When I showed it to you this afternoon, you thought it was funny.'

Reading the note he'd laughed wildly, as if shocked beyond reason that anyone could take such an accusation seriously. Thank God Bel and the other staff hadn't been around. Anger would have been fine, anxiety reasonable. But amazement bordering on disbelief – that cut her to the bone. No wonder she'd wept as she ran out of the restaurant.

'I'm sorry, Kirsty. I was – well, shocked, I suppose. It seemed…'

'Ridiculous?' she asked in a muffled voice.

'Don't cry, Kirsty. It's horrid for you. For both of us. But we mustn't let it knock us off balance.'

'You think it is ridiculous.'

'It's ridiculous to call you…cruel names.'

'You think I'm still just a silly kid, don't you?'

'No, no. We've always been good friends, Kirsty, haven't we?' He leaned forward and rested a palm on her shoulder. His cologne smelled of sandalwood. 'True friends. Friends who care about each other.'

She mopped her eyes with a lacy handkerchief. 'I suppose so.'

'You know so. And I hate seeing you upset.'

The directness of his gaze lifted her spirits. When he concentrated his attention on you, it was as if the rest of the world ceased to exist. Was this how Bel felt, when he looked straight at her? 'So what are we going to do? Tell the police?'

He snatched his hand away as if he'd touched a live wire. 'For goodness sake! How can they do anything? You've thrown away the envelope, we've both handled the message. Even if whoever wrote this left any fingerprints, which I doubt, they will have disappeared by now.'

Her tea had a tang of lemon. She preferred to take milk with it, but Oliver said that ruined the flavour and he was the expert. The song playing in the background was 'Can't Take My Eyes Off You', one of Bel's favourite schmaltzy tracks, yet Oliver had put it on for her. How long would it take to break the spell by which Bel had entranced him? Three times in the past year, he'd kissed her on the cheek by way of greeting or farewell. The kisses were chaste, but each one set her pulse racing.

'I was wondering…there was this programme on Channel 4 the other day, about investigating crime. What about DNA tests?'

'This isn't a hunt for a sniper or a serial killer. The police won't be interested, Kirsty. Trust me.'

Of course she wanted to trust him, but his reaction baffled her. 'You're suggesting we let this…this creature get away with it?'

'With what? Whoever sent that message wants to upset you. Don't give him the satisfaction, Kirsty. The best thing you can do – we can do – is to behave as though nothing's happened. Why should we let some sad person with nothing better to do get under our skin? Let them spin their lies about someone else if they want to spark a reaction.'

She stared at him. 'As simple as that?'

'Of course.' He was breathing hard, as if this meant a lot to him. 'After all, we know there isn't a shred of truth in this note, don't we? You've never laid a finger on me, nor me on you. We're just very good friends – and I swear, we always will be.'

'So this is Paradise?'

'An outpost of Virgin Rail, actually,' Daniel said. 'Don't worry. The Lake District gets better.'

Louise arched her eyebrows and stepped aside to allow him to pick up her suitcases. The train had disappeared north on its journey over the high moors to Carlisle and Glasgow beyond and a group of Swedes with bulging rucksacks were scanning the horizon in a baffled search for the vanished sun. The line below the platform was awash with puddles after a sudden cloudburst, the sky was as grey as the stone station waiting room. Daniel considered mentioning that Oxenholme Station was designed by the man who built the Bank of England, but thought better of it. Louise's arrival had been delayed by fifty minutes (engineering works), the on-train buffet had been closed (staff shortages) and she'd spent the journey sharing a table with three Macbeth-like witches who discussed their digestions at the top of their voices (deafness coupled with contempt for the fit and youthful). She wasn't in the mood to be impressed by local trivia. Not that Louise was often in the mood to be impressed.

As he led his sister down the ramp to the tunnel that linked the parking areas on either side of the station, he stole a sideways glance at her. All at once, her resemblance to their late mother was striking and, as much as he'd loved Mum, he was sorry to recognise the similarities. Gone were the flowing dark tresses, replaced by a severe bob in her natural mousy shade. She'd never liked going out without 'having her face on' but now the make-up was confined to a touch of colour in otherwise pallid cheeks. If she seemed tinier than before, it wasn't merely because of the flat shoes. He guessed she might have lost as much as a stone; there were lines around her mouth that he hadn't seen before. Not even when she'd suffered from anorexia in her late teens, a phase that persisted until an ardent if acned suitor who lived next door helped her recover her self-esteem. He yearned to put his arm around her, but he knew that if he did, chances were that she'd shrug it off with a furious remark.

He'd left his Audi in a marked space on the brow of the hill above Kendal. As they emerged into the light, she halted on the edge of the pavement and took in the prospect of the fells in the distance.

'This is where he lived with her, isn't it, Oxenholme?'

He'd meant to avoid mentioning their father. Her resentment of the old man was excessive, but too deeply ingrained to be smoothed away overnight. He should have known better than to believe that they could gloss over the past.

'Cheryl's in Grange-over-Sands now. She's moved in with someone else.'

'You looked her up?'

Her voice rose; she was too astonished to be angry. For her, Cheryl was the serpent who had tempted their father into destroying his family's happiness and he'd been too weak to resist. She'd never met Cheryl, but like her mother, she hated the woman with blind ferocity.

'I was curious.'

Louise was struggling for calm. 'You were always too curious for your own good.'

He heaved the suitcases into the car and slammed the boot shut. 'Believe it or not, I felt sorry for her.'

Louise swore. 'You're joking!'

'She's not ageing well and the man she lives with is an old misery. He's obviously planning to spend his retirement looking around for errands she can run for him. Waiting for her to mess up so he has something fresh to complain about.'

'Serves her right, the selfish bitch.'

'He used to be her boss.'

Louise grunted. 'That was her modus operandi, wasn't it? Seducing men she worked for.'

They drove through the town in silence. As they turned on to the road that led to Brackdale, she said, 'I know I look a fright.'

'A bit wan, that's all.'

'I've lost a bit of weight too.'

'Not a bad thing.'

'Still not got any manners, then?' She hesitated before saying, 'Thanks for letting me stay with you.'

'I'm glad you came.'

'Who knows, in a couple of weeks people might start mistaking me for a country maid, with pig-tails and cheeks like apples.'

He laughed. 'So this is your first time in the Lakes since that holiday?'

He'd wanted to keep their conversation on safe ground, but with Louise you could never be sure what was safe ground. In a moment, the temperature in the car plummeted.

She said in a low voice, 'Do you ever wonder how he could sleep? How he could live with himself?'

Daniel kept his eyes on the road. 'He's dead now.'

After a pause she said, 'Yes. And I'm sorry about that. And I know how much you cared for him. Like I used to. And I realise I'm a miserable cow, I fully understand. It's just that…'

To his horror, she started to sob. In all the years since their father's departure, Daniel could never remember his sister crying. Not even during those frail anorexic days. Louise didn't yield to emotion, Skiddaw would crumble before she shed a tear. A flame of anger spurted inside him. That smug bastard Rodney, this was his fault.

He pulled off the road and parked on a grassy verge. If ever there was a time to put his arm around her, this was it, but she wiped her eyes with the back of her hand and pushed him away.

'I'm all right.'

'You think so?'

'Happens every day, doesn't it? Woman falls for man, man shags woman, woman gets clingy, man meets another woman and runs away. And the whole cycle begins again. I'll get over it.'

'So you don't like men too much at the moment, big sister?'

'I don't exactly like myself, come to that.'

A sudden instinct made him want to say, 'But I like you, Louise.'

Thank God he bit the words back on his tongue. She'd never forgive him for such a horrendous outburst of sentimentality. For patronising her. For taking pity on her.

In the quiet of the car, as she dried her tears, he realised – with a shock, because he'd never turned his mind to it before, except in the shallowest way – that it was true. For all the years of bickering, for all the gulf between them whenever they discussed their father, there was a bond between them. They were all that remained of their family.

So Kirsty Howe was weeping buckets and the same day, her mother had been accused of killing her father. Hannah leaned back in her chair. She'd been in the job long enough to realise that coincidences, like cock-ups, were commoner than conspiracies. Interesting, though.

Nick looked in. 'See you there in twenty minutes. Mine's half a Guinness.'

She slipped the anonymous message into a plastic wallet and Charlie's irritatingly uninformative crime scene log back in its labelled folder. There were few less exciting virtues in an SIO than tidiness, but Ben Kind had always preached its importance. Mess wasn't merely a nuisance, according to Ben, it could hamper an investigation if it prevented you seeing the facts with a clear eye. It wasn't the end of the world if the facts were incomplete – an occupational hazard in an investigation led by Charlie. Spotting gaps might suggest fresh lines of enquiry. Even the lack of evidence is evidence. Like *The Curious Incident of the Dog in the Night-Time*.

She sat up in her chair, realising it wasn't an original thought. She could hear Daniel Kind quoting those words, in a television programme. A week ago, she'd seen a DVD of his BBC series on special offer and picked up a copy. One evening when Marc was out, she'd watched it for half an hour. The following day, she'd picked up a voicemail message. Daniel, suggesting that they get together again sometime. He wanted her to tell him more about Ben, fill gaps in his knowledge of his father. She hadn't returned the call, wasn't sure it would be a good idea.

He liked to compare the work of historians and detectives. She was reluctant to be convinced, but his arguments defied easy contradiction. Ben might not be an academic, but he had had a sharp mind and was more down to earth than his son. To abandon fame and fortune to get away from it all – even in the Lakes – was daring. Reckless. She could never do what he had done. Yet she couldn't help admiring his nerve in walking away from fame and money, to make a new life with the woman he loved.

At least, she supposed he loved his partner. When they'd last talked, he'd hinted that Miranda was having second thoughts about the move. If he felt let down, he hadn't said so. She was sure he would be loyal, just like his father. Even though Ben, in an aberration, had left his wife and kids to move up here with Cheryl. Something else the Kinds had in common. On occasion, they acted out of character and surrendered to a wild impulse that changed their lives.

Frightening. Yet fascinating.

Chapter Five

The Shroud, officially The Woollen Shroud, was a rambling free house set back from the road out of Kendal. The pub, like the name, dated back centuries, to the days when in an attempt to combat an industrial slump, the authorities forbade people to bury their dead in anything that wasn't made of wool. To this day the Shroud retained a graveyard atmosphere, if graveyards ever smell of stale beer. But the bar boasted a series of secluded alcoves in which you could conduct a conversation with a degree of privacy seldom found outside the confessional, plus an ill-lit passageway leading to a discreet way out at the back of the building. Ideal for a quiet word with a publicity-shy informer, or a chat between colleagues away from the madding and insatiably curious crowd at police HQ.

Nursing his glass of Guinness, Nick said, 'What do you want to know about Chris Gleave?'

Hannah took a sip of traditional recipe lemonade and said, 'What is there to know?'

'Not a lot, if you're looking for a suspect. He had an alibi.'

'A surfeit of those in this case, don't you think? Tina, Sam, Kirsty. Roz Gleave. And now her husband Chris?'

'Yeah, discouraging.'

'Alibis are made to be broken.'

'Charlie never cracked them.'

'That tells us more about Charlie than the strength of the alibis.'

'If I had to name one man who truly would never hurt a fly, it would be Chris Gleave.'

'They used to say Crippen was meek and he still got up the nerve to chop his wife into bits and bury them in the cellar.'

'Even so, he was a sawbones. All Chris cared about was music. He wrote songs and played guitar. Sort of a Cumbrian answer to Paul Simon.'

Succumbing to temptation, Hannah said, 'Don't tell me – 'Bridge Over Troubled Esthwaite Water'?'

Nick groaned. 'Your jokes don't get better. With respect. Anyway, when we were in our teens, we lived a couple of roads apart in Ambleside. We had things in common, though the Gleaves' house was twice the size of ours. His father was an estate agent, his mum a lady who lunched. Sometimes the two of us would walk to school together. As a kid, bullies pushed him around, but by the time he was sixteen, he was able to enjoy the perfect revenge, because most of the girls were swooning after him. A very good-looking lad, I was jealous as hell, but the fact he never showed off made his company bearable. When he went off to Manchester to study music, I missed him.'

'You said you kept in touch.'

'Yes, though we went our separate ways and scarcely saw each other. His grandmother lived at Keepsake Cottage. He was her only grandchild and she doted on him, just as his mum did. When grandma died, she left the house to him. At the funeral, he met Roz Gleave. Within a couple of months they were married. I was invited to the wedding. Despite all that female admiration, it was his first serious relationship with a girl. Roz is someone who knows what she wants and makes sure she gets it. She wanted Chris, so that was that. After a few glasses of champagne, I joked that he couldn't have had much say in the matter. But he made it clear he was head over heels.'

'You said he had a breakdown. When?'

'Three weeks or so before Warren Howe was murdered, Roz called me. She was in a wretched state. Chris had disappeared a few days earlier. She thought he was suffering some sort of psychological collapse. I was one of the first people to hear about it. She and I barely knew each other, but because I was in the police, she thought I might be able to help.'

'And did you?'

'As best I could. Which meant, hardly at all. He left home one morning and never came back. To begin with, she wasn't worried. They didn't live in each other's pockets and it wasn't unusual for him to disappear every now and then. She put it down to the artistic temperament, whatever that was supposed to mean. Only when he didn't get in touch after twenty four hours did she start to worry, make a few calls to friends. By the time she spoke to me, panic had set in.'

'No hint as to why he might have upped and left?'

'They didn't have financial worries. Chris didn't make a fortune from his music, but there was enough family money to make an impoverished sergeant's eyes water. Roz's business was thriving and they didn't live extravagantly. There was no suggestion of strife between them. According to Roz, they never quarrelled.'

'Never? What could be more suspicious than that?'

He grinned. 'I'm sure you and Marc never quarrel.'

Hannah refused to be distracted. 'I know you said he was a sweet guy and all that, but do me a favour.'

'Actually, I found it easy enough to believe her. Chris wasn't one for confrontation. If he found himself in – an impossible situation – he wouldn't want to tough it out. He hated any sort of strife, he'd sooner make himself scarce.'

'Did he have a lady friend on the side that Roz wasn't aware of?'

Nick wiped a trace of froth from his mouth. 'I'm sure he didn't. And before you ask, there was no suggestion his disappearance was involuntary. I could only assume that Roz was on the right lines. Chris's temperament was always fragile. A small independent label had brought out a CD of his music a few months earlier and he'd had high hopes of it. But there were distribution problems and it sank without trace. He'd been a bit quiet about that and Roz thought maybe he was more depressed than he'd admitted to her. Or to their GP. He wasn't taking tranquillisers or anything.'

'Suicidal tendencies?'

'No history of attempts at self-harm and I'd never known him give any hint that he might want to take his own life. But people who kill themselves don't always give any advance warning.'

'No suggestion someone might have wanted to kill him? Bearing in mind what the ACPO manual says?'

'"Every missing person report has the potential to become a homicide investigation".' He was quoting from guidelines issued by the crime committee of the Association of Chief Police Officers. The Murder Investigation Manual was the closest that serious crime squads had to a Bible, but even the Bible didn't tell you everything. 'Sure, but there wasn't a shred of evidence to suggest foul play. He was a likeable man. Still is.'

'So you couldn't help?'

He spread his arms. 'What could I do? There was no role for the police, nothing to suggest that he was a victim of crime. It's a free country, people can come and go as they please, however much distress they leave behind. All she could do was wait – and hope.'

'And then…Warren Howe was killed.'

'No connection.'

'You're sure?'

'Positive.'

'Howe knew your pal?'

'Through Roz, yes. She'd grown up in Old Sawrey and her married home wasn't far away. Her best friend Bel Jenner had a fling with Warren as a teenager, then Roz had a turn. Long in the past, and all three of them had married other people. For good measure, Warren was having it away with Gail Flint. Roz's only interest in the man was as a gardener, I'm sure of that. The cottage grounds were a mess, the old lady had let them become over-run with weeds and nettles and neither Chris nor Roz had green fingers. They liked the idea of a wild garden, but even a wild garden needs to be planned. So they signed up Flint Howe to do the job.'

'No evidence of any hostility between Warren Howe and Chris Gleave?'

'Nothing. The only connection was Roz.'

'Tight-knit community, huh?'

'They don't come tighter.'

Hannah pointed at the empty beer glass and Nick nodded. One compensation of the Shroud's lack of popularity was that it didn't take an age to be served and she was back with fresh drinks inside a couple of minutes.

'When did Chris Gleave reappear on the scene?'

'A month after the murder. He called on his mobile and then minutes later showed up on the doorstep of Keepsake Cottage begging Roz to take him back in. Which she did.'

'No hesitation?'

'If she was in two minds, I never got to hear about it.'

'What was his story?'

Nick indulged in a little crude origami with the beer mat, as if in aid to thought. The Stygian gloom made it hard to read his expression, but Hannah thought he was wondering how much to reveal.

He took in a lungful of musty air and said, 'Basically, he'd lost the plot. The failure of the CD hit him much harder than anyone realised. Harder even than he realised. He felt overwhelmed, his life was spinning out of control, he just needed to get away from it all for a while. Long story short, he ended up down in London, busking on the Northern Line.'

Hannah made a face. On her rare trips to the capital, she'd found the Underground noisy, smelly and claustrophobic. It must have been a severe breakdown for Chris Gleave to be tempted to exchange the serenity of Keepsake Cottage for the subterranean murk of the Tube.

'Takes all sorts, I guess. What brought him back to his senses?'

Nick shrugged. 'His story was that when he managed to straighten out his thinking, he realised he belonged in the Lakes. With Roz. A sad story, but they managed to conjure up a happy ending.'

'Unlike Warren and Tina Howe. Presumably Chris Gleave was questioned about the murder?'

'As soon as he resurfaced. Not by me, of course. I'd declared that Roz and Chris were known to me, but Charlie was happy to keep me on the team. Obviously I took no part in interviewing the Gleaves. As suspects they were a long shot, but by that stage we were desperate. We were all acutely conscious that the best chance of picking up a murderer is within twenty four hours of the crime being committed. After a month had passed, we were clutching at straws.'

'And the alibi?'

'Four hours after Warren Howe was scythed to death at Keepsake Cottage, a Good Samaritan hauled Chris Gleave out of the gutter in a side street near Leicester Square and called an ambulance to take him to Casualty. He'd been mugged and had his wallet stolen by a couple of teenage thugs.'

'What sort of an alibi is that? Four hours might have been long enough for him to do the deed in Cumbria and get back to London.'

'The train times didn't fit and he's never learned to drive.'

'There are other means of travel. He could have made a secret journey, killed Warren Howe and then hot-footed it back to the city, with everyone none the wiser. Who's to say that the breakdown wasn't a part of the plot? A very convenient way of removing him from the scene at the vital moment.'

'Even Charlie had to rule out push-bikes and making a getaway by hot air balloon. Logistically, it didn't make sense that Chris was the killer. Quite apart from the absence of any apparent motive.'

'Perhaps Charlie should have dug deeper.'

'For all his faults, Charlie did at least understand that when you're in a hole, the first rule is to stop digging. We didn't have an infinite budget. Whichever way we turned, we ran into a blank wall. Trouble is, some cases just aren't meant to be solved.'

'All cases are meant to be solved.'

He drained his glass. 'I'm not holding my breath.'

Would Louise and Miranda hit it off together? Daniel had been full of foreboding. Tact wasn't his sister's strong point and Miranda's moods changed like the weather. They could hardly be more different, the sceptical academic lawyer and the free spirit. But they were making an effort. Louise had changed into a svelte new frock and he guessed she'd dropped a dress size since he'd last seen her, with the odious Rodney in tow. She said all the right things about the cottage, while Miranda rhapsodised about his sister's taste in fashion before starting to pump her for embarrassing anecdotes from his childhood. He was content to be the butt of their humour until it was time to sidle off to the kitchen to cook dinner for three.

Later, as they relaxed in the living room, Miranda mentioned

Barrie Gilpin and Daniel found himself having to explain the part he'd played in one of Hannah Scarlett's cases, the murder of the woman found on the Sacrifice Stone.

'As a boy, he could never resist a mystery,' Louise told Miranda. 'That's why he loves unravelling the past. So this police officer was Dad's old sidekick? Or more than that? Was there something between them?'

'She isn't like that.' Before he could stop himself, he added, 'Neither was he.'

Louise's eyebrows arched. 'Surely you haven't forgotten, he had form. Look at the way he left us in the lurch for a young woman on the make.'

Miranda saw his brow clouding and quickly changed the subject to the tribulations of dealing with tradesmen. But the mellow mood had been spoiled and he finished his drink in silence. The slur angered him. He was angry for his father, even more so for Hannah.

'A good haul?' Hannah asked.

'Fantastic.' Marc was sitting cross-legged on the rug in the dining room, marooned in a sea of old books. 'The chap was a connoisseur. I mean, there he was living in this ordinary semi in Ravenglass and up in the spare bedroom he'd assembled this treasure trove. His sister couldn't care less, she had no idea of what he'd collected over the years.'

'I hope you paid a fair price.'

'Of course.' He was all injured innocence. 'You know me.'

Well, yes. When it came to business, he was like every dealer she'd met. Books, antiques, whatever, they were all the same, they took as much pleasure from contriving a little extra profit on the negotiation than from contemplating the rarities they'd bought.

She joined him on the rug and picked up a couple of thin books in gaudy wrappers. She liked to take an interest in his business, just as she was happy to talk when he asked about her latest case. With police work, some things had to remain confidential, but her instinct was to be open. There were too many secrets in the world. He'd kept one or two himself, not least the affair with Leigh's sister that he'd briefly resumed years back, in the early days of their own relationship.

'You're like a pig in muck this evening.'

He beamed. 'I know you worry about this idea of murder for pleasure, but there's wonderful escapism here. Red harvest, green for danger, five red herrings, nine tailors, murder in Mesopotamia and on the Orient Express. See these Inspector French books? Written by a railway engineer whose culprits concocted alibis based on the assumption that trains ran precisely to timetable.'

'Jesus, what murderer in his right mind would risk that?'

'Nostalgic, or what? Those were the days.'

'Actually, I yearn for chance to gather suspects in the library. No worries about reading them their rights. At least in those books you can count on finding out the solution if you battle through the last page.'

He hugged her close. She often forgot how sinewy his arms were. Each time they held her, she was happy to remember.

'Tough day at work?'

'We have a new cold case. A landscape gardener, murdered with his own scythe. Grisly.'

'As it happens, I was talking about gardens in the shop today with your friend Daniel Kind.'

'Oh yes?' Mention of Daniel quickened her pulse, but she mustn't seem too interested. The last thing she wanted was for Marc to get the wrong idea, as he had done about her relationship with Ben. 'More of an acquaintance, really. I've not been in touch with him since the Brackdale file was closed.'

'You've been watching his TV shows. I noticed the DVD in the rack.' For a moment she thought he was going to make an issue of it, but thankfully tonight his good humour was unshakeable. 'His latest passion is the history of his own cottage garden. Maybe you should call him in as a consultant on your murder case. Make the most of having an expert in detecting the past on your doorstep.'

Hannah laughed and flicked through an aged copy of *Busman's Honeymoon*, wrinkling her nose at the title page description, 'A love story with detective interruptions.' One of the chapters was headed 'When You Know How, You Know Who.' A wildly optimistic assertion, not one you'd find in the ACPO manual. Yet so often the key to solving a murder lay in victimology, finding out how a person behaved to find out why they died.

Put it another way. When you know Howe, you'll know who.

Kirsty Howe's bottom lip trembled as she studied the torn scraps of paper. She'd fished them out of the bin-liner and, forgetting that she'd been about to put out the rubbish, she was hunched over the breakfast bar, piecing together the bits like completing a jig-saw.

The roar of the washing machine made it hard to think. She switched it off and focused on her task. The envelope was addressed to Sam. She'd recognised the writing at once – the same horrid stencilled style of the note which had destroyed her day.

He'd screwed up the pieces, making tight little balls, but she smoothed them out with care. Soon the message was staring up at her.

Why did you hate your father? Jealousy?

She'd hardly seen Sam all day. He always left early for work and she mostly came back after he'd gone to bed. This evening was an exception, for he was staying out later than usual. Their mother reckoned he had a girl over in Broughton, but he'd not mentioned anything to Kirsty. His life revolved around football and beer and motor-bikes and women. Throughout her teens, she'd entertained the romantic hope that tragedy would bring them closer together. For all his laziness at school, he was brighter than he liked to make out and she hoped that, once out of his father's shadow, he would reveal a sensitive side. After all these years, she was still waiting. Worse, he was smart enough to have picked up on her liking for Oliver and he never lost a chance to sneer.

As she taped the fragments of the message together, she heard the thundering of a motor-bike for a few moments before the engine died. The smell of alcohol wafted as he strode through the back door, helmet in hand. His eyes might be tired but his skin was glowing. She'd seen that look on the face of a couple of boys from Hawkshead whom she'd slept with. A look of bleary triumph. Her lovers reminded her of Lakeland twitchers excited by the sighting of a rare bird, or train-spotters at Oxenholme who'd ticked a rare number off their list. All they wanted was to bask in their conquest until they targeted a new trophy.

'What's the matter with you?'

'I found this.'

She waved the anonymous message at him. He made as if to snatch the note from her, but she was too quick for him and, evading his lunge, skipped off her stool and stood in the doorway, daring him to hit her. He'd never gone so far as to strike her, at least not since he was a boy and he used to poke her in the ribs or twist her arm behind her back.

He moved forward, the soles of his trainers scraping on the tiled kitchen floor. His mouth was inches from hers. It wasn't only the stale beer that stank, but the pot noodle on his breath. No wonder he hardly ever ate at The Heights, even though he and Peter had been doing some work for Bel in the garden lately. His idea of gourmet dining was curry and chips.

'Hand it over.'

'Why? You didn't want it, obviously. I found it in with the rubbish.'

'Who do you think you are, some kind of detective, sticking all the bits together again so you can have a good laugh?'

'Sam!' Even through the haze of drink, she hoped he might realise he was being unfair. 'I was upset for you. The fact that someone has written something so nasty to you.'

'Who cares about shit like that?'

'I care! Nobody ought to say that about my brother! Do you think we ought to tell the police?'

'What?' He blinked. 'You must be joking, didn't we see enough of them to last a lifetime when…?'

'When Dad was murdered.'

'Well, yeah.'

'I know, but it isn't acceptable, Sam. Who can possibly be doing this?'

'Some interfering scumbag with nothing better to do.'

'I didn't know you had any enemies.'

He scowled. 'You never know what some people might do after a couple of pints.'

'So you think a man sent this?'

'No idea.'

'I thought it might be a woman.'

'Someone I've screwed, you mean? Some bitch trying to get her own back?'

She winced. 'Surely it's someone who knows something about Dad. It's so strange, after all this time.'

He shrugged. 'I've got better things to do than lose sleep over it.'

'You mean you're going to let them get away with this?'

She thought she'd landed a shrewd blow. Turning the other cheek wasn't Sam's style. Again, she watched his fuddled expression while his brain cranked into gear. In the end, he took the easy option. Typical.

'I'll think about it tomorrow. It's been a long day, and I've put my back out. You know what, I've been digging all afternoon, it's a terrible slog.'

Whatever form of exercise had put out his back, Kirsty doubted that it was gardening, but she bit back a waspish retort. They needed to be on the same side over this. Someone wanted to hurt both of them.

'We can't brush this under the carpet. Who could bear such a grudge against us?'

Her brother spread his arms. He didn't have an answer, so much was clear.

'It's me they're getting at, not you.' She didn't speak and he frowned. It was almost possible to watch the jumble of thoughts clattering around inside his brain. 'Hey, did you get one?'

'One what?'

'You know what I mean.' He waved vaguely at the note. 'A creepy thing like this. Poisoned pen letter or whatever you call it.'

'All right.' She put her hands on her hips, wanting to face him down. 'What if one was sent to me?'

A coarse smile. 'How could anyone write anything unkind about sweet little Kirsty? What did it say?'

'It doesn't matter, it was nonsense. A pack of lies.'

'Come on. You shouldn't…' – he was groping for the simplest words – 'you don't want to blush if you're trying to hide something from me.'

He reached out and clamped his hand on her shoulder. She screamed in disgust at his foetid breath, she couldn't stop herself shoving him away with all her might. He lost his balance and finished up on the floor. When he looked into her eyes, he didn't seem to like what he saw. Perhaps it was revulsion; she couldn't disguise how she felt.

'You fucking bitch,' he said thickly.

The next thing she knew, his hands were around her throat.

Chapter Six

A clammy night, too hot to sleep. Daniel sweated under the duvet, battling insomnia for hour after endless hour, Miranda's smooth warm body nestling by his side. She was restless and every now and then, she murmured in her dreams, but he couldn't make out the words. In the end, he eased himself noiselessly out of bed and tiptoed downstairs to find the histories of the Lake District that he'd bought from Marc Amos.

He poured himself a glass of water and settled on the living room sofa. He loved the smell and feel of old books. To hold them was to touch the past. Skimming the pages, he came across a handful of references to Brackdale amongst reams of stuff about better-known valleys like Borrowdale and Langdale. Skeldings had lived at Brack Hall for much of Victoria's reign, it seemed, but there was nothing about the Quiller family. After an hour's browsing, he found a mention of Tarn Fold in a small book with a splitting spine, published locally in 1935.

Tucked away beneath the fell is Tarn Fold, with its old corn mill and, surrounding the tarn itself, an old and melancholic private garden, mysterious and overgrown. For the visitor, the Fold is noteworthy for its proximity to the old coffin trail that wends from Brack Church up towards Priest Edge.

Not much to go on, but at least there was nothing new about the strangeness of the garden. He parted the curtains and was gazing out into the blackness when he heard a sound behind him. Louise was in the doorway, wearing a short red gown.

'Too hot, isn't it?'

'Uh-huh.'

'What are you looking for out there?'

'Wish I knew.'

She came into the room. 'I'm sorry about this evening. I shouldn't harp on about Dad.'

'You still regard him as some sort of monster.'

'You know how hurt Mum was after…'

'Yes,' he interrupted, not wanting to dredge up old quarrels.

She picked up the book. 'What are you reading?'

Glad of the chance to change the subject, he joined her back on the sofa and started talking about the garden. 'There's a story to it, must be, and if the secret was old in the Thirties, I'd guess the explanation dates back to the Quillers. The odds are that the garden was scarcely touched after they died. How come Jacob and Alice died on the same day, supposedly of broken hearts? This paragraph hints that the secret was kept by later owners of the cottage. Like Mrs Gilpin, who lived here till she died? No-one attempted to give the garden a makeover. But why?'

'Respect for the dead?'

'Could be.' He couldn't help laughing at himself. 'Here I go again. Digging into the past, searching for a puzzle to solve.'

'I'm glad, Daniel. When you left Oxford so suddenly, I wondered if you'd had some sort of breakdown. After Aimee and…well, you know.'

'And what do you think now?'

A sheepish grin. 'Could be that we're both finally coming to our senses.'

Kirsty huddled under the duvet after waking from a shallow sleep. Her neck was aching. She slid out of bed and inspected herself in the mirror. The mark was red and vivid. It was bound to bruise, she would have to wear a scarf or something to hide it. And hide her shame that her brother, of all people, should have done this to her.

She got back into bed and listened to Sam blundering around downstairs, banging cupboard doors in search of breakfast things. Sunlight filtered in through gaps in her bedroom curtains, but she buried her face in the pillow and waited for him to go. This house had been home to the family all her life, yet she'd never felt more alone.

How long had he kept squeezing her throat? Only for a few seconds, must have been, and yet it had seemed an eternity. Did he mean to kill her, simply in a flash of temper? Closing her eyes, she had waited for death. Strangely, she felt no fear. She was ready to embrace nothingness. To end life would at least end her despair.

Suddenly he'd released his grip. Perhaps he was more afraid

than her. Perhaps he realised this, perhaps it made him hate her all the more.

'You're mad.' To her horror, he'd made an effort to get the words out straight. Speaking from the heart. 'Off your head, that's you. Of course whoever wrote this shit got it right.'

'What do you mean?'

She was croaking, it was impossible to recognise her own voice.

'I hated his guts. I can't tell you how glad I am that he's dead.'

Studying the photographs from Warren Howe's post-mortem, Hannah felt bile rising in her gullet. The murderer had slashed Warren's body a dozen times, tearing off strips of skin. The pathologist reported that the wounds suggested fury – or desperation – rather than physical might, but through luck or judgement the jugular vein had been ripped open. Warren hadn't stood a chance.

Every time she had investigated a murder, she had forced herself to attend the autopsy and study the corpse with as much detachment as she could muster. The rage welling up inside her helped her to succeed; instead of surrendering to emotion, she channelled it into a fierce resolve to see the murderer brought to trial. Ben's creed, that everyone deserved justice, had become hers. Nobody ought to die like that. It didn't matter that, had she known Warren Howe alive, he would surely have made her flesh crawl.

Nick came in. The photographs spread out on her desk made him grimace.

'Not a pretty sight. You're in even earlier than usual.'

'I wanted to finish reading the files. This morning I'm planning how to take the review forward.'

'What would you like me to do?'

Hannah hadn't been looking forward to this conversation. Best keep it low key. 'You're busy already. Isn't your report on the Brock case due in a couple of days? And then you need to interview those people up in Cockermouth. As for Warren Howe, you've already given me plenty to chew on. I'll take charge and Linz can do the legwork.'

'Maggie Eyre can sort out Cockermouth. I know the Howe

case. And the place. And the people.'

'Yes.' She sucked in a breath. There wasn't an easy way to say this. 'Too well, perhaps. You're friends with the man whose garden the body was found in. You were a member of the original team whose work we're looking at. We need to draw on your knowledge of the background, it's a huge asset, but I don't see you playing a front-line role in this review.'

'I'm too close to it?'

'Correct.'

He was biting his tongue, she could tell, wanting to argue, but knowing that a rant would get him nowhere. She would only be swayed by reason.

'Didn't we agree that the beauty of cold case review is that we can make up our own rules?'

'Spot on.' For all her worries about being sidelined, she relished the opportunity this job gave her to be a detective again. Not just a well-paid pen-pusher.

'There you are, then. Failing to detect the murderer wasn't just a defeat for Charlie, it was a defeat for all of us. Me included.'

'My bet is, you'll soon be sick of my pestering you for information.'

'No more than that?'

'It's enough.'

He weighed up her expression, checking for any sign that she might be prepared to budge. 'Very well, ma'am, if that's the way you'd like to deal with it.'

He strode out of the room without another word. He only called her ma'am in private when he was deeply pissed off. Shit. What was it about Nick and this case? Something to do with Chris and Roz Gleave, she couldn't imagine any other explanation. Whenever a personal relationship existed between a detective and a witness, tensions arose. She just prayed that while Chris was away, Nick hadn't allowed his sympathy for Roz to spill over into something more intimate.

She took another look at the statements made first by Roz Gleave and later, after he turned up again, by Chris Gleave. They'd been interviewed by a pair of DCs whose names she didn't recognise. Neither Roz nor Chris had contributed much of value, even though Roz had found the body. This time around, she'd talk to the couple herself.

A young girl with a ponytail knocked on her door. 'The ACC wanted you to see this, ma'am. She asked if you could action it straight away.'

Paling as her eye caught the photographs, she handed Hannah a sheaf of paper about a clampdown on misuse of emails and the internet. One force had been dragged through the mire in the Press after one group of officers were found sending each other racist and homophobic messages. Another lot devoted half their time to playing an internet game that involved a yeti with a baseball bat trying to hit animated penguins out of sight. Lauren was putting new policies and procedures in place to make sure that Cumbria's computer systems were squeaky clean. Hannah gave a long, low groan. The girl was gone before she realised that her ungracious response had come close to shooting the messenger. It wasn't the sort of mistake she usually made with staff relations. No point in denying it, the brush with Nick had unsettled her.

At moments like this, it was a lonely job. Working for Ben had been tough, he'd been a hard task-master, but ultimate responsibility had lain with him and his superiors. The Cold Case Review Team was her baby and Lauren would judge her by its success or failure. Without making a conscious decision, she found herself checking her organiser for the phone list.

She'd give Daniel Kind a ring. It was about time. Hadn't Marc himself suggested it? As she keyed in his mobile number, she felt her mood lifting. It wasn't a big deal, just a small treat, on a par with nibbling chocolate or buying a new cologne. Nothing more serious than that.

At last Sam slammed the front door shut and revved his van underneath her window for a full minute, the old engine bellowing like a tormented beast. A parting flourish to make sure she'd woken up.

Kirsty lay very still for several minutes. Gathering her

thoughts, and her strength. She told herself he hadn't meant to kill her. He'd had too much to drink, he didn't know his own strength. Perhaps she was partly to blame. Mum often said she let him wind her up too easily.

Life must go on. Clambering out of bed, she paused to look at a photograph on her dressing table. It had been taken at the airfield, the last time she'd jumped there. She was kitted out in her skydiving gear, a broad smile splitting her face. Recalling the excitement of the day lifted her spirits. For years, she'd found it simplest to share the enthusiasms of her current boyfriend. Football, quad biking, skiing, whatever. Trouble was, though she found it easy enough to pick up boyfriends, their enthusiasm for her never seemed to last. Skydiving was a hobby she'd discovered for herself. The *Westmorland Gazette* had carried an article and she decided to give it a go. It looked like fun but she'd never imagined the sheer liberation of jumping from a plane and seeing the world beneath as you sailed through the air. Sam mocked her as a buzz junkie, but she didn't care. Skydiving empowered her, made her feel as though at last she was living life to the full. She'd never felt so free before.

In the bathroom she studied the mark on her neck. No need to panic. Give it a few days and it would disappear. Sluicing herself under the hot shower jet, she considered her body. There was a bit more of it than she'd have liked, but never mind. She kept trying diets but in her opinion restaurants didn't want waitresses to look like stick-insects, it wasn't a good advertisement. If she curved in the right places, a few excess pounds weren't worth worrying about. She'd never match Bel for elegance and glamour, but at least she was still young.

Half way through a self-denying breakfast of muesli and orange juice, she heard the mail drop through the letterbox. *Skydiving Monthly* was due to arrive today. Jumping off her stool, she padded out to collect it, but it wasn't the shrink-wrapped magazine that caused her to freeze as she bent to pick up the delivery, it was an envelope addressed to her mother. The stencilled lettering was unmistakable.

* * *

'It's great to hear from you,' Daniel said into his mobile.

He was up in the tiny third bedroom, staring at a blank computer screen. This was his temporary study until the bothy was converted. He liked to look out on to the peaceful tarn and watch the water birds come and go.

'Sorry I didn't return your call sooner.'

'No problem.'

'Marc tells me you called into the shop.'

'I was looking for books about Brackdale's history. Not that I'll have too much time for research over the next few days. My sister has come to stay.'

'Louise?'

He whistled. 'You have quite a memory.'

'Your father liked to talk about you both. He knew she'd taken the break-up to heart and it hurt him to realise how much pain he'd caused. It's funny, I felt almost as if I knew your family, long before you and I ever met.'

He was beginning to wonder how well he knew his own sister. In the living room, Miranda and Louise were discussing lingerie. Suki wanted a thousand word piece reviving the thong-versus-knickers debate, 'hopefully with a rural lifestyle angle, darling'. When Miranda had complained to his sister that she found G-strings as comfortable as a chastity belt made from piano wire, Louise startled him by saying that she always liked to wear something sexy under the severe suit she wore for work: 'Something lovely, you know? Turquoise, leopardskin, whatever.' He'd escaped upstairs, unable to contain his amazement. Louise the Puritan in leopardskin knickers?

'You must have known him – understood him – better than anyone.'

'Well, perhaps Cheryl…'

He didn't bother to hide his scorn. 'I can't believe she understood him.'

'No, maybe not.'

'I was wondering if we could get together sometime, have another chat. I know you're very busy…'

'OK,' she interrupted. 'Why not? Would you bring Louise along?'

'Christ, no,' he said quickly. 'I mean, she isn't ready to talk objectively about Dad. The wounds are still raw, as far as she's concerned. And she's finished with a boyfriend, that's why she's here in the Lakes, to get away from it all. It wouldn't be a good idea…'

'Just you and me, then?'

'If you don't mind.'

'No,' Hannah said. 'That's fine.'

'Lovely morning!'

A pair of cheery grey-haired walkers greeted Kirsty and she forced a smile in reply. In one sense they were right: the sun was already so fierce that she was wearing her dark glasses and a skimpy T-shirt emblazoned with a picture of an opened parachute and the legend *If at first you don't succeed…maybe skydiving isn't for you.* It turned her on to think of Oliver stealing a glance at her boobs or bare midriff. But the hate mail hung over her like a big black cloud.

She'd borrowed her mother's chiffon scarf to hide the mark on her neck and left her Citroen at home. Walking to The Heights would clear her head. Sam would never have attacked her, but for their row about letters. What had she and her family done to cause someone to be so cruel? They were harmless, ordinary people.

Leaves from an overhanging oak grazed her cheek as she rounded the last bend in the lane. Pushing the branch away, she reminded herself that one extraordinary thing had happened in their lives. Her father's killing. Why would anyone rake the tragedy up after so long? It didn't make sense.

It was as if the Howes were cursed. The Lakes were full of folklore about spells and jinxes: who could say it was all nonsense? Roz had once given her a book she'd published, packed with strange tales. Hidden above these sunlit lanes was the dark domain of the Crier of Claife. Ferrymen of old never took passengers across Windermere at night, for dread of the wailing spectre that prowled the Heights. One boatman who left the safety of the Ferry Inn was struck dumb with terror and died of delirium. In the end, a monk conducted an exorcism and confined the Crier to a rough quarry, where he was to remain 'until a man could walk across Windermere dryshod.' Kirsty remembered a couple of customers swearing they'd heard weird howlings as they walked home in the dark, but Oliver reckoned that had more to do with the whisky they'd been drinking than the Crier of Claife.

Outside the restaurant, Bel was watering the tubs, bending over the pansies, green can in hand. Kirsty stopped in her tracks. For a wild instant she imagined sidling up behind the woman. It would be so easy to slip off the scarf, loop it around her neck – and squeeze.

Oh Jesus, what was happening to her? She would never do it, could never do it. But even to let the idea creep into her brain...

Bel straightened and glanced over her shoulder. When she saw Kirsty, she gave a smile that showed off her flawless teeth. Trust the bloody woman never to have needed a filling in her life.

'I've just taken a booking for noon. Table for eight, a gathering of grandmas. We'd better have them sitting in the window.'

'Fine,' Kirsty murmured. 'I'll put two tables together.'

'Lovely.'

All their conversations were like this. Pleasant, superficial, the same as the movie tunes Bel liked to hum. Sometimes she repeated herself word for word, as when complaining about walkers who didn't take off their muddy boots before entering the restaurant. Her pleasant, softly-spoken manner disguised the fact that, in Kirsty's humble opinion, she really was rather stupid. Thank God she didn't have an inkling of how Kirsty felt about Oliver. Kirsty knew that was how it had to stay; she couldn't risk the sack. Not because it would be difficult to find work elsewhere, but because this job gave her an excuse to spend hours in Oliver's company. Was that pathetic? Sam would say so, but he would be wrong, there was nothing feeble or pathetic about wanting to be close to someone you cared about. Oliver was almost – but not quite – a married man and she'd tried to distract herself with flings, but it was no good. Oliver hadn't encouraged her, but she couldn't help herself. The harder she tried to forget him, the more she yearned to be with him. All the time.

'Has your brother mentioned when he might get round to that work at the back of here?' Bel smiled again. 'I asked Peter Flint, and he said Sam's the one with green fingers.'

Kirsty remembered Sam's warm, chunky fingers, closing around her throat. 'He hasn't said. I expect he'll get round to it soon.'

A car's horn pipped and Bel said, 'Here's Roz. Reliable as always. I phoned and said we were running low on her recipe book and sight-seeing guides. She promised to let me have a few more copies.'

Both of them waved as Roz Gleave jumped out of her little green sports car. Kirsty liked Roz almost as much as she resented Bel and Gail. For a start, Roz never bothered about trying to look glamorous. Bel was uncannily pretty, even Kirsty had to admit that, and Gail disguised mutton as lamb with the help of an army of cosmetic surgeons, while both of them spent a fortune on clothes. In contrast, Roz didn't give a toss about defying the advance of years. Her once-dark hair had turned as grey as Blencathra in the wet; but she never dyed it, and she didn't always bother with a comb. If she fretted about the thread veins on her cheeks or the pouches under her eyes, you'd never guess. This morning, she was wearing dungarees and scuffed trainers. To look at her, you wouldn't dream she ran a business at least as successful as Gail's or Bel's.

A month ago Kirsty had eavesdropped on a conversation in the restaurant between the three friends when Gail asked Roz if she'd thought about investing in implants. To Kirsty's delight, Roz burst out laughing.

'Chris loves me as I am, thanks very much! He's put up with my meagre boobs all these years and I'm a bit too long in the tooth to change them now.'

Another thing Kirsty liked about Roz. She was happily married to a man who might be good looking, but wasn't remotely as exciting as Oliver Cox. In Chris Gleave's company, Kirsty never had the same sense of fierce passions, barely suppressed.

'Half a dozen copies of each title, wasn't it?' Roz lifted a box from the car boot and displayed the contents for Bel to see. 'Hi, Kirsty, how is life?'

Actually, Roz, I'm receiving vindictive anonymous letters and last night my brother tried to strangle me.

Without meaning to, Kirsty rubbed her throat. It was still sore.

'Um, fine, thanks. Absolutely fine.'

'That's good. Love the scarf, by the way. Though aren't you a bit warm on a scorching day like today?'

'No, no, it's OK. I like the feel of it, next to my skin.'

Would Roz understand how she felt about Oliver, would it help to confide in her? Kirsty had known Roz and Bel all her life, even though while her father was alive, the two women kept a distance from the Howes. Presumably because of their past affairs with him. Roz was funny and kind and things hadn't always been easy for her. Chris's breakdown, for instance, there must be a story behind that, though Kirsty didn't know what it was. Surely she could trust Roz to keep a secret. The snag was, Roz was bound to take Bel's side. They were bosom buddies. In fact, everyone liked Bel. They didn't seem to care that she was too bland, too perfect, the same as her home-made apple pie.

While Bel chatted to Roz, Kirsty trudged into the building. She kept her uniform in a locker and soon she'd changed into the short black skirt and white top cut low enough to keep the old blokes from nodding off during the pensioners' discount lunch hour. The scarf stayed on. Through the thin wall of the kitchen, she could hear Oliver talking to the Croatian girls who were here for the summer. Veselka and Danica were lively enough, but scarcely soul mates. All they were interested in was picking up a few quid to take home to their families and seeing how often they could get laid.

Moments after she started lugging the tables into position, Oliver wandered out from the kitchen. He hadn't shaved yet, hadn't even combed his hair. In his sweatshirt and patched-up jeans, he looked nineteen. Too young for Bel, for sure. She'd insist he smartened himself up before any customers arrived. Pointless,

Kirsty thought. People liked chefs to be unconventional, they expected it. If this was her place, she'd change a few things. Liven it up.

'How are you?' He fiddled with a hangnail. 'Got over that hiccup from yesterday?'

'The letter, you mean?'

'That anonymous drivel, yes.'

'My brother received something yesterday, the handwriting's identical. And this morning an envelope has arrived for Mum. She wasn't around to open it, thank goodness.'

His face was ashen. Even in her distress, she felt excitement surging inside her. He was genuinely concerned for her.

'Oh, Jesus, Kirsty. This is dreadful. What – what does the letter to Sam say?'

'It accuses him of hating our father.' Her voice was rising, but she couldn't help it. 'Not that Sam can complain, he admits it's true.'

'Everything all right?'

Bel's voice made Kirsty shudder. She'd breezed back in without either of them noticing. When Kirsty mumbled a reply, Bel said, 'You look a bit off colour.'

'Oh, it's nothing. A touch of hay fever, that's all.'

'You poor girl. Have you been sneezing? I heard on the radio, the pollen count is at an all-time high. I don't know what's best for hay fever. Would a paracetemol help?'

Typical, Kirsty thought, as she murmured thanks. Of course Bel didn't know about hay fever, she'd probably never had a day's illness in her life. But she believed any problem could be magicked away, that there was a quick and easy solution to everything. For all her little acts of kindness, she had no idea of how other people struggled to cope. Even when the woman had lost her husband, she'd fallen straight into Oliver's arms. Her whole bloody life was charmed.

Miranda had joined a yoga class in Staveley and she'd persuaded Louise to come along with her. When Miranda talked about getting in touch with her spiritual side, Daniel expected his sister to cringe. Instead, she started asking Miranda about her take on Indian mystic philosophy.

The old Louise, the Louise he'd grown up with, wouldn't have had any truck with it. She was down-to-earth, focused, practical. As their lives moved in different directions, they'd exchanged a word on the phone here, an email there. He'd never hit it off with Rodney, so contact dwindled. Maybe over the years his sister changed from the girl he'd known, without his even realising it.

Should he mention that he was going to meet Hannah Scarlett? He was tempted not to say a word. He could see Hannah while Miranda and Louise were assuming the lotus position and they would be none the wiser. But it wasn't as if he had a guilty secret to conceal.

He broke the news while the three of them walked around the tarn, but Louise wasn't impressed. 'Oh, Daniel, why don't you let it go? This constant harking back, it doesn't do any good.'

He wondered about reminding her that she'd often spoken of his father's betrayal, she hadn't let that go. But he decided against it.

'I'm a historian,' he said, picking up a pebble and skimming it over the surface of the water. 'Harking back is what I do.'

'Stop being a clever clogs.' How many times had he heard her say that during his teens? 'You know exactly what I mean. I don't mean to seem harsh, Daniel, but Dad is dead. Picking over the past with his old sergeant won't change anything.'

Shielding her eyes from the sun, Miranda said, 'I don't think that's his only motive for seeing Hannah Scarlett.'

He felt his throat drying, but her expression was amused. 'What do you mean?'

'It's the detective thing, isn't it? Louise was telling me that before you took up history, you wanted to be a cop, just like your old man.'

'I was ten years old.'

'But you've never lost it, have you? That's why you wrote the book. You're obsessed with doing justice to history. That's why you're so keen on talking to a cold case detective. You think her line of business is pretty much the same as yours.'

Louise rolled her eyes. 'Well, Daniel, is she right?'

He thought about it. 'Yes, I suppose she is.'

During the dead hours between lunch and dinner, Kirsty's habit was to hang around at The Heights rather than going home. Any chance to spend time with Oliver was worth seizing and Bel didn't mind slipping her a few extra quid for making herself useful. Today was different. The Croatian girls were embroiled in a noisy tug of war over some boyfriend, and Bel asked Oliver to nip over to Ambleside to pick up a set of new menu folders.

Kirsty watched from the corridor as Bel patted his rump and then stuck her tongue down his throat as they shared a parting embrace. Oliver didn't even seem embarrassed, though surely he must be cringing inside. Bel wasn't young or fresh any more, the skin of her neck was definitely loosening; so sad to see a middle-aged woman pretending she was still in her twenties. Kirsty stifled an urge to sob and set off home.

When she arrived back, her mother's big black SUV was parked in the drive. Kirsty hesitated on the doorstep. Should she ask about the latest anonymous letter? She didn't want to tell her mother about the message sent to her. Too embarrassing. Yet how could she sleep, not knowing what the letter-writer had said to Mum? Clenching her fist, she told herself that it would be stupid to keep her mouth shut, for fear of what she might be told. *Go for it.*

Tina Howe was sitting on a high stool next to the breakfast bar, munching an apple while she checked her post. Her skirt showed off her bare legs, her top was even more revealing than Kirsty's waitressing garb. The old, old story: whatever Kirsty tried to do, Mum always did it better.

'Hello, stranger.'

Tina looked up from a gas bill. 'Isn't that what parents are supposed to say to children? Before long, you'll be complaining that I treat this place like a hotel.'

'Don't tell me you're denying it?'

'Well...I have been very busy lately.'

'Oh, yes?'

Tina tossed the apple core into the bin. 'Sorry, sweetheart. I don't want to be a neglectful parent.'

'I'm old enough to look after myself.'

'But?'

Kirsty pointed to the stack of opened mail in front of her mother. 'Something arrived for you today. An envelope with your name and address printed in capitals. What was it?'

Tina swung her legs back and forth. "Why do you ask?'

'It looked – odd. Not the handwriting of any of our friends or relations.'

'As a matter of fact, it was a piece of horrid anonymous rubbish. Not worth talking about.'

'Can I see it?'

'Listen, it was vile, you'd only be upset. As soon as I read it, I ripped it into pieces and shoved it down the waste disposal.'

'What did it say?'

Tina frowned. 'Look, sweetheart, it'd be best…'

'Please, Mum. Tell me.'

'All right. If you really want to know.' Tina took a breath. 'It said something like this. *When you killed your husband, you were screwing his partner.*'

As the words sank in, Kirsty put out a hand to steady herself against the breakfast bar. 'But that's nonsense! I thought you were…you told me you'd only been seeing Peter Flint within the last year or so.'

'Darling, it's bad enough to open a letter and find a message like that. I don't want a Spanish Inquisition on top, OK?' Tina eased off the stool. 'I'd better be getting back to the office. We're still trying to catch up after the computer crashed.'

'Will you be back tonight?'

Tina paused at the kitchen door. 'I doubt it.'

'Are you going to tell him about the letter?'

'Who, Sam?'

'No.' The question was disingenuous. 'Peter.'

'I don't want to think about it any more. I wouldn't have told you if I'd thought you'd make a fuss.' Tina lifted the keys to the

SUV off a rack decorated with little wooden fish and the fading legend Souvenir from Llandudno. 'I'll see you tomorrow, all right?'

As the door banged shut behind her, Kirsty ground her teeth. Her mother hadn't given a straight answer. Was the accusation in the letter really nonsense? Or had the affair with Peter Flint started while Dad was still alive?

Chapter Seven

The morning mist was clearing as Daniel ploughed up the grassy track to the top of Castle Hill. On reaching the summit, he gazed over the lush fields of the Kent valley towards the northern fells on the horizon. A panorama panel named them, but he didn't need it to recognise the flat-topped peaks of the Brackdale Horseshoe. Already he thought of the valley as home.

Kendal Castle was a ruin, with a tumbledown tower and fragments of wall scattered as artistically as if laid out by a heritage artist. There were peepholes and vaults and signs speculating about the precise design of the old fortress, but its defences had been down for half a millennium and now the stone remains enclosed a grassy expanse for recreation. Schoolchildren shouted, terriers barked, mothers with pushchairs gossiped. Tourists fiddled with camcorders, a teenage couple luxuriated in an endless kiss.

Daniel climbed the wooden steps and inspected the view from the top of the tower. Below sprawled the Auld Gray Town of Kendal, with its limestone houses and squat factories. The mountains in the distance would have looked the same to feudal barons eight centuries ago. Returning to ground level, he settled on a bench on the brow of the hill, soaking up the warmth as the sun came out to keep the forecasters' promise.

Butterflies fluttered in his stomach. Why did Hannah Scarlett have this effect on him? He would never admit it to a living soul, but he couldn't drive the woman out of his mind. It was as if he'd persuaded himself that she could unlock a door in his life. But he didn't know what lay on the other side of the door.

At last he saw her, striding briskly up from the road that led back to the river. She always seemed full of purpose, a woman who knew where she was going. The colour of her hair was a shade lighter than he remembered. Catching sight of him, she gave a quick nod.

'You're early,' he said, springing to his feet.

'You've probably read about police officers spending too much time behind their desks. So I have an excuse for getting out and about. Not that I'm expecting to catch any criminals this morning, unless you confess to breaking the speed limit.' She extended her hand. 'How are you, Daniel?'

Her skin was cool to touch. He was seized by the urge to keep hold of her, but conquered it just in time. 'I almost didn't recognise you.'

'You mean the hair?' A suspicion of a blush. 'It's one of my vices. I can never quite make up my mind on what's right for me. I haven't got up the nerve to go blonde. One day, perhaps.'

'It's good.'

'Thanks.' She cleared her throat and jerked a thumb towards the castle. 'So, what's your professional verdict on our ancient pile? Not exactly Windsor, is it? Though there is a Royal connection, with one of Henry VIII's wives. The last and the luckiest, Katharine Parr. Her family lived here, this was her birthplace.'

He smiled. 'I've always loved wandering around old castles. In some ways, the less that survives, the better. Try to picture what life was like six or seven hundred years ago, and there's plenty of scope for the imagination. As for Katharine, the latest thinking is that she was born somewhere else. That's what people don't realise about history. It's not set in concrete, it changes with time. Each time you find new evidence, you're tempted to form a new theory.'

'Like detective work. As you said in your TV series.'

'Good training for a historian to be the son of a policeman.'

'Ben was fascinated by the history of crime investigation, he told me that one of the earliest manuals about procedures for looking into suspicious deaths was compiled in ancient China. They called it Washing Away the Wrong.'

'Washing away the Wrong? Easier said than done.'

'You're telling me.' She eased herself on to the bench and he sat down beside her. Keeping a discreet couple of inches between them. 'So how goes your cottage renovation?'

'Three steps forward and two back, but the place is taking shape. I'm attacking the garden. Since I started digging out weeds and tree roots, I've discovered muscles I never knew I had – and all of them ache. Mind you, I'm allowing myself to be distracted by a puzzle.'

'Last time we met, you told me there was something odd about the cottage grounds.'

He was glad she'd remembered the conversation. 'Nobody would create a garden like that by chance. The answer may be in front of my eyes, but I'm too stupid to see it. Perhaps I ought to consult an expert in garden planning.'

'Do you have anyone in mind?'

He shrugged. 'I've looked in the directories. If you know anybody…'

'There's a company called Flint Howe Garden Design, on the way to Hawkshead. They're supposed to be among the best.'

'You've used their services?'

'I know them by reputation.'

He laughed. 'So long as there's no criminal connection.'

She made as if to say something, then checked herself. 'They are supposed to know their stuff.'

He picked up on the hesitation. 'You came across them at work?'

A wry grin. 'I'm glad you became a historian, not a lawyer. I'm not sure I'd like to be cross-examined by you. Your father was persistent, too. Good at luring people into indiscretions.'

'Persistent, I'd own up to that. I hope you didn't mind my calling you. It's just that…'

As he groped for words, she came to the rescue. 'I should have rung back sooner.'

'I was glad to hear from you.'

'Pleasure.' As if to cover embarrassment, she added, 'I owe a lot to your father. He behaved badly, leaving his family for Cheryl, and I'd say he felt guilty until the day he died. But he was a good man, even so.'

'Are the cold cases warming up?'

'The powers that be have secured extra funding for the project, so they're happy enough.'

'Congratulations.'

'Frankly, it's a mixed blessing. The work fascinates me, but I don't want to spend too long in a career cul-de-sac. For a historian, there may be a future in the past, but I didn't join the police to second-guess mistakes made by long-gone colleagues.'

'So why did you join the police?'

'To make a difference.' She spoke as if stating the obvious, and then gave an incredulous laugh. 'Hark at me, I sound like a politician. Arrogant, puffed up with my own importance. But it's true.'

'Nothing wrong with a bit of idealism.'

'Over the years, you learn to temper it with reality. How much difference can one detective really make? Even so, I suppose a part of me hasn't changed. I like to think I'm helping justice to be done. Perhaps I'm kidding myself. Ben used to warn me I'd grow out of it. Even though he believed in justice as much as me, each time I became too serious, he'd tease me something rotten.'

'He was the same with Louise and me.'

'I can imagine.'

Neither of them spoke for a few moments. An old man in an unseasonal donkey jacket threw a stick for his Golden retriever, a flock of black-headed gulls flapped overhead. Daniel guessed that Hannah was remembering his father. The laconic humour, the quiet resolve that on occasion became unyielding stubbornness. If only he'd seen through Cheryl sooner. The family need never have been torn apart.

'How did you come across these garden designers?'

She studied her short and unvarnished fingernails. There was nothing fussy about Hannah Scarlett. She didn't pretend to be someone she was not.

'A partner in the firm was murdered a few years ago.'

'Hardly a recommendation?'

She grinned. 'I don't think his death had anything to do with the quality of his work.'

'What was it to do with?'

'If only we knew.'

He leaned towards her. 'Is it one of your cold cases?'

'Maybe.'

'I suppose your lips are sealed, you can't tell me anything about it?'

His expression made her laugh and he realised he must look like a spaniel hoping to be taken for a walk. 'I'm not giving away confidential information. The facts are well known, they were all over the newspapers.'

'Was my father was involved?'

'Uh-uh. If he had been, we'd have stood a better chance of getting a result, but the SIO was useless.'

'Who was the victim?'

'Warren Howe. He was murdered while he was making over a client's garden.'

'Even less of a recommendation. The culprit wasn't an unhappy client?'

'Whoever killed him must have had an idea where to find him that particular day. But the client had an alibi and so did several other candidates. Warren Howe was a good gardener but a bad man, as far as I can make out. Motives weren't in short supply, but no-one could be linked to the crime.'

'No forensic evidence?'

'Nothing worthwhile.'

'What made you decide to look into the case again?'

'A bit more information has come to light. Someone has pointed a finger at a possible suspect. Without, unfortunately, giving us any solid evidence to build a case with. The review is a long shot. We don't have infinite resources, but the case interests me.'

'Why?'

'Good question.' She rubbed her chin. 'Perhaps because of the way he died. Or seeing photographs of the man and his family. I've been wondering what it must be like, to have it hanging over you for years. The unsolved murder of a husband and father.'

'What was it about the way he died? Or isn't that in the public domain?'

'Oh yes. The journalists loved it.'

She told him about the scythe and that Warren had dug his own grave. Her features were mobile, expressive; occasionally she used her small hands to make a point. Even some of his cleverest former colleagues at Oxford lacked the knack of conveying their knowledge in a way that captivated their pupils, but he could listen to Hannah Scarlett all day. His father had been a wonderful raconteur, had entertained Louise and him for hours with stories he made up about Sherlock Holmes and an exceptionally inept Dr Watson. His protégée had the same gift of entrancing him.

'I can see why you're fascinated. Solve the crime and you lift the cloud of suspicion from the suspects. From all but one, anyway.'

'My sergeant sees it the opposite way. He doesn't think we'll find the truth and all that will happen is that we'll reopen old wounds.'

'Is his glass always half-empty rather than half-full?'

'No, he's one of the most positive men I know. But this case is different. He was involved in the original inquiry and people he knew were involved.'

'Difficult to be detached if you have a personal connection.'

She shook her head. 'I've decided to do some of the asking around myself. One of the constables in my team can fill in the gaps. First port of call is Warren Howe's client, who found the body. I'm seeing her this afternoon.'

'Poor woman. She wanted a new garden and ended up with a body in a shallow grave.'

'She lives in the house to this day. The crime scene was preserved for a long time, but eventually Warren Howe's partner completed the project.'

'I was about to ask if you thought it suspicious that she never moved. Then I remembered that my cottage was supposedly home to a murderer. So I'm equally weird?'

A couple walked past, on their way to the castle. The young man had a small child over his shoulder, facing behind them. Her ice-cream smeared face was beaming and she waved a small hand at Hannah and Daniel. When Hannah winked and waved back, the child whooped with delight.

'That doubtful grin of yours reminds me of your father.'

Daniel laughed and said, 'Did he ever talk to you about why he left my mother?'

Hannah pursed her lips. 'Well – it was all about Cheryl, wasn't it? He was besotted and she wasn't prepared to be a mistress. She wanted him all for herself.'

'What did he see in her?'

'Use your imagination,' she said dryly. 'I'm not a member of her fan club, but even I'd admit that twenty years ago she must have looked great. And he was a man.'

'That simple?'

'They weren't soul mates, that's for sure. He got to know her through work and she set her cap at him. He became infatuated, they started an affair, the rest you know.'

'What was going on inside his head?'

'I hate to say it, because I was very fond of Ben, but I don't think his head came into it. It was another part of his anatomy altogether. Like I said, he was a man.'

'We're all the same?'

'No, but one thing I did learn a long time ago is that men aren't the same as women. They think differently, behave differently. They compartmentalise their lives in a way that few women do. I'm not even sure they really know what they want like we do. Cheryl wanted Ben. He succumbed to some kind of lustful dream. As time passed, he realised the mistake he'd made.'

'Are you sure?'

'Yes, not that he ever said so in as many words. I'm certain of it. He'd burned his boats, he couldn't go back, but when passion began to fade he saw Cheryl for what she was. Not a bad woman, not even – to be fair – a scheming minx. But behind the pretty face was a person he didn't have much in common with.'

'At least he had things in common with you.'

'Our work, yes.'

'More than that.'

Hannah coloured. As if to cover confusion, she checked her watch and scrambled to her feet. 'God, it's later than I realised. I'd better be on my way.'

He stood up. 'Perhaps we can do this again sometime. You can update me with progress on your cold case.'

She considered him as if checking an ID card. 'You're

fascinated by detective work, aren't you?'

'I'll take that as a "yes", shall I?'

She gave him a sidelong look. 'You can take it as a "maybe", Daniel. Anyway, good to see you again. Sorry I have to dash.'

They shook hands briefly and then she was gone. He stood beside the bench for a couple of minutes and watched her walking down the slope towards the road, brisk and focused as ever. As if determined not to look back.

He'd meant to drive home after seeing Hannah, but their conversation prompted a change of heart. Like a fat man deciding that a single doughnut couldn't do that much harm, he set off over the footbridge across the Kent and past Abbots Hall before heading up the main street towards the Carnegie Library. He'd look up the newspaper records and read up on Warren Howe's murder.

Earlier in the year he'd checked what the papers said about the killing on the Sacrifice Stone and found they devoted more ingenuity to an endless rehashing of facts released by the police at media briefings than to research giving an old story fresh legs. The murder of Warren Howe followed the same pattern. The vision conjured up by the abandonment of the gardener's mutilated corpse in a hole of his own making slaked the thirst of the most ghoulish readers for a few days, but once the initial flurry of excitement died down, there was little else to say. There was no obvious culprit – or, if the reporters believed otherwise, they were too worried by the law of libel to come clean – and few leads to suggest an arrest was about to be made. Those who knew Warren Howe – his business partner, the woman who ran the local restaurant, the client who had found his body – seemed guarded, unwilling to yield anything beyond expressions of shock and horror. Opinion pieces moaned about the state of society and that decent people were no longer safe in their beds (or, presumably, their back gardens) but the arguments, like the police inquiry, lacked conviction. The savage manner of the murder meant nobody could sensibly suggest that he was a victim of random lawlessness. The papers were coy about speaking ill of the dead, but dropped hints that he wasn't exactly an upstanding member of the community. The case migrated from the front page to anorexic paragraphs on page thirteen before disappearing with the emergence of a juicy local government scandal.

Daniel scrutinised grainy photographs of the victim's family and friends. One shot showed Tina Howe dressed in black. The expression on her long face was as bleak as winter on the fells, but whether from grief or guilt he could not divine. Had Hannah received a tip-off suggesting that the widow had killed her husband? This might explain why the pictures had sparked her interest. It was the traditional explanation for murder. Relationship meltdown, one spouse murdering another.

His thoughts strayed. Why hadn't Hannah married Marc Amos? They'd been together for years, but she was a strong woman, she could stand on her own feet. Even so, he couldn't help wondering. He'd seen her smiling at the child up at the castle. She was at ease with kids, did she want some of her own? Plenty of time yet, but the clock never stopped ticking.

'And what might you be looking for, Daniel?'

Good question. He turned to see the amiable moon-like face of a librarian with whom he'd enjoyed a chat on a couple of previous visits. An avid fan of his television series, she had an encyclopaedic knowledge of fell-walks in the South Lakes, Hugh Walpole's novels and the Picturesque Movement of the late eighteenth century. Daniel told her that he'd heard of the murder of Warren Howe and been unable to resist the urge to look it up.

'They never found who did it, you know.'

'It's never too late,' he assured her. 'There's something fascinating about an unsolved crime, don't you think?'

'Oh, absolutely! My husband's family comes from Hawkshead, they know the Gleaves. They're the folk who owned the garden where the man was murdered. Roz publishes local books, we have a selection of her latest titles in the rack over there. Nice woman, she comes in every six months with her new catalogue, she doesn't run to a sales force. Actually, Chris Gleave wasn't around at the time, poor Roz was there on her own.'

'He wasn't around?'

'He's a musician, and arty types can be temperamental, can't they? Mood swings. Well, he disappeared for weeks and it turned out he'd gone off to London and had some sort of mental collapse.'

'So he wasn't even in the Lake District at the time of the murder?'

'No, but then, nobody could ever imagine that Chris Gleave would hurt a fly. I only met him years ago, when he did a gig in Ulverston. I bought a CD of his songs and he autographed it for me. Very meek and mild, not the sort of chap who trashes his hotel room or runs around with young floosies. Roz must have been beside herself when he went off like that, without as much as a by-your-leave, and then she had to cope with all the trauma of policemen tramping through her house and grounds in their size twelves. For all I know, they suspected the poor woman of killing Chris as well and burying his body in the vegetable patch. It must have been hellish. But when he finally showed up and asked for forgiveness, she took him back without a murmur.'

'And they both lived happily ever after?'

The librarian gave him a guileless smile. 'Oh yes. They'd been through so much, it must have drawn them even closer together.'

'Be honest with me, Kirsty,' Bel Jenner said. 'You look washed-out and tired. Are you sure you feel well enough to work this evening?'

'I'll be fine.'

'Because if you're not up to it, you'd be better off going home.'

'No thanks, I'll be OK.'

Bel's face clouded. 'It's just that, if you are sickening for something, we don't want the customers catching a bug, do we? It's not just your welfare, it's a question of health and safety.'

Typical. Bel was generous to a fault, and capable of charming and apparently spontaneous little kindnesses, but she took good care of herself and her business at the same time. Kirsty even wondered if she'd had an ulterior motive in starting her relationship with Oliver in the first place. Bel had lost a good chef around the same time as losing her husband. She'd needed someone to fill the vacancy in her kitchen as well as in her bedroom.

'Honestly, I'll manage.' Kirsty lowered her voice. Confidential, woman to woman. 'It's just my monthly, that's all. Sometimes it hits me very hard. You know how it is.'

'Oh, yes. Of course.'

Bel gave a vague nod and bustled back to the kitchen. Probably to grope Oliver – she was so bloody tactile, that woman, it was past a joke. Kirsty reckoned Bel didn't have the faintest idea how it was. Her life was so serene. It was impossible to imagine her suffering from period pains.

The blackboard listed the desserts in Bel's neat, prissy italics. Kirsty picked up a duster and rubbed out the sticky toffee pudding with frantic zeal. If only she could wipe Bel off the map so easily. There'd been a run on the desserts at lunchtime, thanks to a coachload of wrinklies from Hexham. They were members of a Darby and Joan dancing club, on their way to a tournament in Preston, but judging by the amount of food they'd put away, they'd all keel over the minute they got up for a cha-cha.

Since Mum had told her about the anonymous message, she'd been tormenting herself with unanswerable questions. More than anything, she wanted to talk to Oliver. Share her fears with him, let him comfort and reassure her. But it wasn't going to happen. She wasn't a fool, she had to be realistic. The minute she started talking to him about the murder, he'd back right off. When she'd first worked here, once or twice, she'd mentioned her father, but Warren Howe was a conversational no-go area. Oliver and her father hadn't known each other well, and Kirsty guessed that Oliver's distaste stemmed from the fact that Bel was one of the notches on her father's bedstead. Probably, he was glad that her father was dead. Like Sam.

And like her mother? Kirsty had never been able to read her mind. As a kid, she'd assumed that her parents were deeply in love, that the late night rows and the crockery-throwing were not signs of anything wrong with the marriage, but rather a token of how much they cared. Growing up, she'd assumed that her mother was devastated by the murder. If she'd been sleeping with Peter Flint at the time, that changed everything. What if Dad had found out? His temper was volcanic.

She went down the passageway leading to the customer toilet. Out of hours, it was a sanctuary. She locked herself in the cubicle and dialled Sam on her mobile. It was a lovely afternoon, he should be hard at work, but as soon as he answered, she could tell that he was on the skive. In the background she could hear heavy metal music blaring from a jukebox and shrill drunken female laughter.

'I need to talk to you. It's about Mum. She's had an anonymous letter and it says she was sleeping with Peter at the time Dad was killed.'

'What are you mithering me for?' The disembodied tones combined boredom with bad temper. With each year that passed, he sounded and acted more like their father at his worst. Obviously there was no chance of his apologising for hurting her.

'Is it true?'

'How the fuck should I know? I'm hardly going to ask her, am I?' His voice was faintly slurred. It was still early, but he was a fast drinker. She only hoped he'd left his motorbike at home. One of these days, he'd kill someone. If not himself.

'What about asking Peter?'

'Are you losing your marbles? What do you expect me to do, walk up to my boss and demand to know if he was shagging Mum while Dad was alive? He may be a feeble little wimp, but even he would sack me for that.'

'But don't you see? If it is true, and this person who's sending the letters knows all her secrets, who knows what else is going to come out?'

'It was a long time ago. Who cares?'

'I care, Sam. And so should you. Don't you see? If the police found out, Mum would be a prime suspect.'

For a few moments she could hear nothing except the racket from the pub jukebox. She knew her brother well enough to realise he was scouring his vocabulary for some brutal putdown.

'You're mad. I don't have the foggiest when they first got it together. But if anyone should be shitting himself, it isn't Mum, it's that smug bastard Peter. After all, he finished up with her and the business, didn't he?'

While Daniel visited Kendal, Miranda and Louise had gone to Grasmere, destination Dove Cottage. Returning home, he remembered that he hadn't eaten anything since toast and marmalade for breakfast. Hunger pangs reminded him of Oxford, when he could spend a day delving into the Bodleian archives before thinking of his stomach. Talking to Hannah had made him forget about food but now he was ready for a little self-indulgence. Miranda was on a healthy eating crusade, but her absence gave him a chance to sin with a chunky bacon and egg bap coated in brown sauce. After washing his lunch down with a can of lager, he went upstairs to continue his researches.

The makeshift study would become a spare bedroom once the renovations were completed, although if the builders didn't get a move on, he might be ready for a stair lift by the time the project was finished. Even now most of his books were in crates. A handful of whodunits squatted on low shelves alongside a pile of CDs and a snap he'd taken of Miranda, showing off her long smooth legs as she lazed on a recliner by the tarn. There was nothing to remind him of Oxford, far less of Aimee. He'd wanted to leave his past behind. Though sometimes he wondered if it was madness to believe that might be possible.

A Google search didn't add much to his stock of knowledge about the murder and soon he was navigating the Flint Howe Garden Design website, learning that Peter Flint was a Royal Horticultural Society Chelsea Flower Show medal winner among various other accolades. A gallery of photographs showed 'before' and 'after' shots of drab patches of lawn becoming mini-Sissinghursts. Encomiums abounded from clients whose herbaceous borders, rockeries and patios had been transformed into visions of light, water and colour. The website answered frequently asked questions about the sensitive use of decking in a suburban environment and offered tips on composting and establishing an organic garden. No suggestion that dumping a body in your back yard was recommended for fertilising the ground for years to come.

Daniel clicked on to the site contact details. In the corner of the page was a name in small type. Enquirers were invited to email the firm's 'Client Liaison Partner'. Her name was Tina Howe.

He swivelled in his chair, closing his eyes to let the news sink in. Presumably Tina had inherited her husband's share in the business, but wouldn't most widows take their money and run? Back at the home page, he studied the photo of Peter Flint. Curly, greying hair, spectacles, crooked front teeth. He looked vague and good-natured, not accustomed to getting his hands dirty. Perhaps Tina Howe had tired of her rugged husband and fancied offering his partner a spot of personal assistance? What if...?

Don't go there. He slammed his fist on the desk. He should have learned, it was dangerous to get involved in a case of murder. Not so long ago, he'd looked death in the eye and hadn't liked what he'd seen.

And yet, hunting the truth fired him, it became a obsession impossible to quell, whatever the cost. At last he'd come to understand why his father cared for police work. They shared the need to know.

The front door crashed. He imagined Miranda sniffing the air before calling out, 'Who's been having a fry-up, then?'

He wandered downstairs and they told him about their day. To listen to Miranda badmouthing selfish drivers in Grasmere and the unpredictability of the bus services, one might think she was a native. As she chatted, Daniel kept glancing at Louise. She was on her best behaviour, nodding agreement at suitable intervals and laughing at every witty remark. The perfect guest.

He nodded towards the garden. 'We need help sorting this out. There's a good firm Hawkshead way. I thought I'd give them a ring, ask them to take a look and give us their advice.'

'Fine.'

Miranda resumed her account of what she would show Louise tomorrow. For her, the garden was a place to relax, nothing more. She wouldn't have minded if he'd announced that he meant to dig it all up and replant every square inch. As long as she could sit by the water's edge and soak up the sun, who cared if someone had long ago laid out the grounds according to an unfathomable design?

When she took the tea things back inside, Louise pulled her chair closer to Daniel's. 'So then, what did you get up to in Kendal?'

'I spent an hour in the library. Nothing special.'

'Is that all?'

He frowned at her. 'Meaning?'

'You're wearing your faraway look. Suppressed excitement, something going on in your own little world while you nod your head at appropriate points in the conversation. You weren't listening to Miranda, she doesn't know you well enough yet to realise. I remember that look from when Mum was scolding you for not putting your bike in the garage and all the time you were thinking about that tarty girl from Manor Drive.'

He couldn't help grinning. 'You never liked Simone, did you? Just because she over-did the make-up.'

'It wasn't only the make-up. And don't change the subject. What are you up to?'

He shifted under her steady gaze. 'I've been doing some research.'

Her smile was sceptical. 'It's obviously turning you on.'

'Just because I've escaped from Oxford, that doesn't mean I want my brain to atrophy.'

'It's not your brain I'm wondering about.'

Miranda called from the open kitchen window, 'Anyone fancy a glass of Chablis?'

Louise turned her head and waved her thanks. Softly, she said, 'Miranda's lovely, Daniel. Not your usual type of lady friend, though.'

'Is there a type? Leaving Simone out of it?'

'Well, yes. Pretty, intense, introspective.'

'Christ.' He was startled that she'd given his love life a moment's thought. He'd assumed she was too wrapped up in her own affairs of the heart. 'Actually, I'd say Miranda fits the bill.'

'Mmmmm. Not sure about introspective. I'm not saying that it matters. I just want you to be happy, that's all.'

'We are.'

'Long term, I mean.'

'We will be.'

'Glad to hear it,' she whispered as Miranda approached, bearing a tray laden with wine cooler and glasses.

But he wasn't sure that she believed him.

'Your garden is gorgeous,' Hannah Scarlett said.

Roz Gleave nodded. 'I can see what you're thinking. A lovely place to die.'

Hannah grimaced, not least because she seldom encountered strangers who could read her mind. Even in the heat of the afternoon, Roz was cool and composed in white blouse and jeans. She was a tall woman with decisive movements; it was impossible to imagine her giving a slinky wiggle of the bum. With her thick grey hair and lack of make-up, she made no concessions to vanity, yet there was something about her cast of features and strong jaw-line that was oddly attractive. Not glamorous, but striking. Handsome, even.

They were facing each other across a wrought-iron table on the patio at the back of Keepsake Cottage. Behind them was an extension to the original house, from where Roz ran her publishing business. Through the windows Hannah could see piles of shrink-wrapped books in cardboard boxes. On the slope above the cottage was the spot where Warren Howe's slashed corpse had been dumped in a hole in the earth, but his only memorial was a rose bush with huge yellow blooms. Roz had served Earl Grey and Battenberg cake; de Quincey was snoozing at their feet in a wicker basket. Very civilised: a murder site transformed into a backdrop for a tea party.

'Tell me about finding the body.'

'You must have this in your files.'

'Refresh my memory.'

Roz sighed. 'I spent the day in Lancashire, with a firm of library suppliers. A nerve-shredding presentation of our latest titles. I left home at half seven, to make final preparations at our office before I set off. Warren's van passed me in the lane, he used to say he liked an early start and an early dart. The weather was miserable, but he didn't care.'

'Did you stop for a word?'

'No, I waved, he winked back, and we drove past each other. It was the last time I saw him alive, but I didn't give him another thought until I got home. My main aim was to keep myself busy. Anything to avoid dwelling on what might have happened to Chris. What I dreaded might have happened…'

A frown flitted across Roz Gleave's face as she adjusted her dark glasses. A woman unwilling to surrender to her emotions, or to the urge to colour her hair. If she'd been shaken by the request for a meeting, she'd given no sign of it, agreeing a convenient time with the brisk efficiency of a woman who had succeeded in keeping a small press afloat in an unforgiving business climate.

Hannah said gently, 'You and Warren were friends?'

'We went back a long way.'

'Not the same thing.'

'No.' Roz smiled. 'Come on, this sun is too harsh for a skin as fair as yours, let's sit in the shade.'

She led the way up the sprawling terraced grounds, past lupins jostling with tall ornanmental grasses, towards a teak arbour seat. Hannah sat beside her on the plump cream cushion. Lawns across the county were parched, but this wild garden remained fresh. A stream gurgled down the slope, white butterflies circled a late-flowering mint with a soft lavender haze. Through the branches of an ash tree Hannah could see sunlit patterns on Esthwaite Water. A dark blue wisteria threaded through gaps in the trellis, and she inhaled its perfume.

As if reading her mind, Roz said, 'Special, isn't it? Thanks to Peter Flint – and Warren. You know, Warren used to have a phrase about wild gardens. No moss, no magic.'

'Perhaps he was right.'

'He was no saint, Chief Inspector, but he was no fool, either.'

Hannah was tempted to close her eyes. On the most humid day so far this year, she felt unbearably lethargic, as if she might be going down with flu in the midst of the heatwave. But she must stay focused to glean anything from the conversation. Murder had been committed on Roz's doorstep; she must have ideas about what had led to it. Her original statement was brusque and uninformative. Charlie's team hadn't pressed the right buttons, but this was a second chance.

'You arrived back here that afternoon shortly before five, according to your statement.'

'The first surprise was that I couldn't park in the garage because Warren's van was parked in the drive, blocking the way. I expected him to have gone home by that time. I assumed he was engrossed and didn't want to finish half way through a particular job. I went inside, changed out of my business suit and poured myself a glass of plonk. A tiny celebration. Without Chris, I hadn't had much cause to cheer myself up, but I was in better heart because the people in Lytham had been so positive about our titles. I took a couple of sips and then wandered outside to have a word with Warren. See if he fancied a drink himself.'

'So you were on good terms?'

'If you're wondering whether Warren reckoned his luck was in, working for an old flame whose husband had left her, think again. I'm not exactly a sex goddess these days, I'm not sure I ever was, even in my teens, but he wasn't above trying it on, just for the hell of it. Actually, he was a satyr, but he knew the score. Chris was the only man for me.'

'But you were afraid Chris was dead.'

'Even so.' Roz stared down towards the cottage, and Hannah guessed she was picturing the scene that had greeted her that afternoon. 'I came through that door from the kitchen, made my way up the slope. At first I couldn't see anything untoward. I called his name, but there was no reply. Odd, but no alarm bells rang.'

'Warren wasn't someone you could imagine suffering an accident?'

'That's right. Nothing ever knocked him off stride, stopped him from doing what he wanted to do. I could see where he'd been digging. He'd piled up the turves he'd dug and his wheelbarrow was full of weeds and pebbles. As I moved closer, I saw the ground was streaked with red. When I looked into the trench, for a split second, I didn't realise the bloody lump was

Warren. To tell you the truth, there are still times when I can't quite believe it. For him to be killed like that...'

'How well did you know him?'

'Old Sawrey is a small place. He wasn't easy to avoid.'

'And in your teens you went out with him?'

'For a few weeks. That wasn't easy to avoid, either. I was fourteen, an age when a little flattery goes a long way. One thing about Warren, he was persistent. It was scarcely a remake of *Brief Encounter*. His claim to fame in my life was that he was the first boy to put his hand inside my knickers.'

Roz's wry grin was infectious and Hannah couldn't help smiling. 'Very romantic. And that was why you split up?'

'No, he lost interest. Just as he had done with Bel before me. Thank God, it didn't ruin our friendship. If anything, it brought us closer together. We cried on each other's shoulders.'

'He was a charmer?'

'Oh yes, he could blarney like an Irishman when he was in the mood. Bel and I were young enough and naïve enough to fall for it.'

'You didn't have any qualms about becoming his client?'

'He and Peter were very good at what they did, so it was a no-brainer. Chris and I would have been crazy to look elsewhere, simply because he'd given me the heave-ho all those years earlier. There was no animosity, not that we were close after we broke up, let alone after each of us got married. He and Tina were very different from Chris and me. But so what?'

'Do you ever see Tina?'

'Every now and then we bump into her at The Heights. Chris and I are regulars and since Kirsty started working for Bel, Tina and Peter often go there for a meal.'

'Peter?'

'Peter Flint.' A mischievous grin. 'Don't tell me you didn't know?'

This was the moment that Hannah longed for in any investigation, the rush of excitement when a case took a fresh turn. For all her fatigue, it reminded her why she couldn't conceive of taking any other job. The only comparison was waiting for a lover's touch. With this difference: she had to conceal what she felt inside.

Clearing her throat, she took refuge in the formal jargon of officialdom. 'I'm simply gathering information at present. You're the first person I've spoken to in connection with this crime.'

'Should I feel honoured – or alarmed?'

'No need for alarm, Mrs Gleave.'

'Please, call me Roz.'

OK, Roz, let's hear it. 'Are you telling me that Tina Howe married her husband's old business colleague?'

'Oh no. Peter only got round to divorcing poor old Gail the other week, though they separated ages ago. He and Tina have been a couple in the meantime.'

'They live together?'

'Not permanently. She still keeps the house she used to share with Warren. Sam and Kirsty haven't left home yet. Sam works with Peter.'

'Small world.'

'Village life, Chief Inspector.'

'Any gossip about Tina and Peter getting together?'

'Loads.' Roz giggled. 'What else is juicy enough to natter about during long winter evenings in Old Sawrey? But you must understand, the locals take Gail Flint's side. Not that there are many locals left in the village. Every other house for miles around is a holiday let or a second home for an accountant from Manchester.'

'Gail was born here?'

'Yes, Peter's a foreigner. That is, his family come from Penrith. Might as well be Paraguay as far as the natives of Old Sawrey are concerned.'

'So what do the gossips say about him and Tina?'

'You'll have to ask someone else, Chief Inspector,' Roz said with a smile. 'Me, I never listen to tittle-tattle. Personally, I'm just glad they've found happiness.'

A likely story. Hannah decided against pressing. Roz would reveal exactly what she wanted to reveal, no more, no less. Time to open another front.

'I gather Warren had a high opinion of himself.'

'Part of a man's genetic programming, isn't it? Chris is an honourable exception, he's unbelievably self-effacing, I've never once heard him boast, far less run anyone else down. Warren was the opposite. He never worried if he trod on people's toes.'

'Did he make enemies?'

'Scores, probably. "Take me as you find me," that was his mantra. Most people decided they were better off leaving him. Other than Tina, she stuck with him through thick and thin. Talk about long-suffering.'

'Any hint she might have been looking for an exit route?'

'Divorce? God, no.' Roz raised her thick eyebrows. 'She's not stupid, she went into that marriage with her eyes open. She knew perfectly well what she was letting herself in for.'

'Including infidelity?'

'Part of the package, with Warren. Then again, who knows what really goes on inside someone else's marriage?' Roz glanced at Hannah's ring finger. 'You're single?'

'I have a partner. You're right, it's impossible to be sure what makes other people's relationships tick – but you might hazard a guess. Why would Warren Howe want to tie himself down, if he wanted to keep playing the field? As for Tina, you say she's no fool, so why did she stay married to a serial philanderer?'

Roz stood up and shrugged. 'Sex, presumably. That's the usual answer, isn't it, to most questions?'

Was there a flicker of amused contempt in the words, scorn for those who were slaves to lust? Hannah wondered if the jealousy to which Roz had confessed had faded as quickly as she claimed. Maybe it lingered, maybe she'd still hankered after Warren despite knowing his faults.

She followed Roz along the path. 'Your husband was away from home at the time of the murder. Must have been hard, coping on your own.'

'It was never going to be easy, whatever the circumstances. Imagine, Chief Inspector. Your husband has vanished and you come home from work one day, to find that the bloke you hired to sort out your garden has been scythed to death and deposited in a trench he excavated himself. But that's not all. He wasn't some boring stranger, he was an ex. Someone you got over in your teens, someone you still pass the time of day with. There's always the tug of nostalgia, if hardly romance. How do you think that made me feel, Chief Inspector?'

Hannah didn't have an answer. They strolled on through the wild garden, moving down the terraces towards the house. The fragrance of the roses hung in the air.

Roz broke the silence. 'What makes you think you can solve the case, after so many years?'

'As I said, we've received new information.'

'Which you're not prepared to disclose.'

'Sorry, Mrs Gleave. My job is to ask, not answer. Is your husband due back soon?'

Roz consulted her wrist-watch. 'Chris is a law unto himself. I told you on the phone, he's been recording a show for hospital radio. Could be five minutes, could be five hours. But he was in London when Warren was murdered. He can't help you.'

'I'll judge that, if you don't mind.'

Everyone had a weak spot, every recalcitrant interviewee had a topic they hated talking about. Hannah suspected that with Roz Gleave, it was her husband.

De Quincey had roused himself from his slumbers and was barking enthusiastically, no doubt angling to be taken for a walk. At Roz's invitation, Hannah stroked his rough fur while inspecting the terracotta thermometer hanging on the outside wall. Twenty five degrees Celsius, even at this time of day. No wonder she felt exhausted.

'Had he disappeared before?'

'Not for so long. Once or twice he went away for twenty four hours. But not that length of time.'

'What did you think had happened?'

'If you insist, I thought he was dead. Chris is very sensitive, nobody knows that better than me. I thought the man I loved had killed himself, that marriage to me hadn't been enough to make his life worth living.'

'And then he turned up safe and sound?'

'As you say.' Roz swallowed. 'I was wrong to doubt him. I tell him, he's like a Herdwick sheep, he has the same homing instinct. That's why Herdwicks don't have to be fenced in, isn't it? Well, Chris doesn't need to be fenced in, either. I'd trust him with my life.'

'So you forgave him for causing you such distress?'

'Of course. I swore that I'd never let anything come between us again. And I never have, Chief Inspector. Never will.'

Peter Flint's office was a brick-built extension to the house he had once shared with his wife. Kirsty presumed that the cost of buying out Gail's share was the reason he'd never moved or separated his business premises from his home. Gail had insisted on having her pound of flesh in the divorce settlement – Tina liked to say Peter's ex needed the money to pay for the booze she drank herself instead of selling to her customers. Just as well Flint Howe Garden Design was supposed to be thriving, though there were few obvious signs of affluence. Peter's Renault needed a wash and a paint repair to a scrape on the bumper. In the past, Kirsty had found his lack of ostentation appealing, had been happy for her mother when she'd announced they were seeing each other. But that was before the letters had arrived.

Vertical blinds hung in the window and she could not see inside. A neat label read 'Please ring for reception', but the door wasn't shut properly and Kirsty walked straight in. The walls were covered from floor to ceiling with Tina's photographs of gorgeous gardens. Brilliant orange Chilean firebushes, elaborate mosaic paths of silver and grey, marble water features with concealed lighting and exotic steel sculptures with unexpected peepholes that resembled deformed Polo mints.

Her mother was bending over Peter Flint's desk, handing him a note torn from a telephone pad. The floral leggings were a mistake, Kirsty thought. Their heads were almost touching. Even though they were talking business, the intimacy between them was palpable. Kirsty cringed.

'Here is the address and phone number,' Tina said. 'His name is Kind. The cottage is at the far end of Brackdale, he said. Beyond the Hall.'

'You've booked me in for tomorrow?'

'I told him you were busy, but he insisted that...' Tina spun round. 'Kirsty! Don't you believe in knocking? What on earth are you doing here?'

'I wanted a word.'

'Couldn't it wait till I got back home?'

'I never know when you will be home these days.'

Tina's features hardened. No matter how she tried, she was unable to resist an argument. Perhaps marriage had done that to her, Kirsty thought, perhaps her willingness to stand up for herself had kept Dad interested.

'Sorry, I didn't realise I had to keep to a timetable.'

Peter scrambled to his feet and grabbed a folder from his desk. 'Look, if you two girls fancy a chat in private, I'll make myself scarce.'

'No,' Tina said. 'I don't have secrets from you, darling.'

That *darling* seemed unnecessary. Typical Mum, marking out her territory. Making clear where her loyalties lay. Perhaps they'd lain there for a long, long time.

'This concerns you as well, Peter,' Kirsty said.

'Me?' He blinked behind his glasses. 'I'm sorry, I don't understand.'

Peter Flint's expression suggested an amiable, absent-minded owl. Lately, Kirsty had begun to suspect that his good-natured vagueness about anything unconnected with his work, was a façade. For all his bumbling demeanour, he had a priceless knack of getting whatever he wanted. He must possess hidden reserves of determination.

She turned to her mother. 'Have you told him about the letters?'

Tina gave a long and theatrical sigh. 'So that's what this performance is all about?'

'Have you told him?' Kirsty said again through gritted teeth. Her mother had a flair for moving the goalposts. She'd had a lot of practice when Dad was alive; it was her technique for bringing their quarrels to an end. Sometimes it hadn't worked, sometimes plates had been thrown.

'If you mean the anonymous letters flying around,' Peter Flint said, 'Tina didn't need to tell me about them. I told her as soon as one came to me.'

'What did it say?'

'It was offensive rubbish which deserved to be put through the shredder and that's precisely what I did with it.'

'Because it accused you of having it off with Mum while my father was still alive?'

He blinked again. 'You don't…'

Arms folded, she leaned back. 'All I want you to tell me is whether it's true.'

Tina took a couple of paces forward and seized hold of her wrist. 'Do you want to know, Kirsty? Do you really want to know?'

Her grip hurt, almost as much as Sam's drunken grasp had hurt. All of a sudden, Kirsty wasn't sure any more what she did want to know. Yet could the truth be any more painful than the anguish of guesswork?

'I can imagine,' she said furiously and tugged herself free.

'Kirsty,' Peter said. 'Please listen to me. This is upsetting your mother. You don't understand.'

'You know what, Peter? I'm beginning to understand a great deal about your…relationship.'

Tina folded her arms. 'All right, then. I'll satisfy your curiosity if you want. You've got it all wrong. So has whoever keeps sending these bloody letters. Peter and I never slept together before your father died.'

'I don't believe you.'

'Believe what you want, you stupid little cow. It's the truth.'

Chapter Nine

'You know my sergeant, I gather,' Hannah said. 'Nick Lowther?'

Chris Gleave nodded. 'We were at school together. A good man.'

'Yes.'

'Bright, too. I'd expected him to have made Chief Superintendent by now. If not Chief Constable. But perhaps that's not what he became a policeman for.'

'Perhaps not.'

Chris put his hands behind his head, as if in aid to thought. A slender fair-haired man in a white open neck shirt and beige chinos, he looked younger than his years. Hannah didn't often encounter men as handsome as Marc, but Chris might be a contender. Not that she fancied him. Despite Nick's glowing testimonial, beneath the agreeable exterior, she sensed something cool and distant.

'He had this weird idea that your job is to serve justice, as I remember. I suppose you can do that as easily as a sergeant as a superintendent. Especially if the police service is like most hierarchical organisations. The higher you climb the greasy pole, the more careful you have to be not to upset the people at the top.'

'I couldn't possibly comment,' she said, allowing him a faint smile.

'Nick could be too sardonic for his own good. I remember that one of our rugby teachers really had it in for him and...'

'More tea, Chief Inspector?'

Roz bustled through the door, bearing a crowded tray. From the moment Chris had arrived home, she hadn't left them alone for longer than it took to boil a kettle. She fussed around her husband like an over-protective mother with an only child. Was their marriage like this all the time, Hannah wondered, or was she afraid of what he might say to a detective asking about Warren Howe?

'No, thank you. I don't expect to keep your husband long.'

Roz put the tray down on an occasional table. The furniture in Keepsake Cottage was old and made of pine, the china Crown

Derby. Hannah's chair faced a huge oval mirror, which revealed that she had a ladder in her tights.

After pouring a cup for Chris and herself, Roz sat on the sofa beside him. Their thighs were touching, and she looped an arm around his thin shoulder. Some men would have betrayed embarrassment, but not Chris Gleave. Legs negligently crossed, he gave the impression of a man at ease with himself, unaware of his wife's attentions. Possibly he expected nothing less.

'So what's caused you to investigate what happened?' he asked.

What happened. Hannah remembered the pictures of Warren Howe's from the autopsy. She banished the image. Better not throw up all over such a lovely old Persian rug.

'My team has a brief to review unsolved murders. It's one of a number of cases we're reconsidering.'

'Pure routine, then? No new leads?'

'I'm afraid the details of our inquiry are confidential.'

'I wish you luck. Warren wasn't a nice man, but nobody deserves to die like that. So how can I help?'

'Can we talk about the statement that you gave to the police when you…returned home after the murder?'

'There's nothing to add.'

'I was saying to your wife earlier, it's surprising how often, after a lapse of time, something else springs to mind. Something you might have overlooked previously, or thought too unimportant to mention.'

Chris shook his head. 'Not me. I'm afraid I didn't have anything to contribute to your colleagues' investigation all those years ago and nothing's changed.'

'So you can't cast any light on the case? Even though the murder was committed in your back garden? And the victim was a man you'd known for years?'

'Roz knew him better and longer than me.'

'You were aware that she was Warren Howe's girlfriend in her teens? Until – sorry, Mrs Gleave – he chucked her?'

'All that was history,' Chris said quickly. 'They had a fleeting teenage romance. No lasting significance for either party. Far less me. Water under the bridge.'

Roz's cheeks were rose-pink. 'You're surely not suggesting Chris was jealous? Jealous of Warren?'

'I'm not suggesting anything. You told my colleagues that you had no idea that Warren Howe's body had been found in your garden while you were away, Mr Gleave.'

'Absolutely.'

'Must have been quite a shock.'

Chris exhaled. 'To be honest with you, Chief Inspector, I'd been through a great deal in a short time. I hate to sound cold-blooded, but hearing about the death of a man who was scarcely a friend was the least of my problems. What horrified me was to learn that I'd left my wife to cope on her own with all the sound and fury of a murder investigation. It was a long, long time before I forgave myself for that.'

'But you managed to forgive yourself in the end?'

The barb didn't even graze him. 'Life is short, isn't it? We beat ourselves up all the time, and so often it's for no purpose whatsoever. I've often made the mistake of feeling guilty over something trivial that wasn't even my fault. Perhaps you have yourself, once or twice?'

Hannah prayed she wasn't blushing. 'I'm sorry to pry, but can you tell me about the circumstances of your disappearance?'

Roz made as if to protest, but he silenced her with a sideways glance. 'If you've read the old files, you'll know as much as me.'

For the first time, there was a note of irritation in his voice and Hannah cheered inwardly. She hadn't lost her touch after all; she could still shake the calmest witness. 'Even so, I'd be grateful. Unless you have a particular objection?'

'I didn't hold anything back.'

'Your explanation for your disappearance was that you'd suffered a nervous breakdown.'

'As it happens, that was the doctors' diagnosis. Or whatever medical term they use. Anxiety, depression, stress, whatever. The bottom line is, I was a mess. Overwrought, not thinking straight.'

'Chief Inspector, you don't realise,' Roz muttered.

'I'd slaved night and day over the CD, but the whole project was going pear-shaped. I'd have found it easier if the reviewers had hated my music. Instead they said it was bland, uninspired. Someone compared it to flock wallpaper, for God's sake. The CD was meant to be a turning point, a crowning achievement after years of sweat and tears, but it sank like a stone in a sea of critical indifference. I simply couldn't handle it. Can you understand that, Chief Inspector Scarlett?'

'Well,' Hannah said judiciously, 'I've never brought out a CD.'

'I decided I was a rotten failure, that I'd embarrassed Roz and everyone else who'd believed in me. I just wanted to crawl away somewhere and hide out of sight.'

Roz squeezed his hand. 'You never embarrassed anyone, darling.'

'Why go to London?' Hannah asked.

'It's vast and anonymous. People you pass in the street couldn't care less whether you live or die. Perfect if you want to escape.'

'Did you have friends there?'

He nibbled at his fingernails. 'I told you, it was precisely because I wanted to run from the people I was close to that I headed to a city where no-one knew me. I didn't take much money, little more than the clothes I stood up in. I found a crummy bed-sit and did a bit of busking to pay the rent. Not that I managed to earn enough, even to live in such a hell-hole. I started drinking heavily. God knows, if I'd stayed there much longer, I might have ended up sleeping in a gin-soaked cardboard box under Waterloo Bridge.'

'So why didn't you, what brought you back?'

He took Roz's hand in his. 'My wife saved me, Chief Inspector, simple as that.'

'It was down to you,' Roz said. 'You had the courage to make that phone call.'

Pass the sickbag, Hannah thought. She drummed her fingers against the arm of her chair, wanting them to get on with the story.

'I had too much to drink one night and started getting homesick. I'd been so selfish, so cruel, walking out on Roz without a word. She hadn't a clue where I was, what I was up to.'

'I explained to the Chief Inspector.' Roz paled as the memories returned. ' I realised you were unhappy, but you'd retreated so far inside yourself that not even I could reach you. I was so afraid that one morning I'd wake up and a policeman would be banging on the door, come to break the news that your body had been found in some cave or on a fell.'

Chris said hoarsely, 'The instant I dialled this number, I started to panic. What would I say, how could I make up for all the harm I'd done? Thank the Lord Roz snatched up the receiver. If she hadn't, even Dutch courage wouldn't have let me try a second time. Tell you what, Chief Inspector. Once we'd talked for a couple of minutes, I began to sober up. Come to my senses. I was in tears, mind. But they were happy tears.'

'I told him I still loved him,' Roz said. 'We all make mistakes.'

'I asked if she'd take me back,' Chris said. 'And she didn't hesitate.'

'Not that I've regretted it.' Roz squeezed his hand. 'Not for a moment. I promise you that, Chief Inspector.'

Hannah grunted. Faced with such connubial bliss, she was lost for words. Or at least words that she could decently utter.

And they all lived happily ever after. Except for Warren Howe.

'You're a lucky man, Daniel Kind,' Miranda said.

'Uh-huh.'

An hour ago Louise had announced her intention to go for a walk and explore the far side of Tarn Fold, along the beck beyond the old corn mill. He'd seldom seen her so relaxed; already Rodney was a fading memory. While she was out, he'd been surfing the net, searching in vain for information about the Quillers. He was hunched over his computer screen when Miranda came up behind him and started massaging his shoulders. As the tension trickled away, Miranda took off his shirt. Her long bony fingers were working at his flesh with a steady rhythm.

'I mean,' she murmured, 'you don't just have me. You have a lovely sister of your own as well.'

'No comparison.' He breathed in her musky scent. 'Promise.'

'What I mean is, she's your own flesh and blood. That's so special, you don't realise.'

Miranda had been adopted by an elderly childless couple, who had striven to give her everything she asked for. By her own admission, it was never enough and she'd repaid their idolatry with childhood tantrums, and later a determination to indulge in everything they disapproved of. Within weeks of her twenty-first, both of them were dead and it was too late for guilt about her youthful ingratitude. As for her birth mother, she'd never met the woman, knew nothing of her.

'You could always...'

'Trace her and suggest we get together for a cup of tea? Pray for a tearful reunion with lots of hugs and kisses?' Her fingers stopped moving. 'I don't think so.'

'It might be the best thing you ever did.'

'She rejected me once. That's enough for anyone.'

Above his desk was a framed watercolour of Buttermere in myriad shades of blue and green. Reflected in the glass, her face creased in distress. The pain bit deep, he knew, and yet in her shoes he would not have been able to rest until he had solved the mysteries of the past.

'We all deserve a second chance.'

'Listen, if she shut the door on me again, I don't know what I'd do. It would be more than I could bear.'

He didn't want to let it go. The law had been changed to allow birth mothers to track down the children they'd given away through intermediary agencies. Even though she didn't have to agree to meet, she might yet be contacted out of the blue and then feel guilty for not having made the first move.

'For all you know, somewhere out there you have a ready-made family of your own.'

She raked his skin with her nails. 'Who are quite happy as they are and don't need some neurotic female turning up for a cosy chat by the fireside.'

'You're not neurotic.'

She was breathing hard, he could feel the warmth on his bare neck. 'How old will she be now – forty odd? Presumably she was young when she had me. I must have been a mistake, an accident. A cause of untold angst. She'll have spent the last twenty odd years trying to make a new life. She's probably settled down, scrubbed me out of her mind. Or simply forgotten I was ever born.'

'She won't have forgotten.'

'One thing she won't want is a skeleton climbing out of her cupboard.'

He swivelled in his chair. 'How can you be so sure?'

'Suppose she was very, very young when I was born? Suppose she was raped? It frightens me even to think about it.' Tears were forming in her eyes and he cursed inwardly for pushing too hard. 'You just don't know what it's like, being on your own.'

'Hey, you're not on your own.' He stood up and took her hand in his. 'I'm so sorry, I never meant to...'

'You don't realise, do you? When I see you with Louise, I feel so fucking jealous!'

He stared at her pretty face, contorted with anguish, unsure what to say or do.

The front door banged. Louise's voice floated up the stairs. 'I'm back!'

Oliver, she needed to be with Oliver. If only they could spend long enough together, he would come to understand her better, appreciate that she was ready to give him anything he could ever want. Not money, obviously, she couldn't match Bel on that score. But cash in the bank couldn't compete with a burning desire.

After the disastrous encounter with her mother and her boyfriend, Kirsty hurried straight home. Back at the house, she ran upstairs and stepped under a cold shower. The icy water was a sweet torment, a means of washing away the grubbiness of her family, of her life.

She changed into a purple top with a high neck and set off again for the restaurant. Her long strides took her past a group of middle-aged men in expensive hiking gear. A small bloke with a film of sweat on his brow gave her breasts a lingering look, a man with a serious beer belly whistled at her. It said something about the mess of her life that it was the nicest thing that had happened all day.

As she entered the restaurant car park, she spotted the two Croatian girls, little and large like cartoon characters, loitering near the side door. They were having a quick smoke before getting ready for dinner. Veselka waved. She put on a smile and waved back, thinking: it's your lungs you're ruining. Why didn't people look after their health better? If they didn't watch out they'd finish up in a cancer ward. Sam was even worse; it was as if he had a death wish.

The kitchen windows were open. Kirsty had developed a habit of skirting along the front of the building and past the windows on her way in to the restaurant. Sometimes she heard Oliver and Bel having a private conversation, nothing to do with problems at the wholesalers' or the best place to buy strawberries this summer. It was fascinating to listen to people talk when they didn't know you were there. All the more so when one was the man you yearned for. She might have been a forensic scientist, peering through a microscope for hints of disharmony. Oliver always seemed crazy about her, it had to be a sham. He was trapped like a fly on sticky paper. The relationship with Bel was going nowhere, had nowhere to go.

She trembled at the sound of his voice. A week ago, Veselka had caught her eavesdropping on him in the dining room and given her a mocking smirk, as if to say: *You haven't a hope.* Jealous bitch, just because no matter how high she hitched her little black skirt, Oliver paid no attention.

Kirsty hesitated. Just my luck if Veselka comes out from round the side of the building right now, she thought. But she had to chance it. The opportunity to eavesdrop was irresistible.

'A chief inspector?' Oliver sounded awestruck.

'A woman, too. Roz was saying, you know you're getting older when even the chief inspectors are young and attractive. She said this one was friendly enough, but single-minded. Not easy to fob off.'

'Why would Roz want to fob her off?'

'Darling, who wants to be reminded of a murder?'

Kirsty flinched. The casual intimacy of that *darling* was like being soaked with a wet sponge.

'Besides, it was a thousand times worse for Roz. It was a low point in her life, what with Chris going missing as well. You can't expect her to enjoy being questioned again by the police after all this time. Just because she found the body.'

The body. Kirsty's head swam. Her knees felt as though they were about to buckle. They were discussing her father. She clutched at the window sill, desperate not to lose her balance.

'Why would they send out someone so senior?'

'She's in charge of investigating cold cases, sweetie. Roz said she recognised her from an interview on regional television a while back. They look into old crimes.'

'Why Warren's murder in particular?'

'Look at it from their point of view. No-one arrested or charged, let alone brought to trial. It was a failure, a black mark. Can you remember people being grief-stricken when he died? The police probably took it worse than anyone else.'

I always knew you were heartless. This wasn't just about Bel's insensitivity. First the letters, now a detective asking questions. What was happening in Old Sawrey, why was the past coming back to haunt everyone?

'They must have received some new information.'

'Forensic stuff, maybe, it's all the rage these days.'

'I can't believe that. Not after all this time. Remember, he was found out in the open air after a downpour. What sort of forensic evidence would be left?'

'Oh, I don't know. Roz tried to worm the details out of the chief inspector. But she was keeping her cards close to her chest.'

'So what did she want to find out?'

'Anything and everything. She even gave Chris the third degree when he turned up.'

'But he wasn't even around when Warren was killed.'

'Exactly what Roz said!'

'Sounds as though they don't have any idea.'

'We'll be able to judge for ourselves soon, darling. Roz says the police are going to talk to everyone who knew Warren.'

'Christ. Does Kirsty know?'

'It might explain why she was looking so awful at lunch-time.

I thought she was sickening for something.'

'I'm sure she's fine, it's only…'

As Kirsty craned her neck to listen, Veselka appeared from round the side of the restaurant. Her round face was split by a grin of triumph. Making her look, Kirsty thought, like some kind of manic ventriloquist's doll. With a gap between her front teeth as wide as the Kirkstone Pass. No wonder Oliver never gave her a second glance.

'Everything OK, Kirsty?' Her English was good, although the accent was hard work and she'd developed an irritating habit of making every sentence, however mundane, sound like a question. 'You don't look so happy?'

'I'm fine, thanks.'

'That's good?' Veselka giggled and blew a smoke ring into the soft summer air. 'I was worried about you today? Wondering if you might have – what would you say, boyfriend trouble?'

'So you didn't know that Peter Flint and his partner's widow were in a relationship?'

Nick Lowther shook his head. 'News to me.'

It was half six and they'd bumped into each other in the car park behind the police station. Hannah fiddled with her keys, wondering how much to tell him, and then rebuked herself for having any reservations about candour. They'd known each other a long time and she trusted him as much as any man. Even Marc.

'Who's to say that they weren't having it off at the time Warren was killed?'

'They must have taken enormous care to cover their tracks, then. If Warren Howe had caught them in flagrante, it'd have been Peter Flint's corpse that Roz stumbled over in her back garden.'

'He was the jealous type?'

'We never found any evidence of Tina giving him cause. She was the one who always had to turn a blind eye. Her line was that there's more to a marriage than sexual fidelity.'

Les Bryant, reversing out towards the exit, pipped his horn and she mouthed *goodnight*. 'Perhaps she was thinking about her own behaviour, as well as his.'

'Warren always came back to her, that was what she cared about. Or so she said.'

'He might not have been bothered if she was playing away. Sauce for the goose and all that.'

Nick made a sceptical noise. 'Warren wouldn't fret about inconsistency or double standards. And Peter shagging his missus wouldn't have appealed to his sense of irony. No, he wouldn't have rested until he'd taken revenge.'

'Suppose Tina decided to kill him before he found out?'

He considered her. 'You think she's guilty?'

'Not on the strength of an anonymous tip-off. But Roz Gleave gave me the impression she didn't have much time for Tina.'

'They were never close. Whereas she became friendly with Gail.'

'Linz is due to see Gail tomorrow. She lives near Coniston these days. Peter had to buy her a cottage as part of the divorce settlement.'

'I interviewed her myself.'

'Yes, I saw the statement. Did I read between the lines correctly? You didn't take a shine to her.'

'She's an ice maiden. Very different from Tina Howe. She might have lacked a cast-iron alibi for the murder, but there was nothing to link her to the scene. And there was the question of motive. It was in her interest for her husband's business to flourish and Warren was an integral part of that business.'

'It seems to be flourishing now.'

'Good line to be in, isn't it? Everyone fancies having their own little Eden outside the scullery door.'

'True, but Gail must be worth a second look.'

'Hope Linz gets further with her than I did. Mind you, if Peter's swopped Gail for Tina, Roz will be seriously unimpressed. She'll blame Tina for breaking up the marriage. In her book, that's as serious a crime as murder.'

'She's certainly stayed true to her own husband.'

'Yes.' Nick shuffled his feet on the tarmac. 'What did you make of them, then?'

Hannah chose her words. 'I'd say they look after each other very well.'

'Is that it?'

'You know them better than me.'

'Too well to regard them as suspects.'

'And you assume I do?'

'Don't you?'

'Stop fencing, Nick. If you must know, I liked them, but I thought they were holding back on me. Why, God knows, but there's something they don't want me to find out They're your friends, but I'm sorry, I can't let that influence me. If they're keeping a secret that's relevant to this inquiry, you can bet I'll find it out.'

He didn't answer. The only question in her mind was whether he knew what the Gleaves' secret was, but if he did, he wasn't telling. For a few moments they looked at each other before he gave a curt nod and walked away towards his car.

As she watched his retreating back, an overwhelming sense of loss flooded over her. Whatever was going on in his mind, she was afraid that things between them would never be the same again.

When Kirsty arrived home after work she found her brother asleep on the sofa. The stench of drink and uninhibited flatulence hit her as she walked into the living room. His snoring reminded her of his motorbike's snarl. He was still wearing his muddy trainers and you could see dirt on the cotton throw covering the back of the sofa. Mum would kill him when she found out, but right now she was nowhere to be seen. She would be over at Peter's. Unbidden, an image slid into her mind of Peter Flint's white, stringy body stretched out on top of her mother's fleshy curves.

What's wrong with this picture?

Of course! When she realised, despite herself, she couldn't contain a blast of laughter.

Mum would insist on being on top, no question.

* * *

'You all right?'

Marc had been sitting cross-legged on the carpet, checking a pile of dusty hardbacks for the tiny flaws that would diminish their value to serious collectors and sliding them into protective see-through jackets. Now that the task was completed, he was paying attention to her again. Not for the first time lately, Hannah felt she'd prefer him to remain buried in his own affairs.

She mumbled something non-committal and kept leafing through the latest guidelines for the conduct of staff appraisals that she'd spread over the table. The yearly box-ticking ritual would need to be conducted soon and she was dreading it. Everyone had to pay lip service to the benefits of performance management, but in private everyone ridiculed the whole process. How could you guarantee a level playing field, consistency and an absence of favouritism and score-settling across the whole county? The whole exercise was a time-consuming waste of energy that everyone except the people who mattered thought would be better devoted to real police work. Yet it was becoming ever more important, with scores affecting competency payments and pension benefits for officers at the top end of their salary scale. People like Nick.

'I said, are you all right? You've hardly said a word all evening.'

Guilty, m'lud. She had a raging headache and had economised with effort over their meal, heating up a cheese and salami pizza and disinterring some fruit salad from the fridge. When it was made, she hadn't felt like eating. The encounter with Nick in the car park kept nagging at her and she'd paid little attention as Marc recounted a triumph of internet book dealing. Within hours of his advertising it, someone in Idaho had paid a small fortune for a book by Cecil Waye that he'd found in the job lot from Ravenglass.

'Sorry,' she said. 'Things on my mind.'

'For a change.' Bitterness frosted his voice. 'Work's all you ever think about these days.'

She almost said: for God's sake, stop whining like a caricature of a neglected housewife. Just in time, she bit back the words. For one thing, he was right.

'I am sorry.'

She picked up the appraisal documentation and slung it into her briefcase. It could keep. She walked across the room and bent to kiss him on top of the head. He reached out for her wrists and when he pulled her down on to the floor beside him, she shrieked in mock-protest whilst making no attempt to resist.

But even as he unfastened her blouse, even as he touched her nipples with his cool fingers, in the way that once had driven her to ecstasy, her thoughts began to stray. Marc wasn't entirely right, it wasn't just work that was bothering her. Filed away at the back of her brain was a suspicion so scary that she daren't acknowledge it to herself, far less to Marc.

Kirsty turned up the volume of the television until her brother spluttered and stirred from his torpor. As he came round, he swore repeatedly and with uncharacteristically inventive imagery. For Kirsty, it was water off a duck's back. Their father had been as bad.

'And what the fuck's that?'

On the screen, arrows were being fired at a young Chinese man wearing nothing but boxer shorts who was chained to a vast brick wall.

'New programme. *Brothers from Hell.*'

'You are so hilarious, move over Joan Rivers.'

'Actually, it's one of these endurance programmes. You know, how much can one human being be expected to cope with? Any day now they'll start filming behind the scenes at The Heights.'

Sam snorted in derision. 'You don't have any idea, do you? What it's like in the real world. Your idea of a tough day is when the latest coachload of geriatrics doesn't stump up a single tip.'

She cringed at the smell of the beer fumes on him. 'The real world? Getting pissed and riding motorbikes is your idea of the real world, is it?'

'Why don't you piss off, little waitress?'

Ripping off the scarf, she said, 'See what you did to me?'

'I can hardly see anything.'

'You haven't even said sorry.'

He uttered a long, low groan.

'I suppose that's as close as you'll come to apologising.'

'You shouldn't have provoked me.'

'I didn't...oh God, what's the use? Anyway, I've got news for you, if you'll only break the habit of a lifetime and actually listen.'

'News?'

'The police are re-opening the investigation into Dad's murder.'

'What?' He sat up as though the sofa had been electrified.

'You heard.'

'How do you know?'

'That would be telling. The point is, they are bound to want to interview us, aren't they? His nearest and dearest.'

'Oh, for Chrissake.'

'They'll poke around in our lives. They'll find out about the anonymous letters.'

'So what?' He glanced back at the television screen. A medal was being put around the Chinese man's neck.

'So what if they discover that we lied about the Hardknott Pass?'

'Who's going to tell them?' he demanded.

'They have ways and means.'

He reached towards her and gripped her arm so hard she squealed. 'Listen to me, Kirsty. You'll keep your mouth shut about that day, if you know what's good for you.'

Her arm stung and she could feel tears pricking her eyes. He'd never hurt her like that before. What if he became seriously angry, what if he lost it altogether? Maybe next time he tried to kill her, he'd make a proper job of it.

Chapter Ten

Peter Flint struck Daniel as an easy man to like. Intelligent, affable, articulate. He loved talking about his work, a quality which Daniel always found appealing. And he was honest enough to admit that, although he'd glanced at Daniel's television series, he hadn't watched the programmes all the way through. History was all very well, but he preferred to look forward, not back. What turned him on was creating something fresh for the future.

'I did wonder if you were the BBC man when I heard about the appointment,' he said. 'It's an uncommon name. But I had no idea you owned a second home up here.'

They were sipping home-made elderflower wine beside the tarn. On the table in front of them were fanned out half a dozen pencil sketches by which Peter had illustrated ideas for redesigning the garden.

'This is our one and only home. It's not an investment property, it's where Miranda and I live.'

She'd taken Louise off to the gym in Kendal, leaving him free to see how much he could find out about the fate of Warren Howe without appearing to do so. He was playing a game, and he was sure Hannah would disapprove. Miranda and Louise too, for that matter. But he couldn't resist.

'You've settled here for good?'

'Where better than the Lakes? You come from Beatrix Potter country, don't you?'

'A mile up the road from Near Sawrey, yes. Another lovely spot. Be warned, though, it takes a long time to become accepted by the natives. I'm still seen as an off-comer and I moved to the village from Penrith more years ago than I care to remember. But there's more to the Lakes than the Blessed Beatrix and all those poets. The gardens, for a start. This area is so green – thanks to all our rain.'

'I've almost forgotten what rain is like.' Since the cloudburst greeting Louise's arrival, each day had been hotter than the last. A hosepipe ban was in force and the lawns of Brackdale were starting to yellow.

'You'll remember soon enough,' Peter promised.

Ideas poured out of him like spray from a geyser. How about building a new glass gazebo, connected by a tunnel of hazelnut trees to the water's edge? A garden was like a house, it needed to be split into a series of rooms. The key to success was retaining the element of surprise. You could only get so far with CDs that promised to turn you into a virtual Capability Brown. Even the most sophisticated software lacked creative imagination. You needed vision to see how a drab landscape might be set ablaze with colour. Or, with Tarn Cottage, to see how an unkempt jungle might become a secret paradise.

Vision was Peter Flint's speciality. He drew pictures in the air with his hands, his words tumbling over each other in his enthusiasm. Walkways conjured out of a medley of surfaces – grey slabs, white brick, crazy paving – twisting and turning to reveal new vistas round every bend. Drainpipes cut and stood on end to form containers of culinary herbs and fragrant jonquils. Logs forming stepping stones to lead towards the tarn through sanctuary planting: hawthorn, meadow sweet venusta and loosestrife. For the stretches up to the lower slopes of Tarn Fell, how about ox-eye daisy, meadow cranesbill, cowslip, and quaking grass?

Yet the garden puzzled him as it did Daniel.

'Doesn't make sense,' he said with a frown. 'The choice of planting is odd in itself. Mandrake, hellebore, the monkey puzzle trees. And why lay a path that meanders so aimlessly? Failing to take advantage of a setting like this is almost criminal, frankly. An act of sabotage.'

'Someone, sometime, must have meant it to be like this.'

'Agreed. And a long time ago, I'd guess.'

'The cottage is over a century old.'

'Who knows, the same might be true of this garden? Looks like there have been attempts to keep it up in the past thirty or forty years, but not to much effect. Of course, there are plenty of eccentric English gardens. Think of China and Switzerland captured in miniature at Biddulph Grange, think of the erotic symbolism at West Wycombe Park. Mellor's Garden in Cheshire tells the story of Christian's trials in *The Pilgrim's Progress* and reflects the philosophy of Swedenborg for good measure. But each of those gardens has a meaning. No offence, Daniel, but this is just a tangled mess.'

'Intriguing, though.'

Peter Flint's brow wrinkled. 'Trust me, Daniel, it isn't a recreation of the past you need here. It's a new beginning.'

When Daniel asked about Flint Howe's business, Peter was happy to talk. His partner, Tina, organised the admin; she was the computer wizard, every firm should have one. Her son Sam, the young fellow who had dropped him off in Tarn Fold before taking the van to size up another job, undertook the heavy labouring along with a couple of contract workers. A taciturn lad, Sam, happier astride a motorbike than a sit-down mower, but possessed of a flair for discovering the perfect place for every plant, and that was a gift that couldn't be taught. It was in the genes. Lucky Sam, he'd inherited it from his late father.

'His dad was a gardener, too?'

'We were partners. He was a true plantsman.'

Peter finished his drink and didn't object when Daniel filled the large glass again to the brim. The elderflower wine was an experiment. Miranda had never made it before and it was rather strong. So much the better for loosening tongues, Daniel reckoned, and he was spared qualms of conscience, given that Peter wasn't driving.

'You were in partnership for how long?'

'Ten years. People said we were chalk and cheese, Warren and me. Quite right, but neither of us cared. We didn't socialise, we led separate lives, but we made a damn good team.'

'You must miss him.'

Of course Warren was a sad loss, Peter said. Tina had taken an age to get over his death, perhaps you never get over that sort of thing altogether. But everyone has to move on. While Warren was alive, she worked on the purchase ledger in a Dickensian office in Ulverston, but she'd inherited his stake in the business. Peter had persuaded her that, rather than sell out her interest, or sit back and enjoy the fruits of others' work as a sleeping partner, the best way of capitalising on her investment was to help him grow the firm. As for Sam, if he lacked Warren's work ethic, never mind. He was young, there was time yet.

Savouring the wine, Daniel asked, 'Was it a long illness?'

'Sorry?'

'Your partner, Warren. Cancer, was it? Or heart?'

Peter wiped his mouth. When he spoke again, his voice was pitched lower, as though out of respect for the dead. 'To tell you the truth, Daniel, he didn't die of natural causes. He was murdered.'

Daniel deployed the shocked yet intrigued expression he'd once reserved for financial negotiations with his publisher. Within five minutes he'd gleaned as much as he'd learned from Hannah and his researches in the old newspapers and online.

'So the killer is still walking the streets?'

'Well.' Peter ran his fingers through his hair. 'I suppose you could look at it like that. Unless the person is dead or in prison for some other crime.'

'It sounds premeditated. Which argues that the culprit knew Warren personally, had a particular motive for murder. Random killings are different. Homicidal maniacs don't explore back gardens in search of their victims.'

'True.' Peter's grin revealed crooked teeth. 'Stupid of me. I forgot that you have a professional interest in detective techniques.'

'Presumably Tina lives in hope that one day the police will catch up with the man who killed her husband ? Perhaps if they come across a fresh lead…'

Peter coughed. 'I honestly believe that all she wants is to put the whole dreadful experience behind her. She never likes to be reminded of – what happened. Can't find it in my heart to blame her. She went through so much and then she raised Sam and Kirsty on her own. It's taken her a long time to come to terms with her husband's death. We never speak about it. God knows, the last thing she needs is for the police to start raking over old bones.'

'She doesn't want to come face to face with the man who

murdered her husband?' Daniel racked his brains for a suitable tabloid cliché. The only danger was that he might get carried away and blow it completely. 'To ask him *why?*'

'That wouldn't bring Warren back.' Peter sighed as he struggled for a diplomatic form of words. 'I hate to say this, but he made a habit of getting on the wrong side of people. Tina knew that as well as anyone.'

'Yet she stuck with him.'

'She's an extremely loyal woman.'

'And your partnership with him survived.'

'Warren loved to provoke a fight, but I refused to rise to the bait. He used to say I was boring, but it preserved a sort of harmony. Not everyone who dealt with him was equally patient. Rumour had it that the police investigation was all over the place, simply because he'd antagonised so many people. The detectives didn't know where to start.'

'Must be tough for Tina, knowing that someone killed her husband, but not having a clue who did it.'

'She's a strong woman.' Peter's mouth twisted and for an instant Daniel saw that the friendly, intelligent man was capable of chilly scorn. 'These fashionable notions, closure, bereavement counselling and all that, may be fine for some people. But not Tina. She's embarked on a new life without Warren. Like I said, all she wants is to be left in peace.'

The stillness of the clearing was interrupted by a vehicle reversing down the lane. Sam Howe, back to collect his boss. Peter glanced at his watch and clucked in surprise.

'Your wine is too seductive. I've outstayed my welcome. I'll let you have a few plans soon. I'm sure we can create a garden you and Miranda will love.' He glanced towards the lonely spikes of the monkey puzzle trees. 'Something very different.'

They strolled towards the cottage. As they drew closer, a burly figure in a red and blue rugby shirt and fraying jeans appeared, following the grass track by the side of the building. A young man with a wish-I-wasn't-here demeanour, mouth moving in montonous rhythm as he chewed a piece of gum. The resemblance to the photographs of Warren Howe was unmistakable.

'Sam, meet Daniel Kind. You know, the television historian?'

From Sam's expression, the name meant nothing to him. He offered a shovel-like paw, and grunted something unintelligible.

'Have you time for a quick look round?' Peter suggested. When Sam shrugged in reply, he said, 'Ignore the brambles. Bags of potential, don't you agree ?'

Sam Howe spat out his gum and shambled off to explore the grounds without another word. His indifference to Peter bordered on contempt. Daniel wondered if he didn't believe in kow-towing to the boss. Maybe he just didn't like the boss sleeping with his mother. Or possibly, just possibly, Sam wondered if Peter had murdered his father and got away with it.

Bel was a mobile phone addict. Call herself a businesswoman? Kirsty wasn't impressed. She spent hours each day glued to her tiny Nokia, texting or gossiping with the likes of Roz Gleave and Gail Flint while everyone else sweated their guts out. All very well for a teenager, but pitiful in a woman old enough to be a grandma. Ever since she'd heard from Roz that the police were looking into the case, Bel had talked about little else. Because she took pride in considering the feelings of others, whenever she thought that Kirsty was within earshot, she changed the subject with more haste than finesse. Sometimes it was so obvious as to be embarrassing.

'Had your visit from the police yet?' She was chattering away to Gail. 'Only a detective constable? My God, it's almost a snub. After Roz got the chief inspector! One consolation, they can't regard you as a prime suspect. Though I'm not sure whether you should be flattered. What was she quizzing you about?'

Veselka was coming down the corridor, flip-flops slapping against the vinyl floor. Kirsty bustled out of the kitchen, menu cards in hand, as Bel was putting her phone back in its leather pouch. The Croatian girl smirked at them both; it was becoming her habitual form of greeting. Kirsty ignored her, but treated her boss to a smile. Bel raised her eyebrows and Kirsty wondered if she'd been caught out. Had she come out of the kitchen too quickly and given herself away? Bel would be furious if she thought Kirsty was snooping on her, even if it served her right.

Kirsty distributed the menu cards and wrote up the specials in chalk on the blackboard next to the bar. Her script was large and extravagant, a stark contrast to Bel's neat calligraphy. Bel, Bel, Bel, the bloody woman haunted her. Behind that eternal smile lay the calculating mind of an Olympic gold medallist in the sport of getting her own way. Look at how she'd given Oliver a stake in her business to tie him to her apron strings. Suppose she'd guessed about Kirsty's feelings for him, suppose she feared that, deep down, he felt the same? She was like a Persian cat, gorgeous and pampered. Threaten her, and she'd unsheathe her claws.

Oliver seemed tense and distracted and who could blame him? Falling for the daughter of a murder victim was one thing, falling for the daughter of a woman who had killed her husband was quite another. The anonymous letters might have been designed to wreck Kirsty's chances with him. Bel was agog at the revived inquiry into the murder. What if she'd instigated it, as a means of hurting Kirsty and her family? Perhaps it suited her plan for Kirsty to overhear endless conversations about the police's investigations. Psychological warfare.

Yes, if Bel had written the anonymous letters, the two of them were at war. And Kirsty had nothing to lose. She would fight to the death.

Hannah waved Linz Waller and Les Bryant into vacant chairs around the table in her office. Everyone else in the team was out. Nick was up in Cockermouth all day. Hannah guessed he was glad of the excuse to make himself scarce. She ought to stop worrying about him, but she still felt tense and on edge and she didn't think it was just down to the heat. Better submerge herself in the Warren Howe case.

'So tell us about Gail Flint.'

'Attractive lady,' Linz said, 'at least ten or fifteen years ago, she must have been.'

'Miaow,' Les Bryant said.

'Yeah, probably more your type than mine, Les. Bottle blonde, trim figure. CD collection packed with Abba, Neil Diamond and Barry Manilow. You could make sweet music together, I think.'

'Sounds like a follow-up interview is called for. Conducted by a more mature officer.'

'Mature's the word, is it?' Linz asked sweetly. 'Not semi-retired?'

Les yawned. Thirty years as a cop had given him a hide that any rhino would envy. He'd made it to Detective Superintendent, acting as SIO for the Whitby caravan shootings and the Beast of Leyburn case along the way. After opting for pipe, slippers and pension, he'd discovered that he missed the job; or maybe Mrs Bryant didn't care to have him under her feet so much. Lauren Self had hired him on a short-term contract for the Review Team. They called it Dream Policing, this combination of gurus and young Turks, but managing the generation gap was, Hannah found, occasionally a bit of a nightmare.

'What does Gail say about her affair with Warren Howe?' she asked.

'Her story is that they were just good friends who happened to go to bed with each other a few times.'

'Being married to other people wasn't an obstacle?'

'Obviously there isn't much else to do in Old Sawrey than sleep around. Tell you what, the village has a pretty efficient grapevine. She let it slip that she knew you'd interviewed Roz Gleave, ma'am. I think she was miffed that she only rated a lowly DC.'

That wouldn't have gone down well with Linz, whose ego was as well-nourished as Les Bryant's. Sometimes Hannah wondered if this was where she went wrong. Fast though she'd climbed the ladder, status had never mattered much to her. She cared about meeting her own standards, not other people's.

'Do I get the impression the two of you didn't exactly hit it off?'

Linz made a face. 'She's in the wrong business, if you ask me. The wine trade isn't healthy for someone with a drink problem. She offered me a drink the minute I walked through the door. I said no, but it didn't stop her pouring herself a large one.'

'She's taken the divorce hard?'

'She says it was her decision to split up, but there doesn't seem to be another man around. The booze keeps her company, I'd guess. She did her best to come over as nice as pie, but beneath the pleasantries, she's a cold-hearted bitch. She shagged Tina's husband, now Tina is returning the compliment. Serves her right.'

'Don't sit on the fence,' Les Bryant murmured. 'Tell us how you really feel.'

'That's an objective and professional assessment, actually. She made a point of saying that she and her ex-husband are still best mates, and she doesn't bear him any ill will, but I didn't buy it. Even though she made a joke of it, said what goes around, comes around. She smiles with her mouth, but not her eyes.'

'What did she have to say about Warren?'

'She comes from Hawkshead, just down the road from Old Sawrey, but she hardly knew him until he and Peter set up in business together. Like everyone else she was aware Warren played around, but for years nothing happened between them except for an occasional snog at parties when everyone had had plenty to drink. The Flints and the Howes don't seem to have had much in common and that was true of the wives as well as the husbands. Tina worked in an office and spent her spare time taking photographs, Gail preferred being her own boss. Over time, Gail and Peter drifted apart. Neither of them was interested in kids, so that wasn't an issue, but he wanted a little woman at home to take care of him and she was determined to be her own person.'

'So far,' Hannah said, 'she's got my sympathy.'

'Her story is that Warren chased her. He had the advantage of knowing when Peter would be out of the way. I suppose if you're going to carry on with someone else's wife, it helps if he's a bloke you can keep tabs on. He turned up at the house one evening when Gail was there on her own. Reckoned he expected to find Peter there, but later he admitted he knew Peter was out of harm's way up at Cleator Moor, quoting for a new job. Anyway, she offered him a drink and one thing led to another.'

'How long was this before Warren was killed?'

'Four months, give or take. They both got what they wanted, a bit of no-strings sex. She said he was a terrific lover. Lots of experience, of course. And she enjoyed telling me that it made her realise what she was missing with Peter. As if to rub it in that Tina had got the worst of the bargain. But she said she went into the relationship with her eyes open. She didn't want to settle down with Warren, what she really wanted was her freedom.'

'So why didn't she leave Peter Flint years ago?'

'She claims that Warren's murder horrified them both. In a strange kind of way, it brought them closer together. But they were only papering over the cracks. She'd tasted excitement and she couldn't get enough of that from poor old Peter.' Linz laughed. 'She said that if he was as inventive in bed as he was when it came to designing pergolas and water features, they'd still be together.'

'Why did her affair with Warren end?'

'She said they both recognised it was going nowhere and tongues were wagging in the village. His van had been seen outside her house a bit too often. She was getting cold feet and he didn't want any more grief from Tina. So they parted by mutual agreement.'

Les sniffed. 'That's what they call it when a company sacks an unsuccessful executive or a football club dumps its manager when it's bottom of the league. Pack of lies. Who do you think really finished it?'

'Warren.'

'Would she have been as relaxed about it as she claims?' Hannah asked.

'Not if she wasn't ready to give him up. If you ask me, she isn't one of life's gracious losers. I bet she can scratch and claw with the best of them.'

Les puffed out his cheeks. 'She didn't have much of an alibi for the murder and there's a possible motive. I'll follow up, shall I? If all else fails, mebbe she'll let me listen to her Abba records.'

As he shambled out, Linz said, 'One more thing, ma'am. I did just wonder – is DS Lowther OK?'

'Any reason why he shouldn't be?'

'Only that I was in early this morning, before he set off. He had rings under his eyes as if he hadn't slept and when I said hello, he didn't answer. Yesterday, when I asked him something, he bit my head off. Perhaps it's this weather. So oppressive.'

'You're telling me, I feel shattered...'

As the door shut behind Linz, Hannah thought the trouble with working alongside detectives was that you couldn't hide things for long. On the shelf next to her desk was a dog-eared paperback with an orange cover. *Police Interrogation: a handbook for investigators.* It had been Ben Kind's bible until he'd presented it to her years ago. She turned to the page with a quote from Freud that always rang true:

He that has eyes to see and ears to hear may convince himself that no mortal can keep a secret. If his lips are silent he chatters with his fingertips; betrayal oozes out of him at every pore.

Her mobile rang and she recognised the caller's number on display. Daniel.

'Am I disturbing you?'

'No, it's fine.'

He felt guilty because it wasn't yet five o'clock and she was a busy woman, while he was free to roam the fells. Miranda and Louise were back at the cottage and he'd been seized by the urge to hear her husky voice again. Talking to her was a treat, like an extra glass of Chablis. It would be all too easy to over-indulge.

He'd gone for a walk up Tarn Fell, halting by the stone cairn to take out his phone. The mobile signal from this point was better than usual on the slopes of Lakeland. His new boots were pinching and he sat on the rocky ground to ease them off. In the distance a buzzard hung motionless in the air. It seemed so calm that it was hard to believe it had murder on its mind. He imagined its small dark eyes, scanning the landscape for prey.

'I wanted to let you know I've met Peter Flint. As well as the dead man's son.'

'Is your garden sorted now, then?'

'Far from it. But you might be interested in what Peter told me.'

'You didn't prise a confession out of him, by any chance?'

'No such luck. All the same, he talked freely enough and I found out a few things. Have you got five minutes?'

As he recounted his discussions with Peter and Sam, Daniel pictured her closing her eyes as she listened. As he answered her questions, he guessed she was sifting through the answers, assessing whether there was anything she didn't know already. He liked the way she concentrated her full attention upon him whenever they talked. She didn't disapprove, she took him seriously. He couldn't help finding it flattering.

'I spoke to Tina Howe on the phone and Peter Flint told me the daughter is a waitress at a restaurant called The Heights.'

'The woman she works for, Bel Jenner, was an old flame of her father's.'

'Small world. My sister offered to take Miranda and me out for a meal. I might suggest The Heights.'

Through the crackling, he could make out her laughter. 'You're incorrigible.'

''Fraid so.' Any minute the line would go dead. Time to take a chance. 'I wondered. Would you like to meet up for a drink one evening?'

As he held his breath, the buzzard moved. First it soared into the air, and then it swooped down towards an unsuspecting victim in a patch of gorse. For a long time Hannah didn't speak. Shit. Had the signal gone, or had he simply over-played his hand?

Then he heard her voice again. Faint but clear.

'Yes, why not?'

Chapter Eleven

'Oliver, we need to talk.'

Kirsty dug her nails into her palms. This was a huge risk. If it went wrong, she'd lose him forever. And they didn't have much time before Bel locked the doors for the night. She'd finished blowing out the candles and clearing the tables, but it had taken the last diners fifteen teeth-grinding minutes to agree amongst themselves how to split the bill. Never mind hoping for a tip, she almost volunteered to pay out of her own wages, just to get rid of them. As soon as she managed to bundle them out of the premises, she went in search and bumped into him coming out of the kitchen.

'Talk?' His body language spelled uncertainty. He might have been a quiz contestant, stumped by the simplest question. 'What about?'

'Please. Two minutes, that's all I ask.'

Raised voices were coming from the kitchen. Veselka and Danica, arguing about who should mop up. Bel was in the bar, chatting about nothing in particular to Arthur while they washed the glasses. Once the job was done, Bel would spend five minutes re-stocking the fridge so that enough beer, wine and soft drinks were chilled overnight, and then she would want to lock up. It was now or never.

Oliver brushed a stray hair out of his eyes and focused on her. His eyes were like lasers, she thought, penetrating her soul. She knew she was blushing, but she no longer cared.

'All right, Kirsty, if that's what you want. Two minutes maximum, though, OK?'

'Thank you,' she breathed and led him outside.

The overspill car park at the rear of The Heights was empty except for Arthur's rusty Fiesta. Beyond lay the small garden, separated from the grounds of the house next door by a six foot willow screen. That lazy sod Sam still hadn't got round to doing the work that Bel wanted. Typical, bloody typical. When she clutched Oliver's hand, he didn't resist. His palm was warm. When the moon passed behind a cloud, they were alone in the darkness.

'What is it?'

'Oliver, you're not going to like this, but I have to say it. I think Bel knows about you and me.'

'What are you talking about?' he hissed. 'There's nothing to know.'

She squeezed his hand. So far, so predictable. He never wanted to hear a word against Bel. Of course, that was half the trouble: he was in denial. Loyal and faithful to a fault, he couldn't help still caring for her. He'd never be able to see through her unless she made him understand.

'It's the anonymous letter. I've been thinking about who could have sent it. We've both behaved so discreetly. We've never been anywhere together, we only ever see each other here. Yet the letter told me to keep my hands off you.'

The moon came out again and she could see him, rubbing his beaky nose in bafflement. 'Anyone could have written that. Some spiteful person who saw us chatting together, who knew we were friends. Someone who felt you took too long serving the main course, whatever.'

'No, no, don't you see? There have been other letters, two that I know of for sure. One to my mother, another to Sam. Both of them talking about Dad's murder. Whoever wrote those letters knows our family, Oliver. And wants to hurts us. Me in particular.'

He pulled his hand away and took a step backwards into the shadow. 'You seriously think Bel sent those letters? It's mad, Kirsty. She'd never do it. There isn't a malicious bone in her body.'

Leaves rustled. A squirrel, or more likely a fox. Kirsty swallowed hard. 'She's crazy about you, Oliver. A middle-aged woman clinging on to a much younger man, she'll do anything. You've never married, you're not exactly Mr Commitment. She's afraid she's going to be left on her own, and she can't cope with the prospect. Look at how she chased after you within weeks of burying her husband. The stuff about Dad was a blind. I'm the target.'

'You've got it all wrong.'

She reached out and gripped his wrist. 'Listen to me, Oliver, no other explanation makes sense. I'm not angry with her, I sympathise…'

'No!' He shook her off, like a celebrity detaching himself from an over-familiar fan. 'Kirsty, God knows, I don't want to hurt you, but you must see sense.'

'All I want to see is you,' she said.

'Look, I'm very fond of you, seriously I am.' He closed his eyes. 'Much more than you could ever imagine.'

'Well, then.'

'But we're just friends, that's as far as it goes.'

'No! We can…'

'Listen to me! You say Bel's crazy about me. What you don't seem to understand is this. I'm absolutely crazy about her.'

She recoiled as if he'd slapped her. The moon came out again and she could see his white face, skin taut over those high cheekbones. He was breathing hard, in the way she'd imagined he might when they were making love. But if he meant what he said, they would never make love.

The rusty hinges of the back door screeched. Veselka in sullen mood, bringing rubbish out to put in the bin. She was bound to see them, but Kirsty no longer cared. Oliver was lying, or at least she prayed he was, but he would never admit it. And if he was telling the truth, she no longer cared about anything.

Louise joined Daniel in the kitchen as he took the stopper out of the wine bottle. The smell of chicken curry lingered in the air. The clock on the oven said ten to midnight, but you would never have guessed. This was the hottest night so far.

'Is Miranda OK?'

'She has a migraine, that's all.'

Miranda had been tetchy and monosyllabic all evening. He'd kept quiet, hoping to avoid a row, but in the end she'd gone up to bed, leaving Louise to watch a Julia Roberts DVD while he browsed through a stack of books about the Lakes, searching in vain for clues to the mystery of the garden. Even with the window open, there wasn't a breath of air. He felt like an aged miner, hacking coal out of a poor seam. In the end he gave up and decided to finish off the Sancerre with Louise.

'She blames the weather, but there's more to it than that, isn't there? All day she's been tense and fidgety. Even working out in the gym didn't help.'

'That's Miranda for you.'

'She's missing London, she said so.'

'I don't know why. Whenever she isn't flogging down there on the train, she and the people at the magazine are firing emails back and forth.'

'While we were out, she took a couple of long private calls. From her editor, she said.'

He poured the last of the wine. 'No offence, Louise, but if I wanted relationship counselling, I wouldn't come knocking on your door. Miranda and I are fine.'

In her dream, Hannah was sitting in her car up the lane from Keepsake Cottage, obscured from view by willow trees. Nick Lowther's Mondeo appeared from round the bend, sun glinting on its bonnet, and turned into the drive. He hadn't seen her, but through the leaves she watched him park and jump out. He was in shirt-sleeves and had taken off his tie. The front door opened to reveal Roz Gleave in a well-filled black lace gown. Grey hair, freckled skin, dark eyes and brows. A strong woman, confident of her subtle allure. They embraced and then she took his hand and led him inside. The door shut behind them and Hannah looked up towards the bedroom window. Moments later, she glimpsed two shadows, intertwining.

When she woke up she was sweating. The red digits of the bedside alarm clock blinked at her, as if in reproach. Four twenty; another broken night. She had a tight feeling in her abdomen and her head was throbbing. Marc murmured something unintelligible before rolling over in his sleep. They were both naked. Earlier, they'd made love, but she'd been exhausted and his face had betrayed dismay at her lack of ecstasy. He wasn't to blame for her mind being elsewhere.

She needed to scrub Daniel Kind out of her mind, she should

never have said yes to his suggestion of a drink. It was a mistake, a seeking out of fun and excitement, and a change in fortune, and it was doomed from the start. If she wasn't careful, it might lead to something dangerous, and she didn't want that. At least she didn't think she did.

And then there was Nick. Surely he wasn't having an affair with Roz, surely it was absurd to imagine for one second that he might be covering up the truth about the murder of Warren Howe. He deserved her trust, as Marc deserved her undivided attention. She was letting down the people she cared for most.

She padded downstairs and toasted a couple of slices of bread to assuage pangs of hunger. Catching a glimpse of her pale flesh in the hall mirror didn't make her feel better. Not quite such a pretty sight these days, she thought, whatever Marc might say when he was in the mood for love. She was so accustomed to feeling young and fit and capable of anything, but the years were slipping by. Perhaps she'd risen too fast in the force and hit the ceiling too soon. There was a question she'd regularly asked other people in promotion interviews, but right now she'd hate to have to answer it herself.

Where do you see yourself in ten years' time?

When Kirsty came downstairs, she found her mother and Sam at the breakfast bar. Tina was wearing nothing but a cotton top that scarcely covered her modesty. Unsuitable for a woman her age, in Kirsty's opinion, especially in front of her own son. Kirsty was careful to keep her bits covered when Sam was around, because he wasn't above getting an eyeful, even of his own sister. But she knew that if she said anything, her mother wouldn't be angry, she'd just turn the tables on her and mock her prudishness.

Tina was tucking into milk-drenched cornflakes, but she'd cooked bacon, sausage and eggs for her son. She wouldn't do that for me, Kirsty thought, she'd expect me to look after myself. She's always favoured Sam, and not thanks to anything he's ever bothered to do for her. It's because he's a boy. She's never had much time for her own sex, it's men that matter to her.

'You'll need to make fresh coffee,' Tina said. 'We're almost out of paper filters, by the way, you'd better pick some up from the shop. I didn't fill the machine, it's not like you to grace us with your presence this early.'

'I had a bad night. Couldn't sleep properly.'

'It's the heat.' Tina indulged in an elaborate stretch. Kirsty could see the swell of her breasts straining against the thin cotton. Sam was looking up from his motor cycling magazine to take in the view as well. 'Peter's the same, he's as restless as I don't know what. Anyone would think he had a guilty conscience. That's why I came over here last night, to get a bit of shut-eye. Best not complain about the weather, though. Any day now we'll be soaked to the skin by a thunderstorm. Not that you'll be sorry if it pours down, will you, Sam? He was telling me, Kirsty, when he was digging yesterday it was like trying to drill into Scafell Pike, the ground was that hard.'

Another example of how close they were. He never talked to his sister about his work, not even to grumble. Kirsty reached for the fruit bowl and picked out a banana. At this time of day, healthy eating was easy. It was nibbling at Oliver's chocolate fudge cake during her shift that ruined every attempt at a diet.

'Still going skydiving tomorrow, Kirsty?'

'Yes, why do you ask?'

'No need to bite my head off. You always complain I don't show enough of an interest. It's for charity, isn't it? Peter and I thought we might come along and watch. How about you, Sam?'

Keeping his gaze on a photograph of a semi-naked blonde astride a gleaming Suzuki, he mumbled with his mouth full. 'If I've nothing better to do.'

'Don't feel you have to turn up on my account,' Kirsty said.

'We'd love to,' her mother said. 'I said to Peter, I'll be scared witless, watching you float through mid-air. But he told me it will be wonderful.'

Mum's buttering me up, Kirsty thought. Trying to persuade me that Peter's a regular guy and we can break the habit of a lifetime and become one big happy family. Perhaps the anonymous letter has brought them even closer together. For God's sake, what if they've decided to get married?

She peeled the banana. There was only one way to push the worries out of her mind. Thinking about Oliver didn't work these days, he was just one more thing to worry about. Freedom wasn't down here on earth, you only found it up in the clear blue sky. Staring up at the ceiling, she recalled her first tandem dive.

Ten people, packed like sardines in the tiny plane. Shuffling into position at 10,000 feet and planting her backside in the lap of her partner, a complete stranger, a man who smelled of tobacco and whom she had to trust, because there was no choice. Tightening her harness and remembering a boyfriend who'd tried in vain to persuade her to get into bondage. This was the closest she'd ever come to it. Checking her goggles and hat, waiting for the magic 12,000 to hit on the altimeter.

The door opening. Putting her legs over the side, experiencing the exhilaration as she saw the sky below. Saying a silent prayer as she jumped.

Floating through a cloud, with fluffy whiteness all around. Fighting for breath and freezing cold, yet alive in a way she'd never known before. Alive with excitement and sweet, sweet fear.

Bel Jenner had said on the phone that she and Oliver would meet Hannah at The Heights, rather than in the couple's house next door. Hannah recognised a technique for keeping the investigation at arm's length. No doubt that by now everyone in Old Sawrey knew about the cold case review. The grapevine in a Lakeland village works faster than the latest broadband.

Oliver led them into the bar area, guiding her towards one of a pair of two-seater sofas facing each other across a table with a mosaic top. The place exuded comfort and contentment. The walls were covered with Lake District scenes and in the background Perry Como crooned about magic moments. Oliver waited as his partner took a seat, deferential as a courtier. It wasn't what Hannah expected when a couple had been together for years. What was the old joke – you start by sinking into his arms and end with your arms in his sink?

According to the file, Oliver was fifteen years younger than Bel, but he was as attentive as a man in the first flush of infatuation. To talk to her, Bel was Mrs Ordinary, yet her life had been anything but. In her time, she'd hooked a rich older husband and a sexy young lover. To say nothing of having a teenage fling with a man who was stabbed to death at the home of her oldest friend. Nor was there anything ordinary about her appearance. Posh clothes, lustrous hair and cheekbones to die for. Hannah suppressed a stirring of envy.

'Why the Boggle Bar?' she asked, focusing on the sign above the arch linking the bar with the restaurant.

'After the story of the Waterside Boggle,' Bel said. 'At night a strange creature used to roam by the lake. Some said it resembled a calf, some a dog. Others said it was a beast akin to a donkey. It vanished whenever a passer-by approached, and the only trace of its presence was a sound like a cartload of stones being emptied into Esthwaite Water.'

'Years ago an old man from Far Sawrey told us it wasn't a boggle but a barghest,' Oliver said. 'A much scarier apparition. The sight of a barghest is supposed to foretell a death.'

Bel flashed a nervous smile and said, 'You can see why we prefer to call this the Boggle Bar, Chief Inspector. The Barghest Bar would be rather frightening.'

Oliver stroked her hand with long, slender fingers. Charm seeped out of his every pore. And not only was he fanciable, he could cook. No man ought to be so gorgeous. Hannah consoled herself that he wasn't her type. Good looks and good manners weren't enough. Though she could hear her friend Terri whispering in her ear: but they're a bloody good start.

'Let me organise coffee,' he said. 'Plain filter or cappuccino, Chief Inspector?'

As he busied himself with the machine, the women exchanged pleasantries and Hannah asked how long they had been here. Bel explained that Tom Danson, her late husband, had bought The Heights a few years after their marriage. He had his own building company, but sold it on his fiftieth birthday. His first wife had died of leukaemia ten years earlier and he'd thrown himself into the business as a way of getting over it. They'd met when Bel went to work for the firm as a receptionist and he proposed within a fortnight. She wanted him to ease off and encouraged him to pursue the idle dream he'd had for years, of running a little restaurant out in the countryside.

'By the time we took over, The Heights had become a place to eat, more than a pub. There's more money in selling food than beer. We'd been living in Tom's old house on the outskirts of Grasmere, but it had too many distressing memories of his wife's illness. I'm so glad I persuaded him to make a fresh start here. We had the old cottage next door pulled down and a new home built. At least we had a little time together here before he took ill. An inoperable brain tumour.'

Guilt knifed Hannah. Life hadn't always been kind to Bel. It was wrong to begrudge her some fun with a toy boy.

'It must have been difficult for you.'

'Yes, we needed help. So I brought in a chef called Jason Goddard.'

Oliver fidgeted at the mention of the name, Bel smiled and stroked his hand. Hannah kept quiet. In the background, Dusty Spingfield wailed that she just didn't know what to do with herself.

'Jason introduced an exotic menu. He was desperate for us to get in the Michelin Guide. A delightful young man, but he seemed to believe that to be any good, a chef has to be temperamental. His mood swung like a man on a flying trapeze. What's more, our customers weren't keen on the fancy cooking. I was preoccupied with Tom and shortly before he died, Jason recruited Oliver. He said he needed back-up, but there was an ulterior motive.'

'Jason was gay,' Oliver explained. 'I'd grown up in Preston, but I'd come up to the Lakes after leaving college. I didn't have any ties, or any thought of settling down. As a kid, I'd worked in McDonalds, a country mile from haute cuisine. I wasn't ambitious, I never wanted to be a celebrity chef. One morning I called here, looking for casual work. Nothing had been advertised, but I ran into Jason and he gave me a job after a five minute interview. Not long after Tom died, I discovered why.'

Bel giggled. 'Jason was an outrageous flirt and he fancied

Oliver like mad. Not that I blame him, but it all became very unpleasant. Of course, Oliver wasn't interested, but Jason hated being turned down, it wasn't in the script. He walked out on me and all of a sudden Oliver was in charge of the kitchen. I came to lean on Oliver, he was a tower of strength.'

I bet, Hannah said to herself. The two of them were sitting as close as possible to each other on the opposite sofa, thighs and legs touching. They seemed to fit each other to perfection. Easy to understand what Jason and Bel saw in Oliver. The bitchy part of Hannah thought it even easier to understand what Oliver had seen in Bel. You only had to sink into this armchair. It clutched you like a lover. Sheer luxury, sheer hedonism, sheer expense. If you were going to stop drifting, where better to drop anchor?

'You said in your original statement that you'd known Warren Howe since you were both young.'

'He was a couple of years older than me, lived a couple of hundred yards away in the cottage covered with Virginia creeper. You must have passed it on your way here, a footballer from Blackburn bought it as a holiday home eighteen months back. Warren was a tearaway, but to an innocent of fourteen, he seemed glamorous and exciting.' Bel might have been talking to herself as she recalled the past. 'My parents were strict Methodists, and very old-fashioned Methodists at that. They were both close to forty when I was born and life at home was a bit of a time-warp. They didn't approve of the Howes and they'd have had heart failure if they'd realised I was seeing Warren. I'm afraid I told a lot of lies. But our romance only lasted a month, then he took up with Roz.'

'You must have been devastated.'

'Oh yes. It was all very traumatic and I took a long time getting over it. Looking back, I suppose I ought to be grateful. He helped me to grow up.'

'You fell out with Roz when she took your boyfriend away from you?'

Bel smoothed her hair. 'I didn't blame her. He decided he wanted her and that was that. I never knew anyone so relentless. For him, it was all about the thrill of the chase. Once Roz succumbed, the only question was how long it would take him to dump her. The answer was six weeks.'

'Were you surprised when he settled down with Tina Howe?'

'Depends what you mean by settled down. He liked his home comforts, did Warren, that's why he got married. And Tina was famous for liking sex almost as much as he did. But it didn't stop him wandering. Only death did that.'

'I'm surprised you stayed in touch, after the way he'd treated you.'

'I didn't consciously avoid him, if that's what you mean, Chief Inspector. Why give him the satisfaction of knowing how deeply he'd hurt me? Even if I'd tried to steer clear, it would have been pointless in a place as tiny as Old Sawrey. To a teenager it's as claustrophobic as a prison cell. After leaving school, I found a succession of jobs in Hawkshead and Ambleside. Office junior, a bit of typing and reception work. Truth to tell, I didn't know what I wanted. I had a few boyfriends, but no-one special. After my parents died, I moved out of the village, decided to start again. Shortly afterwards, I met Tom.'

'You told the original inquiry team that you saw more of Warren Howe after you and your husband took over The Heights.'

'He used to drink here. Sometimes the family came for a meal. The last time they ate here was their wedding anniversary, not long before Warren was killed.'

'You got to know them all?'

'Tina and I were never going to be best pals, and Sam was always surly, but Kirsty's sweet. Still is, poor thing.'

'Warren tried it on with you?'

Bel's face was a mask. 'It's no secret. Nothing to be ashamed of. If Warren met a woman he couldn't have, he saw it as a challenge.'

'Yet you turned him down?'

'Of course. Once bitten, you know? I was happy with Tom. After Tom took ill, I was wrapped up with caring for him. Warren's flirting was a distraction. A nuisance. I wasn't flattered, I knew that all he wanted was to get me into bed again. If you'll excuse the expression, I'd been there and done that. He had nothing to offer me.'

'Your husband was dying and he was pestering you to sleep with him.'

'Yes.'

'And after Tom died?'

'He had the brass neck to say it would do me good. Take me out of myself.' Bel kept her eyes on Hannah. 'I hate to say it, but that's the sort of man he was. He never took no for an answer.'

'So how did you deal with that?'

'How would you deal with it, Chief Inspector? I kept repeating myself, kept on saying no.'

'And how did he react?'

'He wasn't happy. Said I might as well be dead myself.'

'Not very nice.'

'That was Warren. He could be cruel.'

'You were very upset, I presume?'

'You presume right. But if you're wondering whether I killed him because of it, the answer is no.'

Hannah turned to Oliver. 'Were you aware that Warren Howe was making a nuisance of himself?'

He shifted under her gaze. 'I hardly knew the man. Once Jason left, I had my hands full, trying to make sure that the restaurant kept afloat. To me, Howe was just another customer. A married man with a roving eye. After my experience with Jason, I suppose I was glad it was women he was interested in, but I did feel sorry for Bel.'

'In case you're wondering,' Bel said, her voice steady, 'there was never anything – personal – between Oliver and me while Tom was alive.'

The coffee was hot and strong. As she sipped it, Hannah wondered if Bel Jenner was telling her the truth. Maybe, maybe not. But what did it matter?

'Later, when we became a couple, there was gossip,' Oliver added. 'Inevitable, I suppose. I overheard people talking behind Bel's back, saying it was a disgrace that she'd become involved with a younger man when her husband was still warm in his grave. It was so unfair. She'd suffered a lot. I'm not an idiot, I realise people round here still say I was only interested in Bel's money. But the honest truth is, Bel was all I was interested in.'

Protesting too much? Hannah let it go. 'Roz was another of Warren's former girlfriends and her husband had left home around this time. Did he try his luck with her again?'

Bel said, 'You've talked to her, Chief Inspector, and I think she's answered your question.'

A quiet, dignified reply. Sometimes this job made you feel uncomfortable, like a voyeur. Or was that, Hannah wondered, part of the appeal of police work, the chance to walk into other people's lives and nose around their most intimate secrets? She recalled Nick's phrase about ordeal by innocence.

'You and she are still very close.'

Bel folded her arms. 'Lifelong friends. We've never had secrets from each other. You know how it is, with your best friend.'

Hannah knew how it was supposed to be, though there was plenty she wouldn't tell Terri. As for Marc, right now there was also something important she wasn't telling him.

'She must have been shocked when her husband disappeared.'

'It was a terrible time for both of us. Losing the men we loved. At least there was a silver lining. In the end I found Oliver, and Chris came back to Roz.'

'You'd assumed Chris was dead?'

'What else could we think? We were afraid he'd committed suicide. He vanished without a word, which seemed so cruel. But he wasn't himself, you have to see it from his point of view. When he had his breakdown, he needed to run away, so he could get his head together.'

'Ever any doubt that the breakdown was genuine?'

Bel's lipsticked mouth curved in distaste. 'Really, Chief Inspector. I'm sure if you check your files, you'll find that poor Chris was interrogated long and hard when he turned up. The very idea that he might have killed Warren is absurd. He wouldn't hurt a fly. Besides, he had an alibi.'

Oliver turned to her. 'Better be careful, darling. Remember, we were never able to come up with watertight alibis for ourselves. If the police run out of other ideas...'

Hannah pulled herself free of the armchair's seductive caress and sat upright. A bowl of nuts sat on the table and she helped herself to a handful. The interview wasn't going well; she'd lost the initiative. Instead of making allies of these people, she was fast antagonising them. Time for an olive branch.

'We worry about people with alibis almost as much as those without. According to your statement, Ms Jenner, you spent most of the day at home next door, sorting through your late husband's business affairs?'

'After he died, the last thing I wanted to do was to bother with paperwork, but the solicitors handling the probate were asking for various bits of information. I set aside that day to get to grips with it.'

'Did you go out?'

'No. The restaurant was closed that day until six thirty. During Tom's illness, and after Jason left, we cut back the opening hours. Bad for business, but money was the least of my worries. I walked over here at half five. Oliver was already hard at work.'

'You'd moved in by that time, Mr Cox?'

Oliver nodded. 'There's a flat upstairs, at present we have a couple of girls over from Croatia for the summer who share it. Jason lived there, but when he left, Bel offered it to me in lieu of a pay rise for my extra responsibilities. I'd been holed up in a crummy bed-sit in a Coniston back street, not far from Coppermines Valley. The first thing I saw when I woke up each day was a damp stain the shape of Africa on the wall. Of course, I jumped at the chance to move. On the day of the murder, I popped next door about nine thirty. To see how Bel was bearing up, I wanted to keep my eye on her after everything she'd been through. I said I'd go into Hawkshead to pick up some food. The rest of the time I spent pottering around this building. No witnesses, I'm afraid.'

'Is there anything you might have overlooked at the time or forgotten to mention to my colleagues?' Bel and Oliver shook their heads in unison. 'When did you first hear about the murder?'

'Roz rang while she was waiting for the police to arrive,' Bel said. 'She's a strong lady, but she was in a dreadful state. First her husband had disappeared, now she'd found a man cut to the pieces in her own back garden.'

'You knew Warren Howe was working for her?'

'She and Chris decided to have the work done and she didn't want to change the plans. Superstition, I suppose. If she acted as if Chris were dead, she'd somehow make her nightmare come true.'

Hannah tried another tack. 'I gather that Gail Flint supplies you with wine?'

'We like to support local business ventures. And of course I've known Gail a long time.'

'She had an affair with Warren not long before he died.'

Bel allowed herself a mischievous smile. 'Well, nobody's perfect.'

'So it wasn't just a rumour?'

'I heard the relationship was over before the murder. And Gail would never have killed him. She can be tough, but she's squeamish. I can't imagine her doing – what the murderer did to Warren.'

'Their affair was over, perhaps she was unhappy?'

'It happens, don't I know it? She'd have got over it in time. As I did, as Roz did.'

'You employ Warren Howe's daughter, don't you?'

'Yes.' Bel glanced at her watch. 'She will be here soon. I don't know whether you want to talk to her?'

'Does she know I'm seeing the two of you this morning?'

Bel shook her head. 'Don't forget, the girl's father was murdered. We tread on eggshells every time the subject comes up when she's around.'

'She's a good worker?'

'Excellent, when she puts her mind to the job.'

Oliver coloured. 'The fact is, Chief Inspector, she has a bit of a crush on me. Of course, she's wasting her time. I don't encourage her, Bel knows all about it.'

Bel snuggled even closer on the sofa. 'Persistence runs in that family, you see. But there's no harm in her, she'll be fine as soon as she finds someone her own age to moon over.'

Wasn't Kirsty closer in age to Oliver than Bel? In a casual tone Hannah asked, 'Who did you think killed Warren?'

'Isn't it your job to find out, Chief Inspector?'

Not helpful. 'You knew the man well. Intimately. Surely you speculated?'

'Of course we did,' Bel said. 'Poor old Warren wasn't short of enemies. Plenty of people had a motive. The one thing we didn't know at the time...'

'Yes?'

She hesitated. 'I...I'm not sure it's fair to say.'

'Come on, Ms Jenner. The man was brutally murdered. And he did mean something to you once.'

She winced. 'Well, we didn't know that Tina and Peter Flint would get involved together – one day.'

'Are you suggesting that they were having an affair at the time of the murder?'

'I'm not suggesting anything, Chief Inspector. After all, Tina had an alibi, didn't she? She couldn't have killed Warren, even if she wanted to.'

Miranda squeezed Daniel's hand as they stood on the shingle at the head of Mardale, looking towards the remains of the drowned village. Holding him tight, as if not wanting him to stray to his sister's side. Louise stood a few feet away, gazing over the bleached and barren stretches left exposed by the receding water. The mountainous ridge known as High Street lined the horizon. In front of them, the preserved remnant of a grey tree stump rose from the stony ground. Other lakes had lush green shores, but Haweswater was different. The drought was revealing a landscape from a lost world.

An elderly couple waved a greeting and stopped to take in the view. The woman's weather-beaten face was a patchwork of wrinkles, her husband reeked of tobacco. They were both wearing white floppy hats and khaki shorts that stretched to their brown, bony knees.

'My grandma came from Mardale Green, y' know,' the old man said out of the blue. 'The buggers flooded the valley seventy years back so folk in Manchester could tap into the reservoir.'

'It's weird,' Miranda breathed.

'Gran told me about the vicar standing in the graveyard, before he was supposed to take the last service. Weeping for his doomed church. When they pulled it down, they used the stones for that draw-off tower, see? The yew trees were eight hundred years old, but did that stop Manchester Corporation taking an axe to 'em?'

'What happened to the bodies?' Louise asked.

The man's wife said, 'Don't get him started, love.'

'Dug 'em up and took 'em to Shap.' The old man took off his hat and wiped his forehead with a yellow-stained hand. 'They were supposed to be reburied, but I bet their ghosts still wander round here at night.'

For all the heat of the morning, Miranda gave a little shiver. She pulled Daniel closer. 'Let's get back to the car.'

'Fascinating, don't you think, Daniel?' Louise was motionless, as though mesmerised by the resurrected walls and pathways. 'The homes of a whole community, deluged and lost forever.'

'They got reservists to dynamite the cottages.' The old man gave a dry smoker's cough. 'Good practice for the war, my grandma used to say.'

As he and his wife pottered away, Miranda jerked Daniel's hand. 'Are you coming?'

'How about we go up the old corpse road?'

'Good idea,' Louise said.

'What's the point?' Miranda made an impatient noise. 'We've got a coffin trail of our own in Brackdale.'

Daniel said, 'OK. Where would you like to go this afternoon? Another walk, or maybe take a look at Beatrix Potter's old house? Hill Top is only a stone's throw from the restaurant I've booked for this evening.'

'I don't mind a bit more exercise,' Louise said.

'Haven't we walked enough in this weather?' Miranda sighed. 'Come on, Hill Top it is.'

Kirsty huddled up in the armchair, as if trying to disappear. Her T-shirt depicted a parachutist coming down to earth. Hannah remembered the girl weeping, the first time she'd seen her. No tears yet, thank God. Her fists were clenched and her eyes darted around, as though trying to spot a pair of hidden handcuffs. For ten minutes she responded in quiet monosyllables to Hannah's attempts to break the ice by asking her about skydiving as well as gentle questions about the murder, before the dam burst under the weight of her resentment.

'This isn't getting anywhere. I can't help you, Chief Inspector, do you understand? My father died a long time ago and I've spent years trying to forget about it, not cast my mind back. I don't want to be hounded any more. Why must you people keep harping on?'

'I explained that my team reviews unsolved cases in the county.'

'You must have plenty to choose from. Why bother with Dad? It's not right, it's not fair on those who have to carry on.'

The ordeal by innocence. But surely you'd want to know who murdered your father – unless you already had a good idea?

'We never close a murder file, Kirsty. The other day, we received an item of new information.'

The girl twitched like a lumpy marionette. 'What do you mean, what new information?'

'I'm afraid that's confidential.'

'But I'm his daughter! I have rights, you know.'

'Of course you have, Kirsty. Including the right to have us try to find out who killed your father.'

'That's rich! A bit late for that, I'd say. Your lot never got anywhere last time. All they did was make our lives a misery.' Her voice faltered. 'They – they didn't seem to trust us. As if they didn't believe we were up on the Hardknott, the day that Dad was killed.'

'And all three of you were?'

'You must have read our statements. We said so right from the start!'

'You went up the Pass with your brother, yes. And – your Mum was with you too?'

'How many times do I have to tell you?'

Soon Hannah would lose count of the lie-signs. Fingers touching the chin, the nervous cough, traces of perspiration on her brow. Poor Kirsty, she was an amateur in deception. Trouble was, if pushed too hard, she'd fall apart.

'OK, Kirsty, if there's nothing else you want to tell me at present, we'll leave it for the time being. Here is my card. Call me any time if you'd like to talk.'

Kirsty thrust the card into the pocket of her jeans. 'Why would I want to talk anything over with the police?'

Hannah luxuriated in a yawn. 'You'd know that better than me, wouldn't you?'

Sam's scornful voice burned into Kirsty's brain as she held the mobile to her ear. He was within earshot of a client, so he couldn't shout, but he didn't hide his anger. She felt tears scratching at her eyelids. Thank God the overflow car park was deserted, and she couldn't be seen or overheard. Hannah Scarlett had driven away, but you couldn't trust anyone. Not even Oliver.

'You stupid cow, I bet you've got her wondering what you're keeping back.'

'Honestly, Sam, I didn't even hint…'

'What did you say to her?'

'Nothing, nothing at all. It was only a short conversation. She gave up in the end, I think she realised she wasn't getting anywhere.'

'Are you sure?'

'Positive, but I don't think she's going to let go.'

'Shit.'

'Listen, Sam, she knows something we don't. You know the anonymous letters? I think whoever sent them has written to the police as well. This Chief Inspector won't let go, she isn't the type. She'll want to talk to you soon, for sure.'

'Fit, is she?'

'You won't get anywhere if you try to chat her up, Sam. Why don't you tell the truth? Please?'

'About what?'

'About what you were doing the day that Dad died.'

'Don't be so fucking stupid.'

'They'll keep asking questions.'

'Hey, if you don't give me away, I'm safe.' His voice softened and in a heartbeat he became the brother she dreamed of. 'I'm depending on you, Kirsty. All right?'

Tina Howe was on her own in the office when Hannah arrived, scanning in photographs of a newly completed garden project. Peter Flint was working over in Hawkshead with Sam, she said, so she was catching up while she had peace and quiet. Her composure was as immaculate as her black business suit. Versace, Armani? Hannah hadn't a clue; the closest she came to designer-wear was leafing through the colour supplements. No-one could doubt that this was Tina's domain, that she was in charge. She nodded Hannah towards a chair with crisp authority, as if greeting a tedious sales rep.

'Matter of fact, Chief Inspector, I was wondering when you might show your face.'

'Is that so?'

'Kirsty called half an hour ago, told me you'd spoken to her about Warren's murder. I guessed you'd make this your next stop.' Tina glared. 'She's in a right state.'

'We only talked for a few minutes, but I'm sorry if she's upset.'

'It's hard for her, she was very close to her father, she went to hell and back after he died.'

Hannah gave a no-harm-done smile. Tina's agenda couldn't have been clearer if typed out in bold twenty-point capitals. The family were victims, not suspects. Put a foot wrong and complaints would come flying in to Lauren.

'When she's slept on our conversation, I'm sure she'll appreciate that it's in everyone's interest for us to review the case. We owe it to you and your family, Mrs Howe. You deserve justice. So does your late husband.'

Tina raised thick dark eyebrows. She wasn't conventionally attractive, yet you scarcely noticed that. For most men, the revealing blouse, short skirt and musky perfume would make up for a lot.

'Why now? What's woken up the guardians of justice?'

Don't let her needle you, Hannah told herself. This isn't the sort of women who likes members of her own sex. Let alone female police officers.

'I explained to your daughter that we've received additional information about the case.'

'An anonymous letter?'

Hannah leaned forward, resting her elbows on the desk that formed a barrier between them, cupping her chin in her hands. Invading Tina's space.

'Why do you ask?'

'I'm right, aren't I?'

'Sorry, Mrs Howe, I can't comment on that. But I would like to know why you mentioned an anonymous letter.'

Tina put her hands behind her head and breathed out. Hannah guessed it was a well-practised pose. Never mind the horsy jaw, Tina exuded confidence. If she'd let something slip by mistake, she wasn't going to let it bother her. She'd seen the police off years ago, she could do it again. Hannah half-expected a couple of buttons on the silk blouse to pop.

'I received one myself this week.'

'Concerning the death of your husband?'

'Correct.'

'What did it say?'

'Can't remember the exact words, it was only a sentence.'

'I'd have thought it would stick in your mind.'

'Frankly, I only glanced at the thing for a couple of seconds.' Tina shrugged. 'Did it say I was a murdering bitch? I'm not sure. Something like that.'

Too smooth, Hannah thought, too much like a disdainful actress, rolling out well-rehearsed lines. Yet why would anyone fib about such an accusation, the same accusation made in the tip-off letter?

'May I see it?'

Tina clicked her tongue. 'Really, Chief Inspector. You don't think I would keep garbage like that? I tore the letter up and put it in our shredder at home.'

'Was the letter typed?'

'Handwritten. A sort of stencilling. I didn't check the postmark, I presume it was local.'

'Who do you think might have sent it?'

'No idea.'

Not true, Hannah thought, looking at Tina's narrowed eyes and the way her lips compressed, as if striving to keep a secret.

'Why would anyone send such a letter to you?'

'I'm not a psychiatrist, Chief Inspector. There are a lot of sick people in the world, you must know that better than me. Mind you, the police don't seem very effective when it comes to making sure they are put somewhere they can't do any harm.'

'You said at the time that you and your children were up on the Hardknott Pass at the time of your husband's murder.'

'Correct.'

'Any points in your original statement that you'd like to clarify with the benefit of hindsight?'

'Absolutely none.'

'Your husband had an affair with Gail Flint.'

Tina snorted with laughter. 'For goodness sake, Chief Inspector, you're going to have to understand my husband better. He had lots of affairs and we never discussed one. They meant nothing to him and so they meant nothing to me.'

'Who do you think killed him?'

'I rather thought it was your job to tell me that.'

'You must have turned it over in your mind.'

'You think it's so simple, do you, Chief Inspector Scarlett? I suppose you believe you can walk into people's lives and throw them into turmoil and then come up with a solution, neatly packed for the media. Fast-tracked for promotion, are you?'

If only you knew. 'Are you saying that you don't have the faintest idea who might have wanted to kill your husband?'

'Ah, that's a different question, isn't it? Fact is, it could have been anyone. A scorned woman, an enraged husband. Warren was careless, that was his downfall. He didn't mind whoever he hurt. I can only assume he hurt the wrong person and paid the price. A terrible price, but people do terrible things in this world. Don't you agree?'

'Simple as that? Person or persons unknown?'

'Well, yes. It will be to do with shagging the wrong woman at the wrong time, if you ask me. When it came to sex, he was insatiable. Believe me, jealousy didn't come into it, I was almost relieved whenever someone else took a turn, it meant I got let off a bit more lightly. But I'll tell you this. Those other women, they would never have had the balls to stay the course with Warren.'

Her head tilted upwards, as if she took pride in having married a Casanova. How could any woman keep so cool when confronted with her man's infidelity? Hannah's thoughts flitted back to Marc's confession of a long ago dalliance with Leigh Moffatt's sister and her own scorching sense of humiliation.

'So you can't confirm that the relationship ended shortly before your husband was killed?'

'Sorry. You'll have to interrogate Gail.'

'Ironic that you are now in a relationship with Mr Flint.'

'For goodness sake. He's a free agent.' Tina smirked. 'A consenting adult.'

'How has Mrs Flint reacted to your relationship?'

Tina picked up a pencil and started doodling on the pad in front of her. It was hard to tell what she was sketching. Perhaps a bed of roses.

'You'd better ask him, I try not to have anything to do with her.'

'Thanks, I will.'

'He'll be back in half an hour. Feel free to hang on here, if you don't mind my getting on with my work. But remember this. Peter's marriage was dead before he and I got together.'

'Is that right?'

'What are you implying, Chief Inspector?'

'Just asking a question, Mrs Howe.'

Tina stabbed the pad so hard with her pencil that its point broke. She tossed it into a black plastic desk tidy beside the computer monitor. Her screensaver, Hannah saw, was a group of well-oiled body-builders in tight tigerskin pants, flexing their muscles in a variety of leering poses. Perhaps her late husband wasn't the only Howe whose appetite was insatiable.

'I must remember, you're only doing your job. You don't mean to be offensive.'

Hannah said nothing. If the woman wanted a battle of wills, fine.

'Only, I wonder if you have any idea what it's like, Chief Inspector? Having your husband murdered? How would you feel in my shoes, if you came home one day to be greeted by a pair of young constables who told you that your man was dead? And not just dead, but butchered? Cut up like an animal in a bloody abattoir?'

There was a catch in her voice, but no tears. The face powder and blue eye shadow made a good mask. Impossible to gauge whether this came from the heart or was a performance worthy of an Academy Award. Hannah waited.

'I'll tell you what it's like, then. It's utterly horrible. Whatever Warren did wrong in his life – and he did plenty – he didn't deserve that.'

'Which is why I ask questions. I don't mean to be intrusive, but I would like to know when your relationship began with Mr Flint.'

Tina gazed straight at her. Wondering what to say next? When she shrugged, Hannah exulted inside.

'All right. The truth is this. Peter and I liked each other from the start. He is so different from Warren. A breath of fresh air. But I didn't think he'd be interested in me. Tarty Tina, put-upon wife of Jack the Lad. After all, he had a good-looking wife of his own, even if she is as tough as granite. It was a long time before I realised he had any feelings for me. Even longer before he did anything about them. Worse luck.'

'And you say this was after your husband was killed?'

'Long after. The murder – knocked us all sideways. You don't come to terms with something like that in five minutes.'

Hannah wasn't convinced. But Tina Howe wasn't going to confess this afternoon. She'd cracked a little, but she'd take time to break.

Kirsty pounded up the path to the front door of Keepsake Cottage and leaned on the bell while she fought to regain her breath. Her sweat-soaked T-shirt was clinging to her, her calves ached, the soles of her feet were screaming. She hadn't stopped running ever since she'd set off from The Heights. A long way, but she ought to be fitter than this, with a jump imminent. She needed to make sense of things before it was too late. This morning she'd read her stars in the *Daily Mirror*. They were uncannily to the point. *You are going to make a decision that will change your life. It's now or never.*

De Quincey was barking inside the cottage. She kept pressing the bell. Roz must be at home, her car was parked in the drive. She glanced around, waving a cloud of midges away from her face. Her father had been killed here, but she'd never made a pilgrimage to the scene of the crime. Keepsake Cottage was a private home and besides, she'd wanted only to forget what had happened.

After what seemed like an hour, the door swung open. Thank

God, it was Roz. She must have been washing her hair. Although she'd wrapped a fluffy towel round her head, a few drops of water were running down her cheeks. She had on a white cotton top and fraying shorts that revealed a wedge of cellulite. At the sight of Kirsty, her eyes opened wide.

'Kirsty! Are you all right?'

'I'm fine. Just give me a moment.'

'You look as though you've been training for the marathon.'

'I've run over from The Heights.'

'But what on earth brings you here? I mean we've never…'

'There's something I need to talk to you about. Please, can we go inside and talk? I hate to bother you, but I've been mulling this over in my mind and you're the one person who can help me. You can tell me what to do.'

'I'm sorry, I don't understand.'

A thought slapped Kirsty. 'Is Chris in?'

'No, he's out in Kendal, talking to someone who runs a folk club. I'm not expecting him back for an hour, longer if he gets engrossed.'

'Thank goodness. We can talk in private.'

'Talk about what?'

'Do you mind if we go in? You see, the thing is, I need to ask you a favour, a big, big favour. Look, I'm ever so sorry to disturb you. I wouldn't do it if I wasn't desperate. But there's nobody else I can turn to.'

Peter Flint talked rapidly, Adam's apple bobbing, hands moving up and down for emphasis. Hannah could understand the appeal of his boyish animation for Tina, even if a bespectacled boffin and a satyr's widow made strange bedfellows.

'It was an appalling business, Chief Inspector, appalling. Warren wasn't everyone's cup of tea, but to die like that…it doesn't bear thinking about. Not even I can quite imagine what it must have been like for Tina and the children. It's taken a long time for them to get over it – if you ever can get over something like that. So it's scarcely surprising that they dread a new inquiry. Utterly dread it. Painful memories are bound to come flooding back.'

Hannah glanced at Tina. Following her lover's arrival, she had emerged from behind her desk and now they were all sitting together in Peter's office. His presence seemed to soothe her. Her body language was mellowing, her smile losing its glacial edge.

'You have to do what you have to do, Chief Inspector,' Tina said. 'Just remember that the murder turned our lives upside down. It wasn't an easy time.'

'We appreciate the sensitivities, Mr Flint, but you'll understand that I have to ask you about your relationship with Warren Howe.'

'Personal or professional?'

'Both.'

Hannah would bet any money that Tina had called him as soon as she'd heard from Kirsty. The party line would already be agreed. She'd be told what they wanted to tell her, no more.

'We both shared the same passion,' Peter Flint said.

Hannah's gaze flicked over to Tina. Yes, I bet. But since when?

'I mean, Warren and I were fascinated by gardens. By gardening.' He spread his arms, reminding Hannah of a magician's stooge trying to fathom an illusion. 'It becomes an addiction. Once you're in its clutches, the tendrils wrap around you like a Russian vine. There's no escape.'

'How about your business – any problems?'

'My goodness, have you ever known any business without problems? As it happens, we were lucky, we had more contracts than we could handle. Above all, we loved the work.'

'With an added bonus,' Tina murmured. 'They divided the tasks, so they could keep out of each other's way.'

Peter grinned. 'Which is probably why we seldom had cross words. I concentrated on design and marketing. Warren was our out-of-doors man. He did the labouring, as well as dealing with the nurseries. We made a damn good team. After Warren died, frankly, our revenue fell off a cliff. It wasn't easy to find a replacement, let alone a plantsman of the same calibre. Customers cancelled agreements, it took years to get the firm back on an even keel.'

'Is that why you wanted Mrs Howe to work for the company?'

'When we were struggling, I couldn't afford to buy out her share. Now, of course, I wouldn't want to.'

'And Sam?'

'He worked for me during his summer holidays as a schoolboy. After he left school, he flitted around from job to job. When I needed another pair of hands, he was the obvious choice. The lad was born with green fingers, it's in the genes. All he needs to do is realise that he needs to put in the hours, bend his back more often.'

'And your personal relationship with Warren Howe?'

'What can I say? He was a rough diamond. The sort of man whose idea of philosophy is: never spend your money on anything that fucks, floats or flies.'

Hannah couldn't help smiling at the gruff impersonation. She would never know whether Peter had captured Warren's tone of voice, but she'd bet he had. 'Not exactly your kind of chap, then?'

'Apart from gardening, we didn't have much in common.'

'What about your wife?'

Two pink spots appeared in Peter's cheeks. 'What about her? I wasn't Gail's keeper. She's always cherished her independence. That's why she devoted her time to her own business ventures rather than Flint Howe. Whatever she got up to was, to coin a phrase, her own affair.'

'Even while you were married?'

'Even then.'

'You were aware of the gossip about the two of them?'

'I take no notice of gossip, Chief Inspector. It's the curse of village life. The idle chatter of small-minded people doesn't interest me.'

'Did you confront her, ask her outright if she was having an affair?'

'Of course not.' He sniffed, as if at a bad smell. 'Listen, we'd married young. I fell head over heels, I don't mind admitting. Gail's an attractive woman, it took many years for me to realise that wasn't enough. That's why we stayed together for so long. Too long, if I'm truthful. Today – I'm just thankful it's over. I'm happier now than ever before.'

Tina reached across the table and patted his hand. They smiled as they looked into each other's eyes. Hannah stifled a sigh of exasperation.

'So you weren't jealous?'

Peter Flint cocked his head. 'I suppose if someone had proved to me that Warren was sleeping with my wife, yes, I would have been unhappy. Thank heaven, it never arose. Warren didn't rub my nose in it, and I'm not plagued by the green-eyed monster.'

Quite a paragon, aren't you? Hear no evil, see no evil.

'Is it true that your wife's involvement with Warren Howe ended a short time before he was killed?'

'If I don't know for sure that there was any involvement, how could I know if and when it ended?'

'How did she react to the news of his death?'

Peter blinked. 'You're surely not wondering whether...'

'All I'm trying to do is to get a clear picture of Warren Howe's life. His relationships.'

'Gail didn't kill him, if that's what you're thinking.'

'I haven't suggested it.'

'She has a tongue like a stiletto, I don't deny it. Especially after she's had a few drinks. But she isn't a murderer.'

Tina frowned and Hannah sensed a warning. Don't overdo it.

'Your divorce, Mr Flint. Was it acrimonious?'

He lifted his chin. 'Aren't all divorces?'

'Was it your decision to part?'

'After Warren's death, it was as if for a time, in some strange way, the tragedy brought us together. But we were only papering over the cracks.' More gesturing with the hands. You're like a politician, Hannah thought, only answering the questions you like. 'We'd become different people since our marriage. Both self-employed, working long hours trying to make ends meet. Between us, we'd sunk every penny into our businesses. We had very little time together. It was never going to work out, we both came to recognise that. A mutual decision, let's say.'

'The anonymous letter, did you see it?'

'Tina destroyed it before she mentioned it to me. Quite right, too. Wicked nonsense.'

Brakes screeched outside. Peter winced and through the window Hannah saw a white van pulling up. A burly figure clambered out and for a shocking instant she thought it was Warren Howe. The shape of the head and the dark tousled hair resembled the old photograph in the file. But of course this must be his son Sam. The dead never came back to life.

Chapter Thirteen

The crowds at Hill Top gave Miranda a headache. Beatrix Potter had stipulated in her will that the old farmhouse should be maintained in its original state, and entry was restricted by a timed ticket system. They waited for an hour to get into the shrine, but within five minutes Miranda declared that she'd seen enough and wandered off to seek refuge from the worshipping sight-seers amongst the whitewashed cottages of Near Sawrey.

Louise lingered in silence over the old bound volumes in the library while Daniel leafed through a pamphlet about the author's life. She'd had an unexpected fondness for mystification, he discovered. It had taken years to crack the secret code in her private journal. He liked the story about her dressing up in sackcloth and being mistaken by a tramp for a fellow traveller. And for all her tales about dear little creatures, Beatrix could be clinical as well as cute. Skinning a rabbit, boiling the bones and then reassembling the skeleton with an autopsy technician's attention to detail, questing for authenticity, determined to give her pencil drawings a cutting edge.

The shaded room offered shelter from the heat and noise. Something was troubling his sister, he could tell; each time the room cleared, she seemed about to speak, but then more visitors came in and the moment passed. Only when they made their way out into the cottage garden did she reveal what was on her mind.

'I'm outstaying my welcome, aren't I?'

'She's tired, that's all.' He screwed up his eyes in the glare of the afternoon sun and reached into his pocket for his dark glasses. 'This weather doesn't suit her.'

'It's not about the weather, Daniel.'

'Don't take it personally. Miranda will be fine.'

'I don't think so.' Louise exhaled. 'I'll check train times.'

'Don't be silly. There's no need. Listen, I enjoy having you here. I don't want you to leave.'

She brushed his cheek with her lips. 'Thanks, Daniel. The break's done me good. But I don't want to come between you and Miranda.'

'Anyone would think you're an old mistress, returning to haunt us. You're reading too much into a few grumpy remarks.'

'She wants you to herself.'

She rested her backside on a low stone wall and he perched beside her, out of the way of people taking pictures of each other, gleefully snapping and posing in Mr Macgregor's flower-filled back yard.

'I want you to be happy together.'

'We are.'

'I'm not just talking about the sex, Daniel.' A rueful smile. 'That sounds pretty good.'

Early that morning, Miranda had woken him up and hauled her warm naked body on top of his. As they made love, she'd cried out in delight. Even with the thick stone walls of Tarn Cottage, it would have been a miracle if Louise in the next-door room had slept through.

He groaned. 'Christ, Louise, I'm sorry.'

'Don't be. All I'm saying is that you need more than fun at bed-time to keep you together. Trust me, Rodney was surprisingly good in that department, but in the long run it wasn't enough.'

'Hey,' he said, determined not to think about Rodney with his sister, 'you and I aren't the only people who've had a rough time. Before we met, Miranda had an affair with a married man that didn't work out. Plus a lesbian boss who made a pass and then victimised her when she didn't say yes. She's been badly bruised. Healing takes time.'

'Don't I know it? But that's the point, Daniel. The two of you need space, a chance to see if you can make this mad idea of running away from the rat race work out for you both.'

'Is it such a mad idea?'

'Not for you,' she said. 'But for Miranda? A different story, I guess.'

'I wouldn't be here if it she hadn't persuaded me we should buy the cottage.'

'Even so.'

'Don't you like her?'

'I do, actually. I'm just not sure she's right for you.'

'What makes you think that?'

'Because I know you.' She hesitated. 'And I can tell that deep down you're not sure either.'

'You specialise in mind-reading now?'

She tapped him on the shoulder. 'You and me, we've spent too many years together to be able to fool each other. Don't let me bother you. After all, you never did when you were younger. I want this to work out for both of you, Daniel, honestly I do. I just think you may have a better chance if I'm not here, getting in the way.'

'You're not getting in the way,' he said stubbornly.

Louise slipped off the wall and disappeared into the throng of camera-toting, ice-cream-licking tourists and National Trust volunteers. He closed his eyes and felt the sun burning his unprotected cheeks. He took in a breath of hot air and then headed out of the garden and in search of Miranda.

Hannah arrived back in Kendal shortly after five. Chris Gleave had presented her with a CD of his songs and she'd been playing it in the car. His voice and guitar-playing were pleasant but unexceptional, his words and music much the same. If he'd ever hoped to earn fame and fortune as a latter day Paul Simon, he'd been deceiving himself. He might entertain an undemanding audience here or in Keswick, but no singer so bland would ever fill Central Park.

As the town baked, tempers frayed. Drivers tooted at pedestrians who took a chance dodging through slothful traffic, mothers yelled at infants and made them wail. Hannah's eyes were dry and sore and her abdomen hurt. She called at a chemist's and a bookshop and then hurried back to the station.

At the water cooler, she bumped into Nick Lowther. They complained to each other about the temperature and he brought her up to speed with progress in the Cockermouth case. The good news was that they'd identified a likely culprit, the bad news was that he'd suffered a severe stroke a year back and would never speak or walk again. No-one seemed to know whether the stats for the review team would record this as a success or a failure.

Nick glanced up and down the corridor and lowered his voice. 'Can we have a word sometime?'

'Of course.'

'I mean, in private. Not here. It's…personal.'

Oh Christ. I'm not sure I want to know.

'No problem.'

'One thing, though, Hannah. This has to be strictly off the record.'

A young woman constable passed them in the corridor and they exchanged a word. As her footsteps receded, Hannah scanned Nick's face. He was an attractive man, she could have fancied him if he wasn't a colleague, but over the past few days he'd aged. The whites of his eyes were bloodshot, his complexion pasty and untouched by the sun.

This is about you and Roz Gleave, isn't it?

'OK.'

'Thanks.' He swallowed. 'I promise I won't compromise you.'

'No worries, Nick.' Should she say this? Not long ago she wouldn't have thought twice. 'I trust you.'

'Thanks,' he said in a tone that told her she'd said the right thing. 'And I trust you. Which is why I need to talk.'

'When?'

He checked his watch. 'I promised not to be late home this evening. The parents-in-law are coming round for a meal and I'll be in big trouble if I don't lend a hand.'

'Call me when you're ready.'

Les Bryant strode around the corner. He was in shirt-sleeves and it was the first time Hannah had seen him without a tie.

'How did you get on?'

Early on after his arrival in the team, he'd made a point of calling her ma'am, in sardonic acknowledgement of his unaccustomed position as a subordinate.At least he'd relaxed since then. One of these days he'd so far forget himself as to use her first name.

'If you have ten minutes, I'll update you.'

'I'll leave you to it,' Nick said. 'I need to be getting off.'

Les filled his paper cup to the brim as Nick walked away. He lapped at the drink like a grizzled old cat and then said, 'Is he all right?'

'What do you mean?'

Les raised his eyebrows to indicate that he recognised a disingenuous reply when he heard one. 'He's not the man he was. Seems hassled about something.'

'Could be the weather.'

'Gets blamed for a lot of things, does the weather. Convenient scapegoat, if you ask me. Any road, Nick Lowther's problems are none of my business. I had enough years worrying about my flock, believe me.'

Despite her other preoccupations, she couldn't help savouring the notion of Les as a caring shepherd. They went back to her office and she switched her new fan to maximum. The whirring set her teeth on edge, and the room seemed hotter than ever. As she summarised her interviews with Warren Howe's family and business partner, Les didn't utter a word. Slumped in his chair, eyes half-closed, he seemed to be dozing off despite the racket from the fan. But Hannah knew better. She'd come to admire his quality of stillness, his ability to focus all his attention on the matter in hand when not playing up to his reputation as a cantankerous Yorkshireman. As a listener, he was up in the Ben Kind class.

'Are they all fibbing?'

She made an exasperated noise. 'It wouldn't surprise me. There are plenty of leads in this case, but none of them seem to go anywhere.'

'You think she did it?'

'Tina?' Hannah considered. 'She would be capable of killing him. And of covering her tracks.'

He plucked a blank sheet of A4 from her desk and waved it in front of his face in the vain hope of creating a current of air. 'Just because a tip-off is anonymous, doesn't mean it's untrue.'

'I'd have more faith if we'd been given some ammunition to fire at Tina. A clear motive, for a start.'

'She was married to the man, for God's sake. What more of a motive do you want?'

'They'd been married a long time. If she snapped all of a sudden, there must have been a reason.'

'The affair with Gail?'

'It was supposed to be over, remember? Anyway, why choose that particular moment to kill him? There's no rhyme or reason. Even so, she has to be the favourite. Which suggests that the alibi her kids gave her is false.'

'Unless she hired someone to do the dirty deed.'

'I can't imagine Tina wanting to put herself at someone else's mercy. I'd say she's a control freak. Besides, there aren't any likely candidates for the role of hit man, are there? The Sawreys aren't exactly awash with contract killers. Poaching rabbits is as wicked as it gets in that neck of the woods.'

'How about Oliver Cox? A young man, newly arrived in the area. A chancer, probably unscrupulous.'

'More rewarding to make a play for Bel Jenner, surely? And a lot easier than carrying out a hit for a woman he hardly knew. Even if he did see Bel as a meal ticket, he's put down roots now. For all the age gap, the two of them are like peas in a pod.'

'Who knows what goes on behind closed doors? Besides, they've never married. Never had kids.'

'You can be happy together even if you're not married, even if you don't have kids,' she murmured.

Realising he'd touched a nerve, Les grunted. An acknowledgement, if far less than an apology. After a pause, Hannah carried on.

'No, if Tina killed Warren, my guess is that she took the scythe to him herself.'

'If you want to break her alibi, sounds like young Kirsty's the weak link.'

'Yes, she's not as hard-faced as her mum or her brother. I felt sorry for her, even though I was sure she was holding out on me.'

'I've never felt sorry for a suspect.'

She could believe him. 'I can't see Kirsty slashing her Dad to pieces.'

'I'm not saying she wouldn't feel bad about it afterwards.'

'If she has a guilty conscience, I don't think it's because she's a murderer. Frankly, if she'd killed Warren, I think even Charlie would have caught her. Kirsty's the sort who would want to get it off her chest. Covering up for her mother might be different. If she was protecting someone else, she might force herself to be strong for their sake.'

'Ask Linz to talk to her. They may have things in common. Pop music, fashion, lads, whatever. She's a similar age to Kirsty, it may give us a way in.'

'So I'm too old to bond with her? Thanks a lot.'

'Horses for courses,' he said, deadpan. 'We're none of us as young as we were. How about brother Sam?'

'I'm certainly past it as far as he's concerned. Talk about a chip off the old block. I bet that every woman he meets, he undresses them with his eyes.'

'That obvious, eh?'

'As a matter of fact, yes. I'm sure he's not as stupid as he likes to make out, but subtlety isn't his strong point. I'm afraid that what he saw when he looked me over mustn't have met his high standards.'

'Can't believe that.'

She grinned. It was the closest she'd ever heard him come to gallantry. Possibly the closest he'd come in years.

'Trust me, the bloke didn't make the slightest effort to make friends or influence me. Even Tina seemed embarrassed by his rudeness.'

'Suppose you prove the alibi is fake. Even if one of them admits that Tina wasn't up on the Pass that day, we'd still be a mile off having a strong enough case to put to the CPS. You know what most prosecutors are like. If you can't give them a video of the mad sniper as he guns down his victims, the file goes straight into the "too difficult" cupboard.'

Hannah sighed. 'For all we know, she and Peter took the opportunity to have a quick shag while Warren was working at Keepsake Cottage.'

'Or maybe Tina persuaded Peter to kill him.'

'I can believe he would be putty in her hands. But if that's what happened, it was an own goal. The business struggled and Peter and Gail didn't split up for years.'

'What if they were playing it long term?'

'Peter might be capable of that,' she admitted. 'But Tina? If she wanted Peter for herself, I can't see her letting him stay with his wife for so long afterwards. Even if they were having it off together on the quiet in the meantime.'

Les glared at the clattering fan. 'Some choice, eh? Either fry or be deafened. All right. We've spoken about Cox. Other candidates?'

'Gail Flint must be worth another look. Bel Jenner – I don't think so. She'd not long since lost her husband and was in the process of seducing Cox. Or being seduced by him, same difference. I'm not sure she's bright enough to get away with murder so successfully. But even if I'm wrong, her relationship with Warren was ancient history.'

'Would he take no for an answer?'

'Depends on what his options were.'

'You'd rule out Chris Gleave?'

'Difficult to see past his alibi. Or find a motive.'

'What if Warren took up with Roz again after finishing with Gail? Suppose he used the garden job as cover for the affair? Could that be what drove her husband away?'

'And then she took a dislike to the way he was planting the hollyhocks?'

'You can't expect me to hand you a solution on a plate like one of them armchair detectives.'

'I'm disappointed in you, Les.'

'All right, then. If you run out of ideas, how about this? All of them were in on it. The whole bloody village.'

She laughed. 'No chance. This is Cumbria, we have narrow-gauge crimes. Not the conspiracy killings you get on the Orient Express.'

The world was turning upside down. Kirsty had been drunk a few times in her life and she remembered the ground tilting under her feet, the dizzy sense of being out of control. Somehow she'd stumbled back home from Keepsake Cottage, but she could recall nothing about the journey except the blaring of a horn when she'd nearly walked under a car's wheels.

Tears stung her eyes. She wandered aimlessly around the kitchen; a couple of times her hips bumped against the edge of the breakfast bar. Her leg hurt; she'd barked her shin and not even noticed. A mirror on the wall distorted her features, like something out of a fairground. How ugly she was. Red-faced, fat and repulsive. How could she ever have imagined that Oliver would want to touch her? They had no future together, that was for certain.

The house seemed like a foreign land, she'd forgotten where everything was. Her stomach hurt; she hadn't had any lunch, but she wasn't in the mood for eating. This was one of those times when even chocolate couldn't solve a thing.

It would have been better all round if that driver hadn't swerved to avoid her. At least before you got drunk you could relish the buzz of the alcohol. She felt dazed, as though someone had clubbed her on the head. In a way, someone had.

Roz Gleave was a friend, how could she be so cruel? What she said, how could it be true?

Yes, she had to cling to that. It couldn't be true.

'Are you sure?' Miranda asked as Daniel kept his eyes on the winding road. 'I mean, you're welcome to stay here for as long as you want. Isn't she, darling?'

'That's very generous of you.' Louise, curled up in the back of the car, spoke over Daniel's muttered assent. 'I'm so grateful for your hospitality, so glad I came. But I ought to get back home. Term will be starting soon.'

'You're going back to the college?'

'It's what I'm paid for. And I need to prepare.'

'Well, if your mind's made up...'

'I just need to check the train times.'

'All right, if you insist. But you will come back and see us again soon?'

'Promise.'

Daniel gripped the steering wheel tight. He sensed Miranda

relaxing beside him and stole a glance at her. A sleek smile of contentment played on her lips.

Hannah's mobile trilled the opening bars of 'I Say A Little Prayer' as Les wandered out of the office. Her home number showed up on the tiny screen. She couldn't resist a frisson of apprehension. Marc rarely called her at work.

'I wanted to let you know, I'll be out till late this evening,' he said.

'What's the matter?'

'Nothing.' He sounded puzzled. 'Remember I told you that Leigh's looking to change the décor in the cafeteria? When I've locked up, we'll be setting off for Morecambe to meet the designer. Don't wait up.'

We're always too busy for each other, she thought. Usually it's my fault. But tonight of all nights…

'Are you OK?'

'Yes, yes. There's – just something I want to discuss with you, that's all.'

'It can keep till tomorrow, can't it?'

'I'd rather we had a word tonight.'

He didn't quite manage to suppress a sigh. 'OK. I'll aim to be back by eleven at the latest. You haven't got to go away on another weekend management course, have you?'

'See you later.' She switched off the phone before he could ask any more questions.

Daniel achieved his aim of arriving early at The Heights and the bar was empty when they walked in. Bel Jenner bustled out to confirm the table reservation and did a double take when she saw him. Another tribute to the reach of television. She'd caught a couple of his programmes, she told him. History had always fascinated her, it was her favourite subject at school, not that she was much of a one for studying.

Oliver was duly brought out for introductions to be performed and he insisted that the first round of drinks was on the house. Bel joined Daniel and Louise on the sofas in the lobby by the restaurant while Miranda indulged in a jokey flirtation with Oliver across the bar counter. The headache had vanished, Daniel noticed. She was back in control and soon her laughter was ringing across the room, drowing the dulcet tones of Astrud Gilberto singing Jobim classics. Louise didn't have much to say, or perhaps she simply struggled to get a word in edgeways. Bel loved to chat and within a quarter of an hour Daniel had learned more about The Heights, Old Sawrey and the local populace than he could have picked up in a hundred internet searches.

Hannah would be proud of me. Maybe so would Dad.

He mentioned working on the cottage garden and consulting a local firm. 'Flint Howe Garden Design. Do you know them?'

'Everyone knows everyone round here, Daniel. Compared to Old Sawrey, Brack is Los Angeles. Tina Howe's daughter Kirsty works for us as a waitress. Lovely girl. You'll meet her later, I hope. She rang an hour ago to say that she's feeling off colour but she still hopes to come in. I told her not to worry, and make sure she gets herself right, but she absolutely insisted. A touch of the sun, I suppose, but that's the kind of person Kirsty is, she hates to let anyone down.'

'I met her brother through Peter Flint.'

Bel pursed her lips. 'Yes, Sam's a bright boy, though you wouldn't necessarily guess it from speaking to him. As Kirsty says, he does like to pretend he's a closer relative of the ape family than the rest of us. He made a mess of his exams and left school at the first opportunity, though if you listen to his mother, he had the brains to go to university. But working for Peter isn't necessarily a waste of talent. You can make decent money out of gardening these days. Nearly as lucrative as plumbing if you're any good. I know when the seal on our upstairs shower perished and the water was trickling down the...'

Unwilling to be diverted into reminiscences about rapacious tradesmen, Daniel said, 'You've known the Howes a long time?'

'As long as I can remember. Kirsty's a super girl. Brave, too. She loves skydiving, she's jumping for charity tomorrow, as it happens. I suppose she felt that if she wasn't fit this evening, I might be cross if she was well enough to fling herself out of an aeroplane tomorrow afternoon. But really, I said to her, if you're not up to working, that's fine. Waitressing isn't an easy job, Daniel. You need your wits about you. As well as doing the work with a smile on your face and making sure you keep your customers satisfied.'

'I gather her father died in – terrible circumstances.'

Bel flushed. 'Did Peter mention that?'

'What happened?' Louise asked.

'He was murdered,' Daniel said, keeping his eyes on Bel. 'Hacked to pieces with his own scythe whilst he was working on a client's garden.'

'Jesus. Not the best advertisement.'

'It was a very unhappy time.' Bel's head was bowed, her tone mournful and subdued, as though she were whispering during prayers. 'You read about that sort of thing in the papers, you might expect it in cities like Leeds or Manchester, I suppose. You never imagine it happening on your own doorstep.'

'You knew Mr Howe?'

'We grew up together.' She paused, for once disinclined to yield information. 'For a while we were friendly, then we drifted apart. You know how it is.'

'He married a local girl?'

'Tina grew up in Hawkshead.'

She made it sound like hailing from Gomorrah. More a reflection of her opinion of Tina Howe than of the pretty little tourist trap, Daniel presumed. He went through a pantomime of working things out in his head.

'Tina? I spoke to her when I booked the appointment. So she works in the office to this day, she's Peter's partner?'

'In both senses, yes.'

'Ah.' Daniel wondered how to keep the conversation going, scrabbled round in his mind for a sentiment that might appeal to Bel. 'She found happiness in the end, then?'

'You could say that. Peter's ex-wife might have different ideas. Poor Gail, she's in the wine trade, we're business colleagues as well as friends.'

'He left her for Tina?'

'Oh, Gail wanted a divorce once she saw the writing on the wall.' She leaned over the table and whispered like a conspirator. 'But I don't believe she's ever got over him. I keep saying, she should forget about him and find someone else. She's a lovely-looking woman, but her confidence has been shot to pieces. It's so sad.'

Louise finished her gin and tonic. 'Men, eh?'

Bel looked across to the bar and Daniel's eyes followed hers. Miranda was in full flow, telling her life story by the look of it, but Oliver's gaze had strayed. He exchanged a glance with Bel before concentrating on Miranda again. Daniel guessed she hadn't even realised she'd lost her audience's attention.

'I suppose I'm lucky.' Bel started humming along to 'The Girl from Ipanema'. 'How many men can you really trust? Well, lovely to have a chat. Let me get you the menus.'

As she moved away, Louise muttered, 'What are you playing at?'

'How do you mean?'

'Come on, you can't fool me. You were pumping her for information. What's going on?'

'Just taking an interest in the everyday lives of rural folk.'

'Lying toad. That innocent expression may work a treat with most ladies, but I've seen it before, remember? You wear it to disguise your ulterior motives.'

'Men, eh?' he mimicked.

She laughed. 'You bastard. For some funny reason I'm going to miss you when I go back home.'

Hannah's dinner consisted of a takeaway Margharita pizza and a glass of Buxton water. Where was the pleasure in cooking for one? She decided against washing it down with half a bottle of wine. For several reasons, not least the need to keep a clear head. Sprawled on the sofa, dressed only in the cotton shirt she sometimes wore in bed, she flicked the television remote control, searching in vain for escape. Escape from Marc, from Nick, from crime, from everything.

She'd scarcely given Daniel a thought all day. Without

knowing it, he'd become a sort of crutch; whenever she was unhappy, she let her imagination roam. In her head they conversed about his father and he listened with his customary intensity as she explained what it was like to work alongside the man who had taught her everything about detecting crime. Today, for the first time, it wasn't enough. She needed to get to grips with reality, remind herself that he had Miranda; her man was Marc.

The television was rubbish. Celebrity mud-wrestling, a sitcom about AIDS, an hour-long documentary about baby-sitters from hell. Marc had bought her a DVD of a Dionne Warwick concert in Syracuse, but she wasn't in the mood. She lifted a framed photograph from the mantelpiece, trying not to think when she'd last dusted the surface. In the picture, Marc's arm wrapped around her as they boarded the liner at Nice. She could still feel the pressure on her shoulder; impossible to believe it was five years since that cruise round the Med. She'd loved going to sleep in one place and waking up in another. They'd lazed around the pool, wandered off on excursions to Taormina and Pompeii. In those days, she'd believed in everlasting love.

Was he up to something with Leigh Moffat, was this meeting with the designer simply a blind? He'd slept with her sister, after all. Dale was younger and prettier, Leigh more of an enigma. Hannah had known the woman for years but still hadn't a clue what went on inside her mind. Perhaps there was nothing personal between them, perhaps Leigh just shared Marc's determination to keep the shop afloat. Then again…

Before she knew it, she was sobbing. She hated herself for showing weakness, even when there was nobody to witness it. Thank God Marc was late, she still had time to compose herself. She wanted to swallow a couple of pills to calm her nerves, but she couldn't do it, she'd have to tough it out. Even though she could no longer dodge the truth. She was frightened that this was the night when she'd lose him forever.

Kirsty served their meals with a smile so bright, so fixed, so forced, that Daniel knew she must be unhappy. Either that or she was one of the Stepford Waitresses. Yes, she assured him, she was fully recovered. No harm done. She'd spent too long in the sun without a hat, more fool her, that was the top and bottom of it. Yes, she was keen on skydiving, and she was doing a jump for charity tomorrow afternoon. But when he said that he'd spoken to her mum on the phone and met her brother, a hunted look came into her eyes and she fled back to the kitchen without another word.

'She only wanted to know whether you wanted anything else with your fish.' Miranda spoke more loudly than usual. By Daniel's calculation, she was on her third large glass of wine. 'It wasn't the opening gambit in a conversation. She's got work to do. Just because her boss can talk for England, it doesn't mean all the staff love a gossip.'

'You seemed to be getting on well with Oliver,' Louise said.

Miranda gave a dreamy smile. 'He's rather nice. We have things in common.'

'Don't tell me,' Daniel said. 'He's into self-help manuals and aromatherapy.'

She kicked him under the table. 'Jealous?'

'Madly.'

She laughed so raucously that an old woman on the next table looked round in alarm. Louise caught Daniel's eye and flashed a wicked grin. He wished she wasn't about to leave him. Without her, he'd feel alone.

'You stayed up, then?'

Marc kicked off his shoes as he walked into the living room. He smelled faintly of old books. Hannah glanced at the clock. Ten to midnight. He was later than expected and she'd had all evening to rehearse, but she hadn't prepared a word of the little speech she meant to make. Her bones were weary, but she was on edge and there'd never been any danger she would fall asleep.

'I said on the phone, I wanted to tell you something.'

'Can't it wait? I'm dog tired, there was a hold-up on the road. Overturned lorry. Ambulance, fire engines, the works.'

'Sit down.'

He stared, then slowly moved to the armchair facing her. 'What?'

'This is important, Marc.'

'The build-up is daunting enough. You've got me shaking in my socks.'

'I'm not in the mood, Marc.'

He screwed up his face, as if trying to read mirror writing. 'You're upset.'

'Not exactly. No, I'm just – wound up, that's all.'

'Go on, then. Tell me.'

Her throat was dry. She couldn't think of an alternative to blurting out her secret.

'I'm pregnant, Marc. We're going to have a baby.'

Chapter Fourteen

Sam belched and said, 'What's up?'

'Nothing,' Kirsty said.

'Come on.' He pushed aside a coffee mug emblazoned with a picture of a pair of bare buttocks. The odour of last night's curry masked the smell of burned bacon. 'You've not said a word since you came down.'

'I'm having my breakfast.'

'Doesn't normally stop you gabbing on. And you've got a face on you like…'

'Like what?' She expected the usual insult, but it could no longer wound her.

'I dunno. Like you're a stranger here, like you don't belong any more.'

She tasted the last of her pineapple juice. Funny he should say that. Was it possible that he was more than an insensitive plank? Too late to find out now. But he was right, she was seeing their home with new eyes. She felt like a traveller wandering through a foreign land without a guidebook. Or even a passport.

'I don't believe it. You're not actually concerned about me?'

'Suit yourself.' The jeering tone reminded her of their father. 'Wetting yourself about jumping out of that plane, are you?'

'No, I'm looking forward to it.'

The phone rang. Waiting for her to pick up the receiver, he leaned back on his stool; he had a circus artist's knack of making it wobble madly, while somehow managing not to fall over. When she didn't move, the phone kept on – they hadn't switched on the voicemail – and in the end he gave a long-suffering sigh and answered the call himself.

'Yeah?' He made a face. 'Roz? Yeah, she's here. Just finished her breakfast.'

Kirsty shook her head vigorously but he stuck his tongue out at her and said, 'Fine, yeah, I'll hand you over.'

She didn't want a conversation, least of all with Roz, but he'd left the handset on the breakfast bar and she couldn't leave the woman hanging on. Even now, even after their conversation yesterday and everything that had passed through her mind since then, her instinct was to show good manners. She'd spent so much of her life waiting on people.

'Hello?'

'Kirsty, thank God! I tried your mobile, but you've switched it off. I was so worried about you.'

'Oh yes?'

'Well yes, of course I was. Look, I know it's dreadful, I know you're angry and hurting…'

'Sorry, Roz, I have to go now.'

She'd never heard panic in Roz's voice, but it was unmistakable. 'You're not going to tell anyone, are you? Please say you won't. Promise?'

That's what she cares about, Kirsty thought. More than whether I'm hurting.

'No, I won't tell anyone,' she said and slammed down the phone.

Saturday was Marc's busiest day. If he wasn't in the shop, he'd be exhibiting at a book fair. Today he'd risen before six to load his car and set off for a fair at the Pavilion Gardens in Buxton. Hannah had still been in bed when he bent over her huddled body and she felt his moist lips touch her brow.

'Let's talk again tonight.' His voice was hoarse.

'Ummmm.'

What's to talk about? she wondered as she picked at a piece of dry toast. Does he think I've hoodwinked him, that the pregnancy was no accident? On the rare occasions they'd talked about having children, they'd both agreed they weren't that bothered. She had her career, he had the bookshop, a screaming baby or two would get in the way. Not that she lacked maternal instincts; when she spent time in the company of friends with young kids, she began to understand the appeal of the small, warm, grubby creatures. She wasn't like Terri, who made it clear to each husband that she wasn't a bloody breeding machine. But she always pushed the idea of starting a family to the back of her mind. Plenty of time yet, she used to tell herself. As for Marc, he was like so many men. Wary about fatherhood in the abstract, but once he held his own child in his arms…

A sick feeling flooded her stomach. Not a symptom of pregnancy, but down to Marc's reaction. The colour had drained from his face as she broke the news. He'd stammered *that's…that's wonderful*, wearing the look of a man about to walk to the scaffold.

Face it, she told herself. You want this to strengthen the relationship, make it secure and work long-term. Forget the daydreams about Daniel Kind, Marc is the man you're with. You've never been hung up about having a ring on your finger, but a child is different. You're committed forever.

But she wasn't naïve. This wasn't guaranteed to finish up happy-ever-after. There could be a dread alternative ending, like those you see as special features on DVD movies, rejected by the producer because they were too dark for the cinema audience's peace of mind. What if having a baby tore them apart?

The ringtone of her mobile pierced the silence.

'Hannah Scarlett.'

'Nick.'

'Oh, hi.'

'Are you OK?'

'Yes, sure.'

'I mean, you sounded…never mind.'

'You wanted to talk?'

'How about this afternoon?'

'I'm off duty but Marc's driving down to Derbyshire. I'd thought of going to a skydiving event. You might like to come along.'

'Are you serious?'

'There's an ulterior motive.'

A laugh. 'Why doesn't that surprise me?'

'Kirsty Howe is one of the parachutists and I'd like to talk to her again. We didn't get off on the right foot. She may be more relaxed if we meet on her home ground.'

'If she's a skydiver, maybe she doesn't do relaxation. But I'm happy to meet you there.'

'We can have a heart to heart.'

Suddenly, she wanted very much to be with a man who cared for her. Not a lover, but someone she could rely on. Would she tell Nick about the baby? Not yet, it was too early. She needed to see her GP to confirm the result from the testing kit, but her guess was that she was a month gone. She wasn't intending to broadcast the news until she'd made it through the first twelve weeks. So much could yet go wrong. She was frightened of tempting fate.

'I couldn't do it,' Louise said. 'I just couldn't do it.'

'I can see the appeal, in a funny kind of way,' Miranda said. 'Skydiving is all about living dangerously, isn't it?'

Behind the wheel, Daniel uttered a silent prayer that she wouldn't develop a new passion for extreme sports. Dodging bikers on the narrow lanes was dangerous enough.

'I'm keen to continue living, I suppose,' Louise said. 'Danger, I can do without.'

Miranda gave a sigh of dissent. Louise was going home the day after tomorrow, Daniel thought, Miranda had won. She didn't need to bite her tongue any more, didn't need to avoid petty disagreements for the sake of diplomatic relations.

'We all need a little danger in our lives, if you ask me. I can see the appeal of jumping out of a plane with nothing to rely on but your parachute, no-one to trust but yourself. Women are supposed to be well-suited to it, Kirsty said so last night when we were leaving. They have the physical flexibility as well as stamina.'

'She didn't look well to me. Pale and drawn. I hope she's going to be all right.'

'Lovesick,' Miranda diagnosed. 'She fancies Oliver.'

'How do you know?'

'I saw the way she looked at him when she thought nobody was watching. Not even him. Poor thing, my bet is, she's doomed to be disappointed. If you ask me, he only has eyes for Bel.'

The airfield stretched across low, flat terrain on the southern tip of the county. It had been an RAF base during the Second World

War, but since then it had seen little action more exciting than the occasional car boot sale. In the Nineties, skydiving enthusiasts from universities and colleges had begun to utilise it and today there was a huge banner above the entrance proclaiming the Lakeland Parachutists' Club Annual Charity Freeflying Day.

The lane skirting the perimeter had been colonised by traders selling ice creams, floppy hats and sun block and a field had been turned into a car park. The Lexus was air-conditioned, but the moment Hannah climbed out, the heat smothered her. The afternoon was so humid that she could scarcely breathe. It was an effort to drag one leg after the other as she crossed the lane. How much of her exhaustion was down to the weather, and how much to pregnancy, she wasn't sure, but she was praying for a thunderstorm to cleanse the atmosphere.

She made a donation to the students rattling tin boxes at the entrance and looked around for Nick. Each of the students wore a sweatshirt bearing the question *Fancy a Jump?* Upwards of two hundred people were milling around on this side of a fence and a signboard labelled – *Danger – Keep Out – Dropzone.* The first face she recognised belonged to Tina Howe. She was wearing a sleeveless top and a short white skirt that displayed long tanned legs. When their eyes met, the older woman stared in surprise, but after a brief pause, she pushed past a group of lager-swilling girls and made her way to Hannah's side.

'I didn't expect to see you, Chief Inspector. What brings you here?'

'Curiosity, I guess, Mrs Howe. I've seen skydiving on TV, but never in real life. I thought it was time to fill the gap in my education.'

'You know Kirsty's freeflying today?'

Hannah nodded. 'Sounds terrifying to me. I did a little research. Freefly involves falling through the air with your head facing down?'

'Twice the speed of conventional skydiving, she tells me.' Tina exhaled. 'I've only dared to watch her once before and my heart was in my mouth when she hit the ground. According to her, the only serious risk is if you try to show off with some hair-raising stunt and miscalculate so that you hit the ground hard instead of skimming over the dropzone and landing perfectly. But when I tell her to take care, she says I'm a whuffo.'

'A whuffo?'

'An American term, it's what skydivers call sane people who ask the obvious question. What for you guys jump out of them aeroplanes? Kirsty reckons skydiving is the best fun she's ever had.' She folded her arms across her breasts. 'Tell you what, I never had hundreds of people watching the best fun I ever had, but it takes all sorts. Are you here with anyone?'

'I might ask you the same question.'

'I sent Sam for ice creams, Peter's gone for a pee. So you're on your own?'

'Looking out for a friend of mine.'

'Another police officer?'

'Why do you ask?'

A scornful noise. 'You're not telling me you've suddenly developed an interest in skydiving. You're here for a reason.'

Hannah held her gaze. 'Kirsty must have stacks of courage. Any skydiver must, I'd say. Yet she seems to me to be worried sick. It's the contradiction that fascinates me.'

'She is a brave girl. Sensitive, too, her feelings are close to the surface. Not like me or her dad. Or her brother, come to that. But you're wasting your time if you think you'll be able to worm something out of her about Warren's murder. She won't tell you anything new. There's nothing to tell.'

'Daniel!' Peter Flint was gorging on his cornet and there was a smear of vanilla ice cream on his chin. His shorts exposed bony knees and made him look like an overgrown schoolboy. 'I didn't expect to see you here.'

'We had a meal at The Heights yesterday evening,' Daniel said. Miranda and Louise had wandered off to look at the bric-a-brac for sale on the stalls. 'Kirsty mentioned that she'd be here today and we decided to take a look.'

'Just as exciting to watch as to participate, if you ask me, and

a hell of a lot safer. Not that Kirsty would agree. She keeps
assuring her mother that freeflying is statistically less risky than
fly-fishing. Anglers are constantly slipping off wet rocks and
drowning in rivers or lakes, it seems. Parachutists come through
thousands of jumps without a scratch.'

Daniel laughed. 'You know what they say about lies, damned
lies…'

'And statistics, yes. Glad to bump into you. I was meaning to
get in touch.'

'I'm still mulling over your sketches.'

'I wasn't meaning to hassle you for business. Sam mentioned
something that I thought would interest you. He once heard his
father talking about a garden at Tarn Fold.'

Daniel stared at him. 'Warren Howe?'

'Yes. According to Sam, he knew people in Brackdale, they
told him the story.'

'What story?'

'Perhaps I was too hasty with my ideas for a re-design. I'd hate
to be accused of vandalism.'

'Sorry, I don't understand.'

'A long time ago, the garden at Tarn Cottage was well-known
in the valley. There was some sort of folk-tale attached to it.
People called it the cipher garden.'

The Cessna 206 Turbo was small and uncomfortable. There was
only room for six passengers, even with all seats except for the
pilot's removed. They were sitting on a mat with their backs to
the pilot, legs splayed with a spectacular lack of dignity that
provoked endless rude jokes. Kirsty's companions were four men
and one other woman, an anorexic redhead who was having an
affair with the pilot. Their eye-line was below the level of the
window, but through the clear plastic roller door she could see
tiny farms and copses and a caravan park. Soon they would circle
over the broad expanse of Morecambe Bay and its bright,
treacherous sands.

The noise inside the plane was drowned by the thoughts
roaring inside her head. Her first instructor had preached that

three-quarters of skydiving took place on the ground. So much depended on how you prepared for the jump.

Flying to altitude would take twenty-five minutes. This was always a time she found peaceful, a time when everything else in her life meant nothing. She'd been taught to relax and visualise herself doing what she had set out to do. Yet whenever the pilot called two minutes, her nerves would fray and over and over again she played through the malfunction procedure in her head. Checking release pins, cut-away and reserve handles, and to make sure that bits of parachute were safely inside the rig. Everyone looked out for each other. If a pilot chute deployed inside the plane with the door open, it could tear off the wings and they would all be dead.

Fear. Skydiving was all about conquering fear. As a raw novice about to make her first jump, Kirsty had found her heart beating faster, she'd taken rapid shallow breaths. The irony was, her trainer said, that survival instinct made your muscles tighten when you needed to relax. Embrace the fear was his mantra, along with hips down, head up. You needed to contain the surge of adrenaline. Over time, she'd learned to focus. Leaving the plane remained the moment of deepest fear, but she would scream out, 'Up, down, go!', breaking the tension in her chest by forcing out the air. And then she would fall.

'I was telling Daniel about the cipher garden,' Peter Flint said.

Sam uttered an unintelligible grunt. Despite the heat, he was tucking into a ketchup-coated burger in a bap and plainly couldn't be bothered with idle chit-chat.

'What can you tell me about it?'

A shrug. 'Not much to tell. I heard my Dad speak about it once when I was a kid. That's all.'

'What did he say?'

They could hear the plane high above, heading towards the bay. Sam spat casually on the ground, then wiped his lips with the back of his sweatshirt sleeve. His breath smelled of fried onions.

'Only that there used to be a cipher garden over at Tarn Fold in Brackdale.'

Peter Flint said, 'He never mentioned it to me.'

'You're an off-comer,' Sam said brutally. 'This was just a local tale. A legend, like. He heard about it when he did a spot of work at Brack Hall.'

'What was the legend?' Daniel asked.

'I dunno exactly. About why the people died, the people that owned the garden? Something like that.'

'A family called Gilpin owned our cottage for years. Originally, it was built by a man called Quiller. In between, it kept changing hands.'

'Maybe people were afraid there was a curse on it.'

Daniel stared. 'A curse?'

'The cipher was about death. There was a message in the garden, it was supposed to explain how the people who lived happened to die.'

'Fascinating, don't you think?' Peter Flint asked. 'And not a little spooky.'

'What else do you know about the cipher?' Daniel demanded.

The young man finished his bap. It was evidently more satisfying than the conversation. 'That's all. I never paid much heed.'

'I'd like to take another look at your garden,' Peter Flint said, 'see if I can make out this cipher. Actually, Daniel, you have some pretty wicked plants growing around the tarn. Venomous plants are like weeds, you know. Give them time and they proliferate. I'm not just talking about all your foxgloves, or the belladonna. Hellebore is seriously toxic, the roots are poisonous as well as the leaves. Even its flowers strike me as sinister. As for mandrake...'

Sam bared his teeth. 'Yeah. Mandrake is supposed to scream when you pull it out of the ground.'

'Sorry I'm late.' Nick was flushed after jogging over from where he'd parked, but Hannah thought he looked good in T-shirt and shorts. She liked his hairy arms and he had much better legs than Peter Flint. 'The old lady who lives next door fainted as I was about to set off and I had to take her to Casualty. It's the heat, none of us are used to it.'

'Let's cool down with a drink after Kirsty's done her thing. Once I've had talked to her, you and I can have a word in private.'

'Hey, someone's waving at you. Don't I know him?'

Hannah turned her head and saw a familiar face. Carefully, she said, 'As a matter of fact, that's Daniel. Ben Kind's son.'

'Of course. I've seen him on the box. Do you know the women with him?'

'I'd hazard a guess at his partner Miranda and his sister. Let's go and say hello.'

As they jostled through the crowd, Hannah caught Daniel's eye. Impossible not to glow at the spontaneity of his smile. As introductions were performed, she considered the women in his life. Miranda was depressingly gorgeous; no longer did she find it so hard to understand why he'd thrown up his career to move to the Lakes with her. As for Louise, at first glance she didn't look much like Daniel. But the resemblance was there if you set about looking for it – not least, she had her brother's cool appraising stare. Ben Kind had it too.

'You look cheerful. I didn't realise you were so keen on skydiving.'

He jerked a thumb in the direction of the plane circling overhead. 'It'll be interesting to watch. But there's no way I'd go up there. A group of students tried to persuade us to book a tandem jump. We had to drag Miranda away.'

'It must be so liberating,' Miranda said dreamily. 'Imagine floating through mid-air.'

Hannah caught Louise's caustic glance. Not much love lost between those two, she guessed. Daniel noticed, as well, and was quick to move the conversation on.

'I've just had some exciting news. From Peter Flint and Sam Howe, of all people.'

Out of the corner of her eye, Hannah spotted Nick's brow furrowing. For once she could read his mind: how come Daniel Kind knows Peter Flint and Sam Howe? Perhaps she was taking more of a risk than Kirsty, up there in that little tin can, but she couldn't just walk away.

'Tell us.'

'Ever heard of a cipher garden?'

When she shook her head, he told them what he'd learned. His animation amused her. He was so natural, not at all her idea of an Oxford don or someone who had presented a television series.

'So what do you think the cipher represents?'

Miranda tugged at Daniel's sleeve. 'Look! They're about to jump!'

They craned their necks. The plane was directly above the field that served as the dropzone. A microscopic figure, little more than a dot, had appeared at the door.

'That's Kirsty,' Hannah said. 'Her mother told me she'd be first to go.'

'How high would you say they are?' Louise asked.

Nick said, 'Nine thousand feet, at a guess. Maybe ten.'

'A long way to fall.'

'Right.'

Kirsty leapt from the plane. She was gliding through the air, elegant as a bird. As she came closer, they could make out her canary yellow jumpsuit. But as they watched, she raised an arm.

'Jesus,' Daniel said. 'What's she doing?'

Nick swore. 'She's taking off her helmet.'

Kirsty pulled the helmet free and it flew away.

Hannah's stomach lurched. She found herself squeezing Nick's hand tight.

Miranda let out a cry. 'What's she doing? Is she mad? She's…'

The figure in the sky was uncoupling her parachute.

'She's not wearing goggles,' Nick said.

The parachute was flapping around the skydiver's legs. It was as if she was dancing, as she tried to wriggle free.

'Shit, she's lost her parachute!'

People screamed as the white parachute billowed and spiralled away. Tears were running down Miranda's cheeks, Louise had covered her eyes.

Kirsty was falling through the air, lying on her back, knees bent towards her chest.

Hannah thought she was going to be sick. She saw Daniel put his arm round Miranda. Their eyes were locked on the girl in the sky.

Kirsty arched her back and put her head down, pointing towards the ground. They could see her long red hair, rippled by a breeze. Her body spun in mid-air and then plunged towards the dropzone.

People were shouting. 'No! Oh God! No!'

As the girl hit the ground, Hannah retched.

Part Two

Chapter Fifteen

Tears filled Daniel's eyes as he stuffed one more sack with clumps of grass and stinging nettles. He'd striven to expel the vision of Kirsty Howe's shattered body from his mind through sheer hard labour, but in vain. However many times he bent his back, the scene at the airfield kept replaying in his mind. That tiny yellow figure in mid-air, intent on destroying herself.

What drove someone to such despair that suicide was the only way out? He'd wrestled with the question a thousand times since Aimee had hurled herself from that tower in Oxford, and never found an answer. To him, life was the most precious gift. To toss it away was unthinkable.

Chaos had engulfed the airfield the instant the girl hit the ground. People were crying out in shock and disbelief, strangers clutched at each other, unable to make sense of what they had witnessed. While Daniel, Miranda and Louise huddled together for comfort, Nick raced off to take charge of the scene. Once Hannah finished vomiting, she followed him. Daniel thanked God he wasn't a police officer, charged with sorting out other people's ruined lives. How had his father coped with the horror?

The three of them drove home in silence and had little to say to each other before going to bed. Kirsty's death had numbed them. All night, he kept waking up, unable to settle. At first light, he headed out into the garden and threw himself into decoding the cipher garden, but his brain wasn't working and he'd resorted to physical graft. Nothing added up, certainly not this eccentric overgrown landscape in the shadow of the fell. What did an old cipher matter, when the young waitress was dead for no reason?

Senseless, senseless, senseless.

He thrust his fork into the hard dry earth and struck something solid buried a few inches under the ground. A large stone. The spikes of a monkey puzzle tree scratched his cheek as he stood up, but he took no notice. Levering with his fork, he brought to the surface a square grey tablet, a foot long and wide. As he brushed off the dirt, he uncovered chiselled indentations. Within a minute an inscription was revealed.

WILL TAKE OUR LEAVE

An anagram? He played around in his mind with the letters, but couldn't come up with anything that wasn't fanciful or meaningless. Perhaps the message wasn't meant to be read in isolation. He'd been clearing the undergrowth from a patch populated by ferns and foxgloves, divided from the rest of the garden by a picket fence and bounded by two monkey puzzle trees, a yew and a small weeping willow.

He leaned on his fork, massaging his back with one hand, listening to the buzzing of the bees. His body was aching, and he'd tweaked the muscles in his ribs, but this wasn't the moment to give up and retreat inside. A current of excitement was flowing through him, a sensation he'd experienced at Oxford. He was on the brink of discovery.

Hannah closed her eyes and let the blast of water from the shower cleanse her. If only she could wash away what had happened. She must clear her mind, the doctor was right, think about the future. Looking back might destroy her.

She stepped out of the cubicle and towelled herself dry. The house was as silent as a crypt. Strange to be here on a weekday. Her instinct was to ring the office, check out what was going on, but she'd promised Marc that she wouldn't make the call, wouldn't allow herself to be sucked straight back into the quicksand of endless meetings and filling in forms.

But it was safer to think about work than the rest of her life. She needed to focus on solving the murder of Warren Howe, it would give her a goal to aim for. Even that was fraught with angst. She couldn't rid herself of the suspicion that Tina Howe had murdered her husband. But she'd watched Tina running towards the dropzone seconds after Kirsty's death. The woman's ravaged face was a sight she would never forget. She might be a murderer, but that was a punishment too far. Nothing was crueller than watching your own child die.

The tablet had lain beneath one of the monkey puzzle trees. Daniel used the fork to test the ground beneath the other. Soon the metal prongs struck another piece of stone. He levered it up and uncovered a second inscription.

LEAVES FROM THE GARDEN

Mosquitoes had stung his bare arms, leaving red tender marks. Sweat was pouring off him, and he'd forgotten to replenish his sun block. None of this mattered. He couldn't stop now. He was on a roll, no question. The pain in his back and ribs meant nothing.

He was driven on by the conviction that at last the cipher was within touching distance. No stopping now. Within ten minutes, he had dug out a third stone from under the drooping willow branches. He cradled it in his hands, as if it were a Ming vase.

The tablet bore a carved question.

WHY DID YOU LEAVE?

The phone trilled. Hannah let it ring. Probably a recorded message, that would try to sell her a timeshare in Spain. But the caller was persistent. In the end she surrendered.

'Hello?'

'Hannah, is that you? You sound strange. Are you all right?'

Terri. Faithful Terri. At least, faithful as a friend if not always as a wife. Hearing her brisk, confident tone was a therapy in itself. Hannah wondered whether to lie and pretend everything was all right. But Terri was no fool. She'd see through the subterfuge. And besides, even detective chief inspectors sometimes needed a shoulder to lean on.

'Well, actually, I've been better...'

There must be another stone. Must be. The message he'd uncovered made little sense. There were four trees and he'd convinced himself there must be four stones. But he couldn't find the missing link.

His skin was burning, but he kept on going. The yew tree had thick, tangled roots that slowed him down, but he was certain there was something to find. Time passed. Twenty minutes, half an hour. What was that, wrapped around by the spreading roots?

He'd found it. Soon he was brushing the dirt from the fourth stone and squinting at its inscription.

TOGETHER AGAIN FOR ETERNITY

Yew trees are often found in cemeteries, he remembered. Christ, did it mean that a corpse was buried here? The thought of it made him grind his teeth. But there was no body in the garden – who could it be? Not Jacob and Alice Quiller, for they had been interred in the churchyard at Brack. Not their son John, whose body had been brought back from South Africa and laid to rest in the same place.

He looked around and saw the cottage grounds with new eyes. Paths leading nowhere, false turnings, dead ends. Belladonna, foxgloves, hellebore. Poisonous plants in a beautiful landscape. Even the loveliest blooms seemed sinister this morning. Weren't lilies by tradition the flowers of funerals?

'Daniel!' Miranda had emerged from the cottage. 'Phone for you. Marc Amos, from the bookshop.'

'You talked about Jacob Quiller.' Marc sounded pleased with himself. 'He's mentioned in a book I picked up in a job lot at a book fair. Riddles of South Lakeland. I spotted his name when I was flicking through a chapter on Brackdale, it talks about Quiller's garden at the cottage in Tarn Fold.'

'The cipher garden.'

'So you know all about it?'

'I wish.'

'This book was published by a local firm, the print run must have been minuscule.'

'Which company?'

'RG Publications, they're based near Hawkshead. A small press, a one-woman band. She's been churning out a title a month for ten or twelve years now. Local interest stuff for tourists rather than the natives. A crowded market, but she keeps her head above water. This isn't a book I recall. Must have been one of her earliest.'

'What does RG stand for?' Daniel asked, although he could guess.

'Roz Gleave, that's the publisher's name. The author is called

Eleanor Sawtell. Never heard of her. According to the blurb, she is – or was – a former primary school teacher. She also boasts that she's a lifelong resident of Staveley and has three children and eleven grandchildren.'

'What does she have to say about the garden?'

'Not a lot, disappointingly. I'll copy the paragraphs and put them in the post to you.'

'Thanks, but I'll call in and pick them up.'

'In a hurry?'

'Puzzling over the garden will take my mind off yesterday.'

'Hannah said you were at the airfield.' He sighed. 'Frankly, she was in hell of a state last night. A horrific business, by the sound of it. That poor young girl. I suppose it couldn't have been an accident?'

'Hannah would know better than me, but the girl's behaviour looked calculated enough from where we were standing. She just ripped off her helmet and parachute and dropped like a stone.'

'My God, how could you hate life enough to want to do that to yourself?'

'Don't ask me. How is Hannah today?'

A pause. 'For once in a blue moon, she's not fit enough to go into work. Though she took some persuading. Of course, she's a workaholic, you must have noticed.'

'She's obviously very committed to the job.'

A brief laugh. 'That's one way of putting it. Between you and me, she takes it all too much to heart. Naturally, she's shocked by what happened. She's not as thick-skinned as most police officers. In fact, she's not thick-skinned at all. God knows what she was doing at the airfield. I've never heard her express an interest in skydiving before.'

'Something to do with work?' Daniel had assumed it was no coincidence that Hannah and her sergeant had shown up at an event featuring Warren Howe's daughter. But he didn't want to say too much.

'Suppose so.' A pause. 'She was on her own, I suppose?'

Daniel hesitated. 'We didn't have time for conversation. But I didn't see her interrogating spectators, if that's what you mean.

And of course the suicide jump stunned all of us. Nobody could have expected that.'

If Marc Amos realised that Daniel had dodged his question, his voice didn't betray it. 'No, the girl must have had mental problems, it's not a rational act. You're coming over to the shop sometime?'

'I'll be with you in half an hour.'

Far below the Sacrifice Stone, the tranquil and secluded corner known as Tarn Fold is associated with a story about the garden created in the late nineteenth century by Jacob Quiller. Quiller's mother was the younger sister of Richard Skelding, whose father had bought Brack Hall fifty years before. The Skeldings and the Quillers were God-fearing folk, much-respected pillars of the Brackdale community and Jacob himself was a churchwarden and staunch supporter of the church at Brack. His wife Alice was a local girl of humble stock who worked at the Hall as a housemaid before catching Jacob's eye. Originally the Fold, like most of the rest of the valley, formed part of the sprawling Brack Estate. Richard, well-known for his generosity, transferred ownership of the Fold to Jacob as a wedding gift, and Jacob built a pretty little cottage in a clearing close to the lower slopes of Tarn Fell. Alice's life revolved around their only child, John, to whom she was utterly devoted.

It was said that the Quillers struggled to keep their faith after John's tragic death. He was a soldier who fought in the Boer War and died one day short of his twenty-first birthday. Neither Jacob nor Alice seems ever to have recovered from that dreadful blow. Indeed, the story goes that after John's funeral, Alice became a recluse who refused to leave the cottage and would not speak to a single soul other than her distraught husband. Before long they were both dead – departing this mortal coil on the very same day. One suspects that in truth their lives ended the moment they received the tragic news from South Africa. The simple epitaph on their gravestone close to the lych gate at their beloved church records poignantly that the couple died of broken hearts.

Jacob Quiller was reputed to have laboured unceasingly in his garden in the months leading up to his demise and it may be that he

over-taxed himself. Village wisdom had it that there is a secret about
their deaths to be discovered by unravelling a cipher that Jacob hid in
the garden, yet little seems to be known about it. The Quillers had no
family other than the Skeldings, to whom the cottage passed back on
their deaths. Richard paid for a memorial to John that can be seen in
the church to this day. He sold the cottage and it remains in private
hands, although the present owner does not encourage sightseers. The
cipher has presumably disappeared, if it ever existed. Possibly it was no
more than a tantalising rural legend. In any event, it seems to this
author to be crass to intrude upon personal grief. How much more
romantic to take at face value the words that the Quillers chose for
their headstone. Let us pause and reflect that, whatever learned
medical men tell us, folk may indeed die from broken hearts.

Daniel handed the book back to Marc Amos. It was a battered
trade paperback. On the back cover was a black and white
photograph of Eleanor Sawtell. Seventy five at a guess, she had
white hair, a kindly expression and a cardigan with a missing
button. An obese and complacent tabby sat on her lap, smirking
as though it had solved the cipher but wasn't telling.

'An unsatisfactory story, really,' Marc said.

'A puzzle without an obvious solution, that's the challenge. I've
been mugging up about gardens and things that grow in them.
Odd, I always thought of gardens as life-enhancing. Plants, too.
Surprising how many of them have macabre connotations.'

Marc shook his head. 'Not my subject, I'm afraid.'

'The monkey puzzle tree, for instance. Originates from Chile,
and guess what? The climate in Cumbria suits it perfectly.'

'It's chilly enough here most of the time. Sorry, terrible joke. I
looked Eleanor Sawtell up in the phone book, but couldn't find
her in Staveley. She might be ex-directory, but...'

'I'll have a word with Roz Gleave, see if she can help.'

A chance too good for someone so obsessively curious to miss,
a chance to kill two birds. To find out more about the cipher –
and the murder of Warren Howe.

Marc grinned. 'Detective work, is it? You'll be competing with
Hannah next.'

On his way to Keepsake Cottage, Daniel decided that he couldn't help liking Marc Amos. How stupid to feel a pang of jealousy because Marc had Hannah all to himself. But was Marc jealous too, did he suspect that something was going on between her and the sergeant? And if so, was he right? Daniel hadn't had time to study Nick Lowther. He seemed amiable and wore a wedding ring, but colleagues at work often had affairs. Hannah Scarlett didn't seem the type to play around, but was there really a type? It was all down to individual chemistry, you never knew what might happen when circumstances thrust two people together.

One more thing he'd rather not think about, like Kirsty's death. He dragged his mind back to the stone tablets. All four were meant to be found, no question. They were so close to the surface that any serious attempt to clear the ground would uncover them. The carved words might be part of an elaborate code – shades of Beatrix Potter's diaries – but he doubted it. His bet was on a simple if cryptic message. He'd start by juggling with the phrases he'd discovered.

Perhaps there was a pattern. Assume that the four stones he'd found – the willow, the two monkey puzzles, and the yew – were connected by the circumference of a rough circle. Start at the willow and move clockwise.

Why did you leave? Leaves from the garden. Will take our leave. Together again for eternity.

Outside the sun was high, but Hannah stayed indoors. Her skin burned too easily in heat this fierce. She gulped down a can of Coke for the sugar boost. Talking to Terri had made her feel half-human again, but she was still tired. She plucked a musty hardback at random from Marc's Ravenglass haul. She reached as far as page 20 before deciding she wasn't in the mood for murder by Italian dagger in a locked room surrounded by snow with not a footprint to be seen. The choice of daytime TV shows was unspeakable and soon she was stretched out on the sofa with eyes shut, forcing herself to focus on whatever had made it necessary for Warren Howe to die.

When you know Howe, you know who – but what else was

there to know about Warren Howe? The picture in her mind was of a man to whom plants meant more than people. With Gail, Bel and Roz among conquests, he was capable of turning on the charm to lure a pretty woman into his bed. He was single-minded and seemed to have mastered the art of getting what he wanted. Every scrap of evidence suggested he didn't have an unselfish bone in his body.

Gail, Bel and Roz. Three old friends. Women could be so close with each other. Closer even than Terri and her. Suppose the trio had nourished a grudge over Warren's treatment of them? Maybe she'd been too hasty in dismissing Les Bryant's suggestion of a conspiracy to kill. But the youthful flings with Bel and Roz were ancient history. There was so much that theory left unexplained. Not least the anonymous accusation of Tina. If one or more of the women had sent it, why resurrect the old case if they had something to hide?

No, Tina was still her suspect of choice. Warren had betrayed her with Gail and it was one betrayal too many. The stumbling block was the Hardknott Pass alibi. But just as locked rooms were meant to be breached, so murderers' alibis were meant to be broken.

The moment Daniel pulled up outside Keepsake Cottage and got out of the car, the heat hit him. It was like walking into a wall. He was about to ring the doorbell when voices came drifting through the air. People must be outside, at the back of the house. He made out the words of a man who sounded frantic.

'Suppose the police find out? That woman, Hannah Scarlett. Roz, this is serious, how can we keep quiet?'

'We must!' A woman's voice, full of anguish.

'But…'

'Oh God, how I wish I'd kept my mouth shut.'

This was fall-out from Kirsty Howe's death, had to be. He waited, but nothing more was said. He pressed the bell. After a minute he rang again and at length he heard footsteps coming round the side of the house. A brisk woman with a helmet of grey hair, wearing a sleeveless top and shorts. When she took off her dark glasses to inspect him, it was obvious that she'd been weeping.

'Mrs Gleave?'

'That's me.'

He extended a hand. 'My name's Daniel Kind.'

'I recognise you, don't I? You were on the television.'

'A while back, yes.'

She raised her eyebrows and Daniel sensed that, for all her distress, this was a woman of considerable strength of mind. 'What on earth brings you to my house?'

'I live in Brackdale and I've been reading your book about the riddles of South Lakeland.'

'Not my book, really,' she said. 'I'm only a humble publisher.'

He grinned. 'A humble publisher? Some people would say that's a contradiction in terms.'

'Not if they know anything about the realities of running a small press.' She mustered a tired smile. 'I don't do long expense-account lunches or six-figure advances. In fact, I don't do advances at all. Our authors write for love rather than money. An occasional royalty cheque is a bonus. The book you're talking about was written by – let me see, Eleanor Sawtell? Nice lady, primary school teacher. She'd been collecting curious tales from her neck of the woods for donkey's years.'

'I was wondering how to make contact with her. Is she still alive?'

Roz sighed. 'Yes – but the last I heard from her daughter, poor Eleanor was suffering from Alzheimer's. Her husband had died and she'd moved into a care home in Kendal.'

Shit. 'In that case, could I pick your brains?'

'To be honest, it's not convenient.'

He assumed a doleful expression. 'Of course, I'm happy to make an appointment and come back another time.'

'No, no.' She took a breath. 'It isn't every day that a television personality shows up on my doorstep. Do come in. On second thoughts, let's sit out in the garden. This weather won't last forever. Might as well make the most of it. My husband's doing just that.'

He followed her round to the back of the cottage. Chris Gleave was sitting on the edge of a low stone wall. He was wearing brief shorts and nothing else, his body was slim and brown. Daniel noticed the look of proprietorial pleasure on Roz's face, as she considered her husband while introducing them.

'I saw some of your programmes on the box,' Chris said. 'History as detective work. Neat concept.'

'Now,' Roz said, evidently reluctant to become distracted by chit-chat with their unexpected visitor. 'What is it you want to know about Eleanor's book?'

He explained about Jacob Quiller and the garden at Tarn Cottage. 'Did Eleanor have any inkling about the cipher?'

'If she did, I don't remember her sharing it with me. She wasn't a professional researcher, I think she relied on anecdotes that she'd gathered over decades for most of her tales. As most of my authors do.'

'Only when I've asked about the Quillers in Brack, nobody seems to know anything about them.'

'It was a long time ago. Eleanor's scraps of knowledge might date back as far as the Forties or Fifties.'

'If that's right, there's not much chance of my finding out much more about them.'

A bleak smile. 'A test of your prowess as a historian, then.'

'Or as a detective.' He sighed. 'Your own garden is gorgeous. Did you create it yourselves?'

'Not exactly,' Roz said. 'We used a professional firm.'

'I've called in experts to look at our garden too. They are based near here. Flint Howe. You know them?'

She nodded, unwilling to commit herself to words. Daniel saw that Chris had paled beneath his tan.

'Have you heard about Sam Howe's sister?'

Roz blinked. 'You know about Kirsty?'

'I was at the airfield yesterday.'

Chris whispered, 'Jesus.'

He looked as though he too was about to burst into tears. Roz fired him a nervous glance.

'I'm sorry. We've known Kirsty since she was so high. The news has come as a terrible shock to both of us. Really, it's not something either of us can bear to talk about. Now, if you don't mind, I really ought to be catching up with some work.'

'On a Sunday?'

She moved forward, waving him back to the front of the cottage, like a farmer trying to shift cattle from his field. 'Running a small business from home is a seven day a week affair, I'm afraid. Sorry I can't be more help.'

The church was a cool refuge from the heat outside. A couple of elderly ladies were up near the altar, arranging flowers and enjoying a good moan about the weather. On a table near the door were scattered a selection of leaflets about fair trade and third world poverty. Nothing about the history of the parish or the denizens of the graveyard. But at least the rector had got his priorities right, Daniel thought as he ambled down a side aisle, inspecting the plaques set into the wall. The memorial to the Quillers' son was easy to find. A large rectangular cast bronze panel, bearing an embossed inscription.

To the glory of God and in memory of a much-loved son of Brackdale who lost his life in the war in South Africa. Major John Quiller, of the 1st Northumberland Fusiliers, died of enteric fever, 5 April 1902. Faithful unto death.

He heard footsteps echoing on the stone floor and someone humming an approximation of 'Praise my soul, the King of Heaven'.

'Mr Kind, how good to see you again. Still on the detective trail?'

Daniel turned to face the rector of Brack, a tiny man with sparse grey hair and half-moon spectacles perched on a pointed nose. His manner suggested a gregarious church mouse.

'You remember my interest in the fellow who built our cottage? This is his son.'

'Ah.' The rector peered so closely at the panel that Daniel thought he was going to rub his little snout against it. 'A tragic business. Death in war is so futile, don't you agree? Take this young fellow, for instance. If I'm not much mistaken, the war was over within weeks of his death. He'd survived everything the enemy could throw at him – only to die of natural causes. So sad.'

'His parents never got over it. A local legend grew up about them.'

As Daniel explained about the cipher garden, the rector's eyes widened with excitement. 'Dear me, dear me, how very intriguing. I once had a parish in Norfolk, with an elderly monkey puzzle growing by the edge of the graveyard. Not an attractive tree to my mind, I much prefer the good old English oak myself. But there was no question of chopping it down, my parishioners wouldn't have heard of it. Would you happen to know why?'

Daniel shook his head.

'By tradition, the sparse foliage is meant to deprive the Devil of a hiding place. If the branches were leafy, he might be able to spy on funerals and steal the souls of the dead.'

'What about yew trees and weeping willows – any symbolism there?'

'Most certainly.' The rector twittered with delight at the opportunity to display his expertise. 'Yews are supposed to represent immortality. Weeping willows, as you might guess, are associated with sorrow and bereavement. So how do you interpret the cipher, may I ask?'

'Strictly speaking, I don't think it is a cipher. Ciphers involve the substitution of letters. This just looks like a cryptic message.'

The rector wagged his forefinger in playful rebuke. 'Ah, there speaks the Oxford don!'

'Pedantic to a fault, I know. Trouble is, breaking a code may require more than precise, minute analysis. Sometimes imagination is called for.'

'Goodness, do I take it that you have solved the conundrum?'

'Yes.' Daniel stared at the bronze panel. 'Unfortunately, I think I have.'

Chapter Sixteen

'Are you all right?' Marc asked.

Hannah contemplated several possible answers before saying, 'Yes, I'm fine.'

'We could go away somewhere.' He chewed a last mouthful of burnt bacon before slinging his plate and cutlery into the dishwasher with a crash. 'Spend a bit of time together. You're due plenty of leave.'

The coffee he'd made was bitter on her tongue but she drained the cup anyway. Better make the most of his solicitude; it wouldn't last. At once she rebuked herself for cynicism. He was making an effort. She slid off the stool. All she'd felt like eating for breakfast was a single slice of unbuttered toast.

'What about the shop?'

'Tim and Melanie can look after things for a few days. I'll cancel the Haydock Park fair.'

'OK, let's talk about it tonight.'

'I'll call you later.'

'No need. I thought I'd go into work later this morning.'

'Are you serious?' He caught her hand, squeezed her fingers between his. 'You've had a miscarriage, for Christ's sake!'

Miscarriage. It sounded so dramatic. Actually, what had happened was more like a painful and very heavy period. Her GP, a severe woman whose no-nonsense manner wouldn't have been out of place in a sergeant-major, was brisk to the point of being dismissive. These things were commonplace in the early weeks. Nature's way of telling you that something wasn't quite right. Hannah fled from the surgery before she could be told that her loss was a blessing in disguise.

'The sooner I get back to normal, the better.'

'You need to look after yourself! Work can wait. You're not indispensable.'

The kitchen tiles were cool under her bare feet. Already the sun was beating down outside. When was the weather going to break? She wasn't an invalid and she had no intention of succumbing to self-indulgence. Right now, she needed the job more than the job needed her. Better to drag her mind away from what had happened and bury herself in that overflowing in-tray. But she couldn't face an argument.

'All right.'

'Great.' When he smiled, the white even teeth and laughter lines around his mouth reminded her why she found him so difficult to resist. 'You'll feel like a different person once you've had a proper rest.'

A different person? Confident and in control, not diminished by emptiness and loss?

'Yes.'

His dry lips brushed her cheek. 'Listen, Hannah. I'm so sorry about this. Perhaps – it just wasn't meant to be.'

The doctor had said the same, but Marc's meaning was different. His sympathy was genuine, yet she detected a lightness in his manner that had been absent after she'd told him she was pregnant. As if he'd been granted a reprieve.

Unworthy, unworthy, unworthy. She hated herself for thinking he was selfish. But even as she felt his fingers ruffling her hair, she knew she was right. Sifting out the truth from a jumble of confusing evidence was what she was supposed to be good at, after all.

'So Kirsty's father was murdered.'

Miranda was gasping as she dragged herself up to the top of the path leading up the slope of Tarn Fell. Daniel pulled his floppy hat down over his eyes. The sun had disappeared behind clouds and the air was heavy. The heat had become a physical presence, an unseen oppressor. Each stride forward felt as though you were pulling against a ball and chain. He'd hoped it would be cooler on Priest Edge, but there wasn't a hint of breeze.

'Hacked to death with a scythe,' she continued. 'Mrs Tasker was regaling a customer with the story when I went to the shop first thing. The papers are full of it. Maybe Kirsty was killed by someone with a grudge against the family.'

As Louise moved along the narrow stony ridge, Daniel muttered, 'She ripped off her own helmet, unhooked her own parachute.'

'What if she'd been drugged?'

'Do the reports suggest that?'

'No, but the police might not be telling.'

'They'd drop a hint to the journalists, off the record. You know how they work.'

Louise came to a stop where the path broadened out. 'Wasn't there a skydiver once who staged his suicide to make it look like murder?'

'Allegedly,' Daniel said. 'Nobody knew for sure and the inquest recorded an open verdict. This is different. We all saw what happened.'

For all the heat of the morning, Louise shivered. 'Unspeakable. I'm not surprised you're not sleeping, Miranda.'

Miranda took no notice. She'd had another bad night, but over breakfast they'd agreed that a walk would do them good. 'Remember how uptight she was in the restaurant? What if she was frightened of someone? Suppose she'd been threatened? Darling, are you planning to talk to Hannah Scarlett?'

'There's no way she'd share confidential information with me.'

'Come on. She's taken a shine to you. It was written all over her when we met at the airfield.'

He threw her a sharp glance, but her expression was mocking rather than suspicious. 'I spoke to Marc Amos yesterday when I was checking out the history of the garden and he told me Hannah wasn't in work. She's off sick.'

'You don't imagine police officers being stressed out by an encounter with sudden death, do you? You'd think they were hardened to it.'

'They're only human,' Louise snapped.

They walked on in silence. Daniel thought: you weren't so forbearing when Dad made his great mistake. He knew better than to voice what was passing through his mind. Lately, he'd felt closer to his sister than ever, but in a few hours she would be leaving for home. This wasn't a good time to re-open old wounds.

Miranda mopped her brow. 'This humidity – I can scarcely get any oxygen into my lungs. Thank God the forecasts are promising a drop of rain. Shall we turn back?'

The Sacrifice Stone lay ahead, a dour grey boulder. As they approached, Louise said, 'Close up, it looks smaller than when you look up from the cottage. But my God, what a view!'

Brackdale stretched out below them. Daniel's eyes travelled along the thin ribbon of road that ran through the village, past the church and the last resting place of the Quillers, beyond the Hall and Tarn Fold, towards the abandoned quarry workings and the stern crags that closed off the far end of the valley. A small, enclosed world. He imagined living here a century ago. John and Alice Quiller would have felt bereft after the death of their only child. Lifelong believers, they must have found that John's death tested their faith to destruction. How could they not feel betrayed by God?

In their horror and confusion, he was convinced, lay the secret of the cipher garden.

'Hannah? This is Nick. How are you?'

He sounded as anxious as a first time offender. Touched by his concern, she said into the cordless handset, 'Much better, thanks. I'll be in tomorrow.'

'Nobody hear can remember you taking a day off sick.'

'I'm becoming a hypochondriac in my old age. Probably could have made it today, but Marc came over all protective.'

'Thank God you listened to him. You push yourself too hard.'

'I don't need wrapping up in cotton wool. The doctor tells me I'm suffering from a touch of sunstroke. It's the fashion.'

It was an off-the-cuff lie. She trusted Nick, but she hadn't figured out how to handle the miscarriage in her own mind, whether to talk about it with friends or simply behave as though it had never happened. For now she wanted to keep both options open.

'What happened to Kirsty Howe was grisly. Enough to knock anyone sideways.'

'Maybe that was a factor, I don't know.' Nor did she know whether it had played a part in the miscarriage. 'What's the latest on her death? Any suggestion of anything untoward?'

'I spoke to a couple of guys working on the investigation. The forensic gurus are crawling all over her kit, but witnesses saw her checking it herself, as per standard procedures. The jump was routine, she'd done it hundreds of times before.'

'Remember what the good book says. Think murder.'

'Pity the *Murder Investigation Manual* doesn't go into detail about death by skydiving. There's not a shred of evidence to suggest sabotage. She died because she ripped off her gear and didn't take any of the precautions that might have saved her life.'

'No doubt it was suicide?'

'None. A spectacular way to choose to die, but it's happened before.'

'A new trend, killing yourself in front of an audience?'

'Gone are the days of discreetly sticking your head in a gas oven. Now even people who want to end it all fancy their fifteen minutes of fame.'

She was draped over the sofa, phone wedged between head and shoulder, determined to think about anything except the sight of Kirsty's remains spread across the dropzone. When Nick called, she'd been watching daytime TV. A fast-talking presenter was urging a surly sixteen year old to identify which of three tattooed boyfriends was the father of her baby girl. Even with the sound muted, the kids' faces told the story more eloquently than any words they might mumble.

'What do the other skydivers say?'

'They never picked up a hint that she anything untoward in mind. But they didn't know her well, she was someone who lurked on the edge of things. Skydivers party hard, presumably because they never know if the next jump might be their last. She'd had a couple of one-night stands with fellow skydivers, but nothing recent. Several chaps had tried it on with her, and got nowhere. They reckoned she'd found a lover who wasn't part of their community.'

'Perhaps she was just sick of men.'

'By the sound of it, none of the skydivers could imagine how a woman could ever get sick of men.'

'Charming.'

'She was very quiet before the jump, even by her standards. In the plane, someone asked if she was feeling under the weather, but she said she'd never felt better. She looked haggard, but the guys put it down to a night on the tiles. In fact, she was working at The Heights the previous evening.'

'Anything out of the ordinary there?'

'If so, Bel Jenner and Oliver Cox aren't telling. Her death has stunned them. Bel was in tears and Oliver looked as though he'd been run over by a truck. Mind you, good waitresses aren't that easy to find.'

'You're so cynical. How about her family?'

'Tina Howe says Kirsty had mood swings and she'd seemed down in the dumps, but there's no history of her threatening to do away with herself. No overdoses, no self-harming. She wasn't the sort to cry for attention. This suicide came literally out of the blue.'

'Spur of the moment decision?'

'Looks like it. She wasn't a heavy drinker and there's no evidence she ever so much as smoked a joint. Plenty of work to be done yet, but they haven't found anything that links in with our investigation.'

'Doesn't mean there's nothing to find.'

'It is a coincidence that she dies shortly after we receive the anonymous tip-off pointing the finger at Tina.'

'Suppose she discovered something that proved her mother killed her dad?'

'Such as?'

'If she and Sam lied to give Tina an alibi, they must have had suspicions from the outset. Perhaps Kirsty wrote the anonymous letter herself.'

'And the letter that Tina received?'

'Attempting to put her under pressure, force her to cough? Or maybe Tina made up the letter. Peter never saw it, remember.'

'What if Sam was the culprit and Tina and Kirsty lied to save his neck? He might have sent the letters to divert attention from himself.'

'Why resurrect the case if for years he'd got away with murder?'

'Your guess is as good as mine.'

Hannah scowled at the television screen. The girl was snivelling and her mascara had started to run. Motherhood wasn't all it was cracked up to be, perhaps. Even so, Hannah wanted to find out for herself one day. The putative fathers were smirking with a mixture of cockiness and embarrassment as they waited for the presenter to reveal the answer.

'We need a fresh angle. Instead of focusing on who killed Warren, let's ask who might have given us the tip-off and work forward from there.'

'Isn't that a blind alley, without any forensic evidence from the letter?'

If Nick hadn't been such a good friend, she wouldn't have restrained the impulse to snap back at him. Ben Kind often complained that technological advance discourages even the best cops from reasoning for themselves.

'Think laterally. Who might want to stick the knife into Tina?'

Nick pondered. 'Leaving aside her kids?'

'Uh-huh.'

'Gail Flint,' he said. 'Revenge for taking her husband?'

One of the lads on TV grinned stupidly at the news that he was a father. The girl was still crying as the presenter led the audience in a round of enthusiastic applause. Hannah felt like joining in. She'd come to the same conclusion as Nick.

'Let's talk to her tomorrow.'

'Thanks for everything,' Louise said.

'Sorry about Saturday,' Daniel said.

She hesitated. 'I suppose it brought back memories?'

She was, he knew, talking about Aimee's suicide.

'Maybe.'

'You're still hurting, aren't you?'

'I'm not looking for sympathy.'

'You never do. But everyone needs a bit of comfort sometimes.'

'Well.' He cleared his throat. 'I should never have dragged you out to the airfield.'

'You weren't to know she was going to kill herself.'

Confession time. He cleared his throat. 'No, but I knew about her father's murder from Hannah Scarlett. It's a cold case she's investigating. That's why I asked Peter Flint for advice about the garden. I knew he was Warren Howe's business partner.'

Louise groaned. 'As a kid, you wanted to be a detective. Just like Dad.'

'Maybe I haven't grown up as much as I'd like to think.'

'Which of us has?'

They were killing time with a coffee and cake in the platform buffet at Oxenholme. The latest announcement warned that the train from Glasgow was running forty minutes late. Miranda wasn't with them. She'd elected to chase the builders on the phone rather than come along to see off their guest. At the door of the cottage, she and Louise exchanged pecks on the cheek and promised to keep in touch, but these were the meaningless formalities of English good manners. Daniel knew it wouldn't break their hearts if they never clapped eyes on each other again.

'No need to wait for the train.'

'I enjoy your company.'

She blinked. 'You've never said that to me before.'

'It's never occurred to me before,' he said with a grin.

She stuck out her tongue at him. 'It's best that I disappear. Miranda's not comfortable when I'm around.'

'It's nothing personal. She's just...'

'Insecure?'

'Unaccustomed to family life. Her adoptive parents were elderly, no kids of their own, she became accustomed to being the centre of attention. Since they died, she feels the lack of a past. That's why she seems jealous of you and me. There's so much stuff that she isn't part of. But – you do like her?'

Louise laughed. 'Now who's insecure? Of course I do. You're not stupid enough to fall for just a pretty face. Though I must admit I wondered if it was too soon for you – after Aimee, I mean. Don't take this the wrong way, but I'm not sure you've ever faced up to how hard her death hit you.'

'We can't plan our lives like train timetables. Pick the perfect moment to fall for someone new.'

'No, of course not. And she's a lot of fun when she's so inclined. But you'll have to persuade her – either she lives the dream up here with you, or she does the London journalist thing.'

'She can combine the two.'

Louise shrugged. 'I hope you're right.'

Me too. He devoured the last piece of cream cake and said nothing.

'So where does Hannah Scarlett fit in?'

He felt colour rising in his cheeks. 'What do you mean?'

'I saw the way she looked at you, Daniel. You said yourself, she told you about that old murder.'

'She worked with Dad, he was her mentor. She's talked to me about him. That's all.'

'And she's married to this chap you went to see, the bookshop owner?'

'Not married. They live together, have done for years.'

'What about the cipher garden, then? You kept your cards close to your chest when you got home.'

'Was it that obvious?'

'Let me share something with you, Daniel. The air of casual unconcern you cultivate when you're trying to hide something isn't as convincing as you'd like to think. Perhaps it fools Miranda, but not me. I've known you a long time, remember.'

He managed a rueful grin. 'Probably as well you're leaving, then.'

She kicked him under the table. 'Yes, you and I would soon be at each other's throats if I hung around. Now – the garden.'

He recounted his discoveries of the previous day. When he told her about the fragment of conversation he'd overheard between Chris and Roz Gleave, she wanted to know what he thought they were talking about.

'Presumably Roz has an idea about what drove Kirsty to take her own life.'

'Are you intending to tell the police?'

'I'm hoping the Gleaves will save me the trouble.'

'You should mention what you heard to your mate Hannah.'

He gave her a sharp look, but her expression was all innocence. 'When she's fit again, perhaps I will.'

'Carry on with the story.'

When he'd finished, she pulled a face. 'It's weird. People don't die of broken hearts.'

'You never were much of a romantic, were you?'

'Come on. They expired on the same day, which just happened to be the anniversary of their son's death?'

'Too much of a coincidence, but a hundred years after they were buried, there's not much to go on. You need to make a leap of imagination to have a chance of making sense of it.'

She laughed. 'You used to wear that expression when you figured out the solution to an Agatha Christie five chapters before that old Belgian big-head. Let's hear about where the leap has taken you.'

A disembodied voice announced that the train would be arriving shortly and apologised for any inconvenience. Daniel swallowed the last of his drink.

'Suppose you are Alice Quiller. Brought up to fear God. Perhaps you've seldom ventured far outside the valley you were born in. For upwards of half a century, your faith is unquestioning. Until tragedy tears your small, comfortable world apart. Your only child, the apple of your eye, dies in a foreign land. No good reason for his death, you can't even console yourself with the fiction that he sacrificed his life defending freedom. The stupid war he's been fighting is as good as over, but he succumbs to sickness and dies a rotten, miserable death. You've devoted your life to the boy, you're crazy about him. Obsessed, maybe. All of a sudden, the world becomes worthless. You cut yourself off from it. Your husband is the only person you will speak to, but even he can't reason with you, even he can't make everything right. Nothing can make it right. You're left not knowing what to believe any more. Not wishing to live any more. What do you do?'

She said slowly, 'I might not want to go on living.'

He mimed applause. 'Spot on.'

'You're suggesting they decided – or Alice persuaded her

husband – that they should kill themselves? To take part in a suicide pact?'

'For her, death must have seemed the only way out.'

She winced. 'Shit.'

'Only one snag. In those days, suicide was a mortal sin. Worse than that, a crime. The rector reminded me, suicides weren't even permitted the dignity of burial in consecrated ground. In those days, you were expected to cope with whatever lousy hand life dealt you. No therapy, no bereavement counselling, just get on with it. In England it was still the age of the stiff upper lip. For the Quillers, the public disgrace of a double suicide would have been intolerable. Not to be contemplated.'

'So they disguised their intentions?'

'A triumph of appearance over reality. As prominent Brackdale folk, well-respected, they'd have been on good terms with the local medics. So long as there was an opportunity to write off their deaths as due to natural causes, honour would be satisfied all round. Jacob and Alice Quiller could be buried in the same grave as their beloved son John.'

'And the garden?'

'I'd guess Jacob was familiar with the Victorian fashion for gardens that conveyed messages. Often to celebrate religious beliefs, or represent Bible stories or mystical revelations. Jacob turned all that upside down. His mind was in turmoil. While his wife pined away inside the cottage, he transformed their garden to simulate a kind of spiritual anarchy. No "paths of life" for the Quillers. Instead, nothing but tracks that wound back on themselves, false turnings and dead ends.'

'The pattern was that there was no pattern?'

'Jacob was mocking the pious certainties that he'd subscribed to all his life. Yet even in his dark despair, he couldn't abandon every last vestige of faith. He couldn't help minding what happened after he died. Perhaps Alice felt the same, perhaps she was past caring, who knows? One thing's for sure, it was impossible for them to write a straightforward letter declaring their intention. But they could leave a hidden message in the garden for anyone who cared to know what they'd done.'

'Such as Richard Skelding?'

'The man who inherited his land back, yes. My guess is that he discovered the truth. A handful of people in the valley kept the legend alive.'

'Including later owners of the cottage?'

'Notably the Gilpins. They didn't disturb the cipher garden, or betray the Quillers' secret. Why should they? It was a private sorrow. For all I know, Eleanor Sawtell tried to pump Mrs Gilpin for information. I can't imagine her giving any change to a nosey parker.'

Louise tapped her spoon against her saucer. 'You're right. All this does require a leap of the imagination.'

'There is a crazy logic to the garden. The monkey puzzles symbolised Jacob and Alice and the weeping willow John. The yew tree stood for the eternal life that Jacob hoped against hope might yet await all three of them in Heaven.'

'And the death from broken hearts?'

'The clue to the means of suicide is in the planting, as well as the words on the tablets. Of course, those foxgloves have spread far and wide over the past hundred years. They grow like weeds, you find them everywhere. But you have to treat them with care.'

Her eyes opened wide. 'They're poisonous, aren't they?'

'That's right, foxglove leaves are the source of digitalis. In small quantities it stimulates the heart, but a large dose is apt to be fatal.'

'Leaves from the garden,' she quoted.

He nodded. 'Will take our leave.'

The train was pulling in. Time to go. Daniel picked up Louise's cases and they hurried outside. Once she'd scrambled into the carriage, she opened the window.

'How are you going to break the news to Miranda?'

He sighed. 'That her dream cottage boasts a garden that celebrates death and hides a coded suicide note?'

She contrived a wry smile. 'Tricky, huh? Best of luck.'

The doors closed and Louise waved. He blew a kiss and called out to her as the train pulled away from the platform.

'I may need more than luck.'

Gail Flint stood in the doorway of her grey cottage, tightly wrapped in a silk kimono, screwing up her eyes against the early morning sunlight. It was only half seven and she hadn't had a chance to disguise her bleariness with make-up.

'May we come in?'

Hannah caught a fruity whiff of stale gin on Gail's breath as she squinted at the warrant card. 'The organ grinder as well as the monkey? My, my. I suppose I ought to be honoured, Chief Inspector, but it's really not a good time.'

'We'll only take a few minutes, Mrs Flint.'

Hannah glanced past Gail into the hallway. A large blue nylon jacket, bearing the legend Allin of Esthwaite Drains and Rodding Services, hung from a coat-stand. A rusting Ford van similarly emblazoned was parked on a yellow line outside the cottage. A thud came from upstairs. Someone overweight, clambering out of bed.

'Sorry to interrupt.'

'You're not interrupting anything at all,' Gail muttered. 'Though couldn't you make an appointment? I do have a business to run, as I told DC Waller here the other day.'

'We thought an informal conversation might be preferable to asking if you'd come to the police station with us.'

Gail glared. 'This is about Kirsty Howe?'

'It would be easier to talk indoors, Mrs Flint.'

'Oh, for goodness sake.' Upstairs, a lavatory flushed. 'All right, have it your own way.'

She padded unsteadily along the hall carpet, shepherding Hannah and Linz into a large and crowded sitting room. A leather suite jostled with a couple of filing cabinets, a desk and a computer. A Bang and Olufsen hi-fi system gleamed in one corner, a plasma television screen was suspended from the wall in another. On the table by the sofa were a couple of empty bottles of Rioja, two unwashed glasses and a CD of Barry Manilow's Greatest Hits. She drew the curtains to reveal a pergola hung with fronds of Virginia creeper. The patio commanded a view of a lawn cut in immaculate stripes and in the distance the brooding bulk of the Old Man of Coniston.

'I insist on Peter mowing for me personally,' she said. 'I made my lawyer include it in the terms of settlement.'

'You didn't prefer a clean break?'

'Where's the fun in that? He may not have been the ideal husband, but he is a bloody good gardener. Besides, a monthly alimony cheque didn't seem penance enough.' Gail waved the detectives towards the armchairs. 'Go on, then. Take the weight off your feet.'

Hannah nodded at the PC. 'You run your business from home?'

'Why spend precious cash on fancy office premises? I've survived one or two business mishaps over the years, but Roz Gleave has given me good advice on keeping control of cashflow. I don't hold too much stock.' She bared her teeth. 'Besides, I'd be tempted to guzzle it, and that would never do, would it?'

Hannah heard someone – or perhaps a small army – tramping down the stairs. Gail shuddered and called out, 'And don't think you can send me an invoice, Tod Allin!'

The front door slammed and moments later the van's engine started up. Gail curled up on the sofa, tucking her bare legs beneath her, and pouted at the two women.

'Tradesmen are so unreliable these days, aren't they? Tod assured me that blocked passages were his speciality.' A rictus smile. 'Very well, Chief Inspector, what can I do for you?'

'A few days ago, we received information about the murder of Warren Howe. An anonymous message accused his wife Tina of the crime.'

'So what, she's the obvious suspect, isn't she?'

The skin seemed to have been stretched too tightly over Gail's cheekbones. On close inspection, not a marvellous advertisement for cosmetic surgery. The main benefit of entrusting your face to the surgeon's knife, Hannah decided, is to make it difficult for people to figure out when you are lying.

'You believe Tina killed Warren?'

'Your colleagues never came up with a better solution.'

'And the motive?'

'Jealousy, rage, a combination of the two, how would I know?'

'No reason for her to be jealous of your affair with Warren, was there?' Hannah asked softly. 'It was over.'

'He didn't dump me! It was a joint decision, perfectly amicable. Our relationship had run its course, that's all. The affair might not have been going anywhere, but then neither was his marriage.'

'And yours?'

'I went back to Peter, didn't I?'

'How did he feel about being cuckolded by his business partner?'

'Cuckolded?' Gail savoured the word as though it were a vintage wine. 'Oh, poor Peter. He didn't murder Warren, if that's what you're hinting. There was no need. He turned a blind eye, he knew I cared for him more than Warren.'

'So why the affair?'

'I wanted a change, a touch of passion in my life. Is that so terrible? Excitement's in short supply after you've been married a number of years.' Gail's high-pitched giggle set Hannah's teeth on edge. 'The temptation to sample forbidden fruit becomes impossible to resist. Perhaps you find that yourself, Chief Inspector?'

Hannah wasn't going there. 'The excitement died for both you and your husband, didn't it? Hence the divorce.'

Gail made a dismissive movement with her shoulders. 'These things happen.'

'You didn't want it to happen, though.'

'As a matter of fact, the divorce was my suggestion.'

'Anticipating the inevitable, surely? When you realised that your husband had fallen for Tina Howe.'

'She started working in the business. Called herself a personal assistant, but she was no more than a shorthand typist with attitude. And a skirt short enough to let the boss catch a glimpse of knickers. Flaunt yourself long enough and you'll hook your man. It's the oldest trick in the book.'

'You were the jealous one, not Tina.'

Gail sat upright. 'Rubbish!'

'She has the settled relationship. With a man you still care for.'

Linz said, 'While you're left – waiting for your annual service from the plumber.'

Gail folded her arms. 'Don't think your sidekick can rattle me, Chief Inspector. I've got a pretty thick skin, you know.'

'I can tell.' Hannah's gaze lingered on the chiselled features. 'Is this why the divorce took so long to finalise – you were fighting a rearguard action, trying to slow it down, hoping he'd change his mind?'

'Bollocks!'

'And when everything was finalised, you took revenge. Not against Peter, but against Tina and her family. You accused her of murdering Warren.'

Gail lifted her chin. It was as pointed as a dagger. 'If you think I'm going to admit writing anonymous letters, you're mistaken.'

'You know there have been several letters, then?'

Gail's eyes darted from Hannah to Linz. 'Watch my lips, will you? I can't help you.'

'Can't or won't, Mrs Flint? I believe the person who sent us the tip-off also wrote to Kirsty Howe.'

'Oh no, you don't! You're not blaming me for that stupid girl's death.'

'Why do you think she killed herself?'

'De mortuis, Chief Inspector.'

'Sorry, they don't do Latin at police college.'

Gail's withering look suggested that this in itself explained the rise in crime. 'I don't care to speak ill of the dead.'

Hannah said coolly, 'Try to overcome your finer feelings.'

'Listen, then. The plain truth is, she was an ungainly lump who couldn't keep a man. A waitress mooning after a man who was devoted to someone else. A shame, but she really didn't have too much going for her.'

'She was young,' Linz said. 'She had the whole of her life ahead of her.'

Gail hissed, 'Try this, before you get too dewy-eyed. Her

mother killed her father. Isn't that reason enough?'

'You're forgetting that she gave her mother an alibi.'

'Oh yes, the watertight alibi.' Gail gave a scratchy laugh. 'Tina, Kirsty and Sam, the three of them were supposed to be together, weren't they? But they were telling fibs.'

'How can you be so sure?'

'Because while Tina was taking a scythe to her husband, I was in bed teaching Sam Howe a thing or two.'

'So at the time of the murder, Sam wasn't up the Hardknott Pass…' Linz chortled as they turned into Tilberthwaite Avenue.

Hannah kept her eyes on the road and resisted the temptation to supply a punch-line. 'If Gail is telling the truth.'

'Do you doubt it?'

'Reluctant as I am to believe a word she says, the story hangs together. Gail didn't want her latest peccadillo to wreck her marriage. Peter overlooked her sleeping with the father, but he might have drawn the line at her bedding the teenage son. The sprained ankle didn't prevent her misbehaving with Sam, but with a little exaggeration it sufficed for an alibi. Quite right, she never left the cottage that day. Why would she want to?'

According to Gail, it was the one and only time she'd slept with Sam. It hadn't exactly been a match made in Heaven. Just a bit of a laugh, really. The two of them had been flirting for a while. When he'd rung to commiserate over her sprained ankle and asked if she'd like him to kiss it better, she'd said it was the best offer she'd had in ages. Probably he fancied a slice of what his dad had been having, but Gail wasn't bothered about his motives. She knew too much about men to entertain illusions. As a lover, the son didn't compare to the father. Youth and virility were all very well, but no match for experience, in her book.

The three-way alibi was Tina's idea. Neither Tina nor Kirsty knew what Sam had been up to and at first he refused to say. They panicked out of fear that his tense relationship with Warren might make him a suspect. Only later did it strike Gail that, just as Tina had persuaded Sam to lie about his whereabouts, so she might have inveigled Kirsty into shielding her from a murder charge.

'Gail sent us the note about Tina, didn't she?'

'Racing certainty,' Hannah said. 'Not that we can prove it.'

'God, she's a bitch.'

All of a sudden, and against all logic, Hannah felt sympathy stabbing at her.

'Yes,' she said. 'But a very unhappy bitch.'

Linz's brow creased in disapproval – keen young DCs didn't do sympathy. She'd learn. They drove on for a few minutes until Linz broke the silence.

'On the radio this morning, the forecaster said that humidity levels have never been so high in this country. I'm sweating like a pig.'

'They've promised a storm before the end of today.'

'Can't come a moment too soon, as far as I'm concerned. All right, ma'am, where do we go from here?'

'To Old Sawrey. Time for another word with Tina Howe.'

'Gail Flint? *Gail Flint?*'

If Hannah had accused her son of having had his wicked way with the late Myra Hindley, Tina Howe might have been more relaxed. Gail Flint? This was sleeping with the enemy.

'The bastard told me she was a tourist from Sweden. Just passing through on her way to Scotland, that's why she wasn't around to back up his story. And you're telling me it was that hatchet-tongued lush! A natural blonde, he said!'

Natural? At least a sense of irony must lurk beneath Sam's sullen exterior. Hannah asked when he would be back and Tina spread her arms.

'He's supposed to be working, but he's just as likely to be propping up some bar or having a leg-over with some scrubber in a caravan park. He doesn't bother about keeping appointments. We're trying to keep going as best we can after – what happened to poor Kirsty, but he isn't helping. We've had loads of complaints, haven't we, Peter?'

Peter Flint gave a nervous cough of assent. The four of them were in his office; this was his domain, but he'd hardly uttered a word since their arrival. His bony frame was squashed up in his chair and Hannah supposed this was how he'd managed to stay married to Gail for so many years. When the going got tough, he pretended to be invisible.

Tina shook her head. 'There's only one thing that lad seems to care about, and it isn't his work, I can tell you. He takes after Warren, and he won't pay attention to what I say any more. Just like his dad.'

'We'll talk to Sam later.'

Tina put her elbows on the table and cupped her chin in her hands. 'Go on, then. Who told you this?'

'I'm sorry, Mrs Howe, we can't…'

'Well, it wouldn't be Sam, would it?' Tina's voice rose. 'Not exactly something to boast about, having it off with Ms Nip and Tuck. It was her, wasn't it? That reconstructed cow.'

'You'll appreciate the implications of the information we've received,' Hannah said. 'You and your children maintained that you were together when your husband was killed. If your son was – otherwise engaged – then the question is obvious. Were you with Kirsty at all?'

'How do you think we managed to take the fucking photographs?' Tina was almost screeching.

'Photographs?' Hannah shrugged. 'Of course, in this day and age, all kinds of technological jiggery-pokery is possible. Isn't that right, DC Waller?'

Linz nodded sagely. 'Dead right, ma'am.'

'For Christ's sake, we were there! Up at the old Roman fort, on the Hardknott Pass, just as we said!'

Hannah felt a surge of triumph. *She's losing it.*

'Who precisely was there?'

Tina swallowed. 'OK, let's just assume that Sam didn't come along that day. What does it prove?'

'You're going to tell me you're still protected by Kirsty's statement, that she was with you all the time?' Hannah turned to Linz. 'Any thoughts?'

'Trouble is, ma'am, Kirsty's not here to corroborate the story any more.'

Tina said in a low voice, 'My daughter died two days ago, Chief Inspector.'

'I was there, Mrs Howe.'

A bitten-off laugh. 'Yeah, I remember you puking your guts out.'

'Tina!' Peter Flint's tone was despairing rather than authoritative. 'I know you're upset...'

Tina turned on him, crimson with anger. 'That bloody old sow Gail, you've always let her walk all over you. All those years you were married, and now you're paying through the nose for the privilege of divorcing her. You've let her get away with murder.'

Hannah said, 'One thing is for sure, Mrs Howe. For years someone did just that. They got away with your husband's murder.'

'Seems like you're no nearer to finding out who did it than on the day he died.'

The horsy face crumpled and Tina Howe started to weep. All of a sudden, her whole body was convulsing. As they watched, she wailed and beat down on the table with her hands. Linz put out a hand to her, but Tina shoved it back. Hannah's surge of triumph ebbed away as Peter Flint got to his feet. He went over and wrapped his arms around Tina, murmuring words of comfort. But it was no use. She would not be stilled, could not be silenced.

Peter treated Hannah to a glare of reproach. Christ, she thought, I deserve it.

Grief had deadened her own emotions. Burying herself in the cold case worked as a means of coping. But it didn't give her the right to torment a woman who had watched her own daughter plunge to her death a couple of days ago. Even if that woman had killed the girl's father by cutting him up with a scythe.

'You think she's guilty, ma'am?' Linz asked as they drove into the car park at Headquarters.

Hannah had spent the journey swathed in gloom as she weighed up that very question. 'I suppose she's still my prime suspect.'

'Uh-huh.'

'What do you think?'

Linz took a breath. 'How about Peter Flint?'

'Why him?'

'Humiliating enough if your wife shags your business partner. How must it feel if she seduces the same bloke's son for good measure?'

'Isn't that a reason for murdering your wife rather than your business partner?'

'But he wanted her back. Must have done. This was before he and Tina got it together, don't forget. And what if Warren encouraged Sam to take a turn with Gail? If Peter realised, wouldn't he want to take revenge?'

Hannah locked the car and led the way inside the main building. At length she said, 'Of course, it's possible. But you saw how his jaw hit the floor when I told them about Sam and Gail? I'd say he was even more shocked than Tina. If he knew beforehand, he's the next Olivier.'

They turned a corner and saw Nick and Les Bryant striding down the corridor towards them. Les grunted at the sight of Hannah and said, 'Nasty business at that airfield, by all accounts. Messy. I heard you'd been signed off for a week.'

'I have amazing powers of recovery.'

'You reckon?'

'We've had a busy morning.'

'Fresh developments in the Warren Howe case?'

'Have we got news for you. Come to my office, Linz will debrief to you.'

'Am I included?' Nick asked.

'Of course. Didn't you tell me that Cockermouth is sorted?'

They headed for Hannah's room via the water cooler. When Linz had summarised their interviews with Gail, Tina and Peter, Nick asked, 'Is Gail telling the truth?'

Hannah said, 'Why should she lie?'

'To firm up her own alibi?'

'Not clever if Sam denies her story. Which might yet happen.'

'Or to hurt Tina?'

'That's more like it,' Hannah admitted. 'The pair of them hate each other, but I'd say Gail's the more vindictive. I can see Tina killing Warren in a fit of temper. As for Gail, no doubt she's capable of murder, but I'd expect subtlety from her. A slow-acting poison would be her weapon of choice. Good old-fashioned arsenic, maybe. Not something as crude as a scythe.'

'I still fancy Peter,' Linz said.

'Rather old for you, isn't he?' Les Bryant murmured. 'For all you know, he may be a lifelong devotee of Abba and Neil Diamond.'

Hannah said, 'OK, that'll do for the time being. I need to catch up on my emails. But before I become engrossed, DS Lowther, can you spare me a minute?'

When they were alone, Hannah switched off her mobile and put her phone on divert. 'Fine, I'm all ears.'

'Before I start, I don't mean to be rude, Hannah, but I have to say, you look like death warmed up.'

'You always did wonders for my confidence.'

'Sorry, but you need to know. I'm only seeing what everyone else is seeing. You'd be far better recuperating at home for a few days instead of getting up at the crack of dawn to interview sad women like Gail Flint and Tina Howe.'

'They'd claw your eyes out if they heard you describing them as sad.'

'True, though, isn't it?'

'Show me someone over thirty who isn't a bit sad.'

He sighed. 'Not having a good day?'

'Pretty shitty, since you ask. I finished up with my heart going out to Tina Howe. Which wasn't in the plan. God, I hate this job sometimes.'

'Me too.'

'All right, fire away. The suspense is killing me.'

'Don't get too excited.' He licked his lips. 'Actually, this is very difficult for me.'

'We go back a long way. No need for any secrets between us.'

'You may change your mind once I've had my say.'

'Don't worry. By now I ought to be unshockable.'

He bowed his head. 'I suppose you've guessed already.'

Hannah took a breath. The fan was whirring sluggishly, exhausted by its losing battle against the heat. 'This is about your relationship with Roz Gleave?'

'Oh, no.' No mistaking the astonishment on his clean-cut features. 'It's about my relationship with her husband. You see, Chris and I were lovers.'

The grey heron stood motionless by the edge of the water, head resting between its shoulders. It surveyed the tarn and the tangled grounds at the foot of Tarn Fell, as if contemplating Jacob Quiller's testament to shattered faith. Daniel and Miranda paused on the winding path, not wishing to disturb its reverie.

'It's as mystified as you and me,' she whispered. 'Daniel, isn't it time to give up on trying to make sense of the garden? This place is so lovely, let's just appreciate what we see.'

'You're right.' He put his arm around her slim shoulders. 'I've been making the historian's mistake. Conjecturing too much about the past, not making enough of the present.'

'Life's short.' She trembled under his touch. 'I dreamed of Kirsty again last night. Watching her fall in slow motion, unable to do anything to save her.'

'There was nothing any of us could do.'

'What could make her so unhappy? What was so bad that she couldn't bear to carry on any longer? If only I'd talked to her more at the restaurant, perhaps I could...'

'You can't blame yourself. It's crazy. We didn't know her, didn't have a clue what was going on inside her head.'

'It was such a lovely evening,' Miranda said. 'Louise was good company, I'm sorry I was mean about her. As soon as she said she was leaving, I realised I'd been selfish.'

'Don't worry about it.'

She cleared her throat. 'There's something I wanted to tell you.'

The air had chilled and at last you could believe that the heatwave might be drawing to an end. He slipped his arm off her.

'What is it?'

'Wipe that frown off your face, you ought to be pleased after all your nagging. I've decided you were right. We all need to be sure of our roots. I must set about tracing my birth mother.'

'Seriously?'

His voice rose in surprise. As if alerted to their presence, the heron drew back its long neck and took flight. Within an instant it had disappeared among the trees.

'Yes. It's ridiculous, this fear of rejection. If she doesn't want to know me, fine. I'll survive. But I'd hate to think she was yearning to hear from me, and I froze her out of my life because she made one mistake, a long, long time ago.'

'Why the sudden change of heart?'

'There's a bond between parent and child, it's unique.' Her voice was dreamy, her eyes far away. 'The blood-tie.'

This was precisely how he felt about his own father, and why he needed to learn more about the man's life, what he was really like. Yet her words didn't ring true. Whenever they'd talked about this before, Miranda had been resolute. The words, the sentiment, didn't seem to belong to her. She'd been talked round. But not by him. And certainly not by Louise.

A phrase of Miranda's came back into his mind as they set off back to the cottage. *We have things in common.*

'You've talked to someone about this?'

'It doesn't matter.'

'I'm interested, that's all.'

'As it happens, I have had a conversation…'

'With Oliver Cox?'

She stared. 'Right first time. How on earth did you figure that out?'

'You were chatting with him in the bar at The Heights. He persuaded you, but what I'm wondering is – how did he manage it?' He closed his eyes, breathing in her perfume. 'Was it because Oliver was adopted too? He understood the dilemma better than the rest of us.'

'He didn't want to talk about it to begin with. I found it so encouraging when he urged me to trace my mum that I asked him outright if he was adopted. Typical, huh, putting my foot right in my mouth?'

'What did he say?'

'At first he backed right off. He's lovely, but he's easily knocked off balance. He actually denied it, would you believe? Said I'd put two and two together and made five.'

His face was very close to hers, but he'd shut his eyes. He was picturing her at the bar, determined not to let Oliver off the hook. 'Go on.'

'Well, I'd had a couple of large glasses of wine and I'd talked him into having one himself, even though he said he never drank on duty because it soon went to his head. I suppose the booze loosened both our tongues. He tried to brush me off, change the subject, make a joke of the whole thing. But I begged him to be straight with me, told him how much it mattered.'

'And in the end he gave in.' That was what people did with Miranda. It was always easier to surrender than to fight.

'Yes, he finally admitted he was adopted. Even then he said he didn't want to make it out to be such a big deal.'

'Did he tell you about his own experience?'

'I dragged it out of him. He said he was riven with doubt about tracing his blood-family. Once he'd dropped out of uni, he hadn't been able to settle to anything. As a last resort, he decided to look for his real mother. He was frightened of how she would react, his dread of rejection was as intense as mine. But when at last he found her, it changed his life. No question, he told me, it was the best thing he'd ever done.'

'Where did he meet his mother?'

'No idea. He clammed up after that and I didn't want to make any more of a nuisance of myself. I was grateful for his honesty.'

They were taking a short cut across the grassy area that he'd cleared. Leaving behind the yew and the monkey puzzles and the weeping willow. He was determined that they shouldn't become trapped in the maze of the Quillers' despair. As he walked, he was delving into the undergrowth of useless information in his mind, striving to make out what lay beneath.

He wasn't sure of the precise chronology, but from what Hannah and Bel Jenner had told him, two things had happened shortly before Warren Howe's murder. Oliver Cox had turned up in Old Sawrey, and Chris Gleave had disappeared. What if a young man turned up on their doorstep one fine morning and announced that Roz was his mother? If so, then judging by her age, she could only have been fourteen or fifteen when she gave birth. Chris and Roz didn't have kids; if Chris was incapable of being a father, how might he react if a stranger blundered into their cosy little marriage and revealed something his wife had never got up the nerve to mention? He was a sensitive soul, self-consciously artistic. Perhaps he might run away and hide.

'What do you think?' Miranda asked.

'Sorry?'

'You're miles away, aren't you, darling? Not very flattering. I was saying, if we're going to ask those garden designers to give this place a makeover, perhaps we should take a few photographs so that we can remember how it used to be. Before and After shots.'

'I want to keep the basic lay-out intact. The garden's odd, but...'

'You like it as it is?'

He groped for the right words. 'It deserves...respect.'

'Darling, it's a garden, not a shrine.'

'Even so.'

'All right, but we need a new theme. And lots more colour. It's drab and dark here. Except for the foxgloves. They're starting to die off, but they are so pretty in full bloom.'

Daniel gazed at the purple flowers shaped like bells. The means by which Jacob and Alice Quiller had killed themselves.

'You know their leaves are poisonous?'

She laughed. 'Typical. You always have to look on the dark side.'

'Sorry. You're right, we need a fresh start. As for a theme – how about celebrating a new life?'

She smiled with almost childlike delight. 'Wonderful.'

The scent of the roses was heady, butterflies were fluttering to and fro. A picture came into Daniel's mind. Jacob Quiller bent over the ground, grim in his determination to convey a confession through his work. Back-breaking labour, but an escape from sitting inside by the fire, while his guts churned in despair. No such escape for Alice, as the clock ticked on towards the anniversary of John's passing, the date they had fixed for ending it all. Both of them were obsessed, Jacob with macabre garden patterns, Alice with the loss of her only son. It was on Alice, of whom he knew so little, that his thoughts lingered. The housemaid who became mistress of the little cottage in the clearing, proud mother of a young man who left his native shores to fight for Queen and country, never to return.

The love between mother and child could break down all restraints and scrape away the coat of varnish that protects from raw emotion, rage, and violence. Bees buzzed in the background, Miranda ducked her head to smell the flowers, and Daniel tossed possibilities around in his mind.

Suppose Oliver had not only found his long lost mother, but his father as well. Who was a more likely candidate to impregnate a young girl in the village than the late and unlamented Warren Howe? Consider it from Chris Gleave's perspective. What if he was driven by jealousy, what if he hated the man who had given Roz a son, when he had not?

It might add up to a motive for murder.

'You don't have to tell me this,' Hannah said.

'You're wrong, ma'am.'

She bent forward. 'Ma'am? What happened to Hannah and Nick?'

'Sorry.' A threadbare smile. 'You're wrong, Hannah. You need to know this. What you do with the information is up to you.'

She poured two cups of coffee, marvelling at the steadiness of her hand while her stomach was somersaulting. She dreaded what Nick might confess. A breach of regulations, perhaps even a crime, something that would destroy his career. That he'd had a gay relationship didn't matter, even though learning of it had floored her. Even as she watched him deliberate, working out how much to say and how much to leave out, she realised how many clues she'd missed. Nick was a good actor, but there were limits to his ability to pretend. She recalled an interview she and Nick had conducted with a man called Allardyce, not long after she'd first met Daniel Kind.

'You know what women are like. Or maybe you don't, eh?'

She remembered her sergeant colouring at the gibe. At the

time, she'd dismissed it, but although Allardyce was a brute, he'd sussed Nick out in a matter of minutes. She'd been fooled for years. Call herself a detective?

If he was a closet gay, no wonder he'd never tried it on with her. It was one of the differences, she understood now, between her relationship with Nick and that with Ben Kind. With Ben, she'd always had this sense that he wanted to touch her, but held back, perhaps because he was afraid of rejection, perhaps because he knew it was wrong to start an affair with a young subordinate. With Nick, the friendship never threatened to become more than platonic. For all her occasional wishful thinking in bed or in the bath as she recalled his smooth features and long lean limbs.

'It's not such an unusual story,' he said at length. 'A teenage boy, uncertain about his sexuality. Chris and I were each in the same boat. Conventional upbringing and outlook, desperate to be part of the crowd, but aware of secret longings too dangerous to acknowledge. No wonder we were drawn together. I'm not going to give you all the gory details, OK? Let's just say we enjoyed each other for several months. But both of us were riddled by guilt. Especially me. Pathetic, really. In my defence, I was only seventeen. Trouble was, that was below the age of consent. Another reason for feeling bad.'

'Who cares?' she said. 'Didn't we pass a couple of posters for the Gay and Lesbian Police Association as we walked down the corridor?'

'Do me a favour. I never wanted to be a pink policeman.'

'All I mean is, times have changed. So have attitudes.'

'On the surface. But that's beside the point. I've no desire to join a protected species, I'm just an ordinary bloke. Which is why Chris and I split up. The angst was more than I could handle. I'd set my heart on joining the force and I wanted the orthodox life everyone in my family had. A pretty wife and two point four children, a modest mortgage and a decent pension. Boring, boring, boring, as far as Chris was concerned. He wanted to make music. Money didn't matter to him.'

'He had the luxury of inheriting it.'

'Fair comment. We went our separate ways. I joined the force, got married. You know the rest.'

Do I? 'It was your decision to break up?'

'Yes, but Chris wasn't bitter. We kept in touch. I went along to his concerts, every now and then. He told me he'd had a few other boyfriends, but nobody special.'

'He wanted you to get back together again?'

'I suppose so, but it was out of the question. I'd made my choice and so far as I was concerned, he had to respect it. Which he did. Next thing I knew, he was engaged to Roz. I didn't know what to expect when I met her. When I found out it was a genuine love match, I was thrilled for him.'

'All's well that ends well?'

Nick nodded. 'Until I heard that he'd disappeared from home, and while he was missing, Warren Howe was killed in his back garden.'

While Miranda absorbed herself with the laptop, working on a first draft of her latest article for Ethan Tiatto, Daniel stayed outside. He yearned to talk to Hannah, share his ideas about the murder with her. He took out his mobile and dialled her number. Straight to voicemail. Shit. Better to try later rather than leave a message. How to explain in a couple of crisp sentences the speculation swirling around inside his brain?

He paced up and down the path outside his own front door, striving to reconcile the known facts with his guesswork. When he'd called at Keepsake Cottage, he'd overheard the Gleaves discussing whether a secret could be kept. He'd assumed it was connected with Kirsty's death, but there might be a link to the murder of Warren Howe.

Would there be harm in a return visit to the Gleaves' home? Hannah might insist he shouldn't poke his nose in, but he might have more luck than a police officer in gleaning crucial information.

He went back inside and told Miranda that he'd be out for an hour or two. She nodded, but didn't look up from her work in progress. On his way out, he tried Hannah again. Still no answer.

Weaving through the country lanes, he stretched his brain, refining his theory that Chris Gleave had killed Warren Howe. He'd spent such a short time in the man's company, he found it impossible to do more than guess at what made him tick. By instinct he rebelled against the idea of a likeable musician committing a savage murder, but it made sense as a crime of passion, fuelled by jealousy and loathing.

Rounding a bend, he found his way blocked by a farm boy standing in the middle of the road, with upraised hand. Behind him plodded a herd of cattle, on their way from one field to another. Daniel breathed out. His reasoning had also run into a jam. How had Chris contrived his alibi? He must have been in the frame for the murder, yet the police hadn't come close to pinning him to the scene. A bizarre location for a murderer to choose, if there was any degree of planning. Why kill someone in your own back garden? It had to be a crime born of panic, yet that didn't square with an alibi strong enough to defy intensive scrutiny from a team of detectives under pressure to solve a high profile crime.

While he waited, he tried Hannah's number again. Her disembodied voice once more invited him to leave a message; once more he decided not to bother. He fancied setting up another meeting with her to reveal the ingenuity of his theory. If she doused it with cold water, he wouldn't care. What he wanted most was a fresh excuse to share her company.

He was asking himself what this said about his relationship with Miranda when the last cow trudged through the gate and the boy waved his thanks. Daniel returned his smile. A chance to put his foot down and dodge a mystery even more awkward than Warren Howe's murder.

'Did Roz know about you and Chris?'

'If she did, she never dropped a hint.'

'And when he left home?'

'I kept my mouth shut.' Nick bowed his head. 'To this day, I'm not sure if that was right or wrong. I didn't have a clue what had happened to him. There was no reason to believe his past had any bearing on his disappearance. Of course, I couldn't help wondering. Had he picked someone up in a park or public toilet and been bashed over the head for his pains? Anything was possible. But there was no body. So I hoped against hope that he would come home to Keepsake Cottage.'

'Which he did.'

'Eventually. I must say I didn't buy his explanation for going AWOL. I mean, his music was important to him, and the poor response to his CD must have been disheartening. But vanishing from sight seemed like a massive over-reaction, even if he'd had a nervous breakdown.'

'Did you talk to him?'

'Not officially. I wasn't supposed to discuss the Howe murder with him, but keeping to the rules didn't prove difficult. Ten days after he came back, he agreed to go out with me for a couple of beers. We went to a pub in Barrow where neither of us were likely to be recognised. Before he'd downed his first half pint of Stella, he was spilling the beans. Poor bastard, he was desperate to talk to someone who might understand.'

'Which you did?'

Nick nodded. 'He told me he'd fallen in love for the first time in his life.'

Hannah opened her eyes wide. 'With?'

'Oliver Cox's predecessor as chef at The Heights. A Scots lad called Jason Goddard, utterly gorgeous if Chris was to be believed. Probably he wasn't, given that love is blind. And Chris was head over heels, that was for sure. He was willing to give up everything for this kid, he just couldn't contemplate losing him. It was a mid-life crisis, not really love at all. Wild infatuation would be nearer the mark. There was only one snag.'

'Don't tell me,' Hannah groaned. 'The devotion wasn't reciprocated.'

'Life's so unfair. Jason was notoriously camp and promiscuous. I heard all this long before I had any idea that Chris had fallen for him. My take is, Jason led Chris on and Chris was more than willing to be led. The trouble was that Jason fancied a bit of fun, not a lifelong union. When Chris started getting heavy and spoke about leaving Roz so the two of them could be together, Jason couldn't handle it and took fright. There was nothing tying him to the Lake District, so he ran off to London. What he didn't bargain for was Chris following him.'

'And the nervous breakdown?'

'He told the truth about that. Down in London, everything became messy. Chris haunting Jason's footsteps, Jason threatening to sue Chris for harassment. In the end, Jason lost his cool and resorted to more direct methods. He arranged for a couple of thugs to beat Chris up.'

'On the day Warren Howe was murdered in his garden back home?' Hannah shook her head at the irony of it. 'Because of the attack, no-one had a chance of proving he was guilty of murder. Talk about a blessing in disguise.'

Roz Gleave seemed calmer today. Was this because Chris wasn't around? He had left an hour earlier, she said, on his way to Lancaster to negotiate with the manager of a folk club. She cast a wary glance at the darkening sky as she led Daniel round the back of Keepsake Cottage, and suggested they make the most of the weather before they were drenched by the thunderstorm the Met. Office had threatened. They sat on opposite sides of the teak table at the rear of the house, looking up towards the terrace where Warren Howe had been cut down.

'Sorry I was so abrupt last time we met. We weren't in the mood to be hospitable after the terrible news about poor Kirsty. Now, if you don't mind, I can only spare you ten minutes. I'm expecting a friend to call round for a cup of tea and a chat.'

'Ten minutes is all I ask.'

'Were your ears burning yesterday? I was talking about you to Marc Amos. He sang your praises, tells me you're a valued customer.'

'Marc's a friend of yours?'

'We scarcely know each other. Both of us make a living from books, but in different parts of the market. He sells them second hand, I'm rather keen to make a profit the first time my publications leave the shelves. We don't get a percentage the second time around. I met Hannah, his partner, the other day. Young for a chief inspector, I thought. Or perhaps that just shows my own advancing years.'

'It was Marc who told me about the book by Eleanor Sawtell.'

'So I gather. Any progress with your garden mystery?'

'A little.'

She looked him in the eye. 'Marc mentioned you were involved with one of his partner's cases not so long ago.'

'Hannah heads the county's cold case team. I like to think there's a parallel between her work and historical research. Not sure I've persuaded her, mind.'

'And you were at the airfield when Kirsty died.'

'I'd met her at the restaurant the previous day.'

'Quite a coincidence.'

Time to break cover, Daniel decided. 'Not really, Roz. Truth is, I'm incurably inquisitive. So I can't help being intrigued by what I've heard about the murder of Warren Howe.'

The temperature was plunging with every word he uttered. She pursed her lips. 'I see.'

'Must be painful for you, having the whole business resurrected after all these years.'

'We could do without it. That was a difficult time for Chris and me.'

'All the more so because Warren was a former boyfriend?'

'We went out a few times as kids,' she snapped. 'Nothing more. It was buried in the past, it didn't mean a thing. I was sorry he died such a brutal death, but candidly, I was sorrier still that it happened here. I won't pretend that I spent much time in mourning. Warren wasn't a nice man. Not like his daughter. Poor Kirsty.'

'One thing I've learned about history is that things we believed were buried in the past can reach out and poke us in the eye today.'

'What are you talking about?'

'Your relationship with Warren. I hate to be intrusive, but I've found out that Oliver Cox is adopted. He told my partner, Miranda, and I couldn't help wondering...'

Roz Gleave's face contorted with dismay, bordering on disbelief. 'He discussed his past with someone he hardly knew?'

'She's adopted as well. She was confiding in him.'

'My God, he always said he would never...'

'She's a journalist. Very accomplished at worming information out of people. I'm sure when Oliver told her a little about his own past, he didn't mean to cause any embarrassment.'

'Meaning what?'

Daniel said softly, 'Meaning that I'm sure he didn't intend anyone to suspect that you might be his mother.'

She put a hand to her mouth and he thought she was going to faint. But when she spoke, it wasn't to admit that he'd seen through to the truth.

'Have you taken leave of your senses?'

He'd expected outrage or evasion. Not amazement. It felt like being hosed with cold water. 'You're denying it?'

'You bet I'm bloody well denying it!' She stood up. 'You'd better go.'

No-one could feign such shock. Her face was reddening, astonishment giving way to anger. And yet he couldn't imagine that his theory was so wide of the mark.

'Oliver said that meeting his birth mother changed his life. Until then he'd been a drifter...'

Roz's hands were on her hips. She nodded towards the path that led around the cottage.

'Please don't outstay your welcome, Mr Kind.'

Oh Jesus. He got to his feet. 'I'm wrong, aren't I? Oliver isn't your son.'

She said hoarsely, 'I'm not able to have children. It's been a great sadness, but at least I have a marvellous husband. Now – please go.'

Hannah said, 'You talked to Chris after he came back to the Lakes?'

'He asked if we could meet. When he heard about the murder, he was overwhelmed by guilt, for having left Roz to endure the trauma on her own. He was afraid Charlie would find some way of pinning the crime on her, but that was never an option. Her alibi was as unbreakable as his. I wanted to know if he had any idea of who was responsible, but if he had, he wasn't telling. He hadn't wished Warren dead, but his only concern was to return a semblance of normality to his life.'

'So he settled for domestic bliss rather than chasing after unsuitable young men?'

Nick gave her a sharp glance. 'I've never asked if he's strayed since then, and he hasn't told me. One thing he did make clear, he didn't care if Warren's murder was never solved. I said it would only take a single stroke of luck, and he said he hoped we never got it. Whoever had been driven to such violence must have had good reason to kill Warren. We'd never argued until then. I thought he was wrong to side with the murderer, when the crime had put Roz and everyone in Old Sawrey under the microscope.'

'The ordeal by innocence?'

'Yes.' Nick exhaled. 'I suppose things were never the same between us afterwards. Since then we've not spoken more than once or twice a year. But he promised that he'd never told anyone we'd been lovers. Not even Roz.'

'Did she know he was gay?'

'Not according to Chris. Until he explained about Jason, she didn't have the foggiest.'

'Did you believe him?'

'Yes.' He looked her in the eye. 'If you told Janice I was gay, she'd never believe you.'

Hannah shrugged. 'You and Chris, it was a long time ago. You were kids, experimenting. He may have played around since, but...'

'I haven't?' Nick's face was desolate. 'That doesn't mean I haven't been tempted. Which is what I'm afraid of, Hannah, if you really want to know. Janice might not have guessed and you might not have guessed. But I know who I am and what's in my heart and mind. What keeps me awake at night is the fear that I'm living a lie.'

* * *

As Daniel walked back to his car, he felt Roz's eyes boring into his back. She had retreated into her cottage, only to stand at the window of the front room and keep watch, making sure that he didn't hang around.

For all his hot embarrassment, he didn't mean to be hurried. There was too much to think over. He unwound the sunroof. The air was heavy, soon there would be the first drops of rain. As he changed the CD, his brain was racing. How could he have made such a mistake?

In the distance, he heard a car engine. Someone was coming to Keepsake Cottage. The friend Roz had mentioned? He glanced back at the house and caught sight of Roz's face. It was haggard with fear.

He fastened his seatbelt, taking an age over it, wanting to see who visited Roz. Within a minute, his time-wasting was rewarded as Bel Jenner's BMW glided to a halt alongside his Audi.

She opened her door and treated him to a guileless smile. 'Hello again. Small world.'

He unbuckled the seatbelt and got out too. The cottage door opened, in a moment Roz would join them and try to shoo him away. But he only had eyes for Bel.

The dark hair, high cheekbones and beaky nose were clues, of course. The resemblance wasn't obvious, but it was there if you searched hard.

Small world was right. This time he was sure. Oliver Cox was Bel Jenner's son.

Chapter Nineteen

'Is everything all right?' Bel asked.

Daniel shook his head. It was as if he'd been kicked in the solar plexus. Speech was beyond him. He needed to take this in.

She doesn't know. Jesus. She doesn't have the faintest idea that for years she's been sleeping with her son.

Bel was a woman who liked things comfortable about her. Pleasant. Very English. She'd used her money to create a secure little world. And she indulged herself with a passionate devotion to the young man who had sought her out and then fallen in love with her. But he had kept secrets from her. He'd understood that she couldn't cope with the truth.

Daniel heard the door of the cottage open behind him. He spun round to see Roz advancing towards them. Her gaze was focused on him and he could tell that she realised he'd worked it out. She might have been Eve, contemplating the serpent.

'I asked you to leave.' Her voice was a croak.

'What's wrong?' Bel asked.

Roz's breath was coming in short jerky gasps. When she spoke, her voice was stripped of pride. She was begging.

'Don't say another word, Mr Kind! Just go!'

'Nobody else knows, is that right? Just the two of you?'

Roz and Oliver, he meant. She understood and gave a quick nod.

'How come?'

Roz stood within an arm's reach of him. Her mouth was clamped shut.

Bel put her hands on her hips. 'Will someone please tell me what on earth is going on?'

Daniel ground his teeth, his gaze flicking from one woman to the other.

I can't do it. I'm not the police, it's not for me to play games with people's lives. Much as I want to know everything that is to be known. If I push on, it would be like taking an axe to a doll's house.

He bent towards Roz and murmured, 'Did Warren know that Bel had fallen pregnant?'

Her eyes were as hard as pebbles. When she whispered in reply, her lips scarcely moved.

'She told him the baby had died.'

The door closed behind Nick, leaving Hannah alone with the fan, gasping with mechanical emphysema. So many years of friendship and shared gossip, and yet she hadn't really known her sergeant after all. This affable, laid-back man was quietly torturing himself and she'd never had a clue.

It had taken courage for him to bare his soul to her, but surely he'd read too much into an intense teenage relationship? Schoolgirl crushes of her own had, thank God, faded into the vaguest memories. Nick needed to liberate himself from the past and look to the future. With Janice.

She checked her mobile for messages. Lauren had called, wanting to know when the latest stats recording the cold case team's endeavours would be on her desk. And she heard Daniel Kind's voice, breathless and jerky.

Can you call me? I've found out something you need to know.

Hannah's brain hummed as she turned the last bend and caught a glimpse of The Heights. The restaurant wouldn't be open for a couple more hours. She took the fork in the drive leading to the house next door. There wasn't a sign of life at the windows. She hurried up the front path and leaned hard on the bell. No answer.

At the side of the house, a fence separated the back garden from the front. Six feet of willow screen, guarding the privacy of Bel Jenner and Oliver Cox. A gate beneath a wisteria-draped arch barred the way. She tested the handle and found it wasn't locked. Without a pause, she shoved it open and strode around the side of the house. Daniel was right, she was sure of it. But if they were wrong, it was too late to worry about making a fool of herself.

A white canvas hammock stretched between a pair of beech trees. Oliver Cox lay on it, dozing. In T-shirt and shorts; with bare feet and black hair flopping over his face, he might have passed for a boy. Tall, handsome, innocent. His legs were long and smooth, like Marc's.

On hearing footsteps, he stirred and looked round. 'DCI Scarlett. I was expecting Bel. What can I do for you?'

'Sorry to butt in.'

Oliver yawned and slid off the hammock. 'You look hot and bothered. I hear you were there at the airfield. Poor Kirsty. It must have been horrific.'

'I'll never forget it.'

'I can imagine.'

'Can you?' Hannah didn't try to hide her scorn. 'Will you miss her?'

'Well, yes.' A wary expression crept across Oliver's face. 'She was a lovely girl. An enthusiastic waitress, keen to learn.'

'And that's all?'

'I don't know what you want me to say.'

'Surely she meant something more to you?'

'She was a sweet kid, all right?'

The heat had sucked out all Hannah's energy. It was too late for subtlety.

'She was your sister. Half-sister. You shared the same father.'

'What?' Oliver's features contorted, as if she'd slapped his cheek. 'Who – who have you been talking to?'

'I'm right, aren't I?'

'You know – about Bel?'

Hannah heard a rustle behind the willow screen, but she didn't care who might be listening. Presumably it was the Croatian kids who worked in the restaurant; they wouldn't have a clue what was going on. Bel was still at Keepsake Cottage, according to Daniel, as Roz attempted the impossible and tried to comfort her.

'You fell in love with your mother.'

After a long pause, Oliver said in a scratchy voice, 'Sorry if you disapprove.'

'You misunderstand. What I disapprove of is what you did to your father.'

'My father, what are you talking about?'

'Your father, Warren Howe.'

Oliver was breathing hard. Not speaking.

'I'm right, aren't I? You found out that he was your father.'

'So what?'

'So when Roz Gleave told Kirsty that she was wasting her time with you because you were family, your sister had nothing more to live for.'

'It wasn't my fault! Not that she killed herself. That was the last thing I wanted.'

'And why did she kill herself? Not just the heartbreak, is my guess. She realised that you must have confronted Warren Howe.'

'What if I did?'

'Was it like this?' Hannah watched the muscles of Oliver's cheeks fluttering beneath the flesh. 'You approached your father, but he didn't want to know. He'd spent the years in between believing you were dead, and that suited him fine.'

'I didn't need him,' Oliver whispered.

'But you did need Bel. The catastrophe came when Warren told you he wanted her, was determined to have her again, come what may. If you didn't back off, he'd make sure she knew who you were. The shame of what she'd done would destroy her. That's why you murdered him, isn't it? Not because your father rejected you, but to save the woman you loved?'

'Guesswork.' Oliver was backing away, but he was backing himself into a corner too, in between Hannah and the fence that barred access to the garden from the open countryside. 'This isn't detective work. It's pure imagination. Your colleagues investigated thoroughly. There's never been any suggestion of evidence linking me with the scene of the crime.'

'They didn't know you were Warren's son, or that Bel was your mother.'

'Even if they did, nothing could be proved.'

The shaking hands belied the confident words. And yet he was right, wasn't he? The Crown Prosecutors would demand clear evidence of guilt before authorising a trial. Hannah felt a splash of wet on her cheek, then another on her hair. Rain, at long last rain. As she watched Oliver Cox, unmoving as the raindrops fell faster, she felt overwhelmed by a tidal wave of sadness. Kirsty was dead and soon the lives of Oliver and Bel would be wrecked forever.

A thunderous voice ruptured the silence.

'Listening to you is all the proof I need.'

Hannah heard footsteps from behind the willow screen. She didn't need to look to know who was coming. *Oh God, what have I done?*

Oliver's eyes widened in terror. Hannah clenched her fists and looked round. Approaching them was Sam Howe. He must have been working in the restaurant garden, behind the willow screen. Chances were, he'd heard everything. In his hand was a garden fork. Its prongs were pointing at Oliver's heart.

'Put it down,' Hannah said.

'He killed my father. You know what he fucking did? Threw lilies over the body and a strip of sacking. Murder wasn't enough, he had to bury him as well.'

Play for time, play for time. The rain was falling faster, Hannah needed to blink it out of his eyes.

'You loved your father?'

'He killed my sister too.'

'Did you bother much with her?'

'He's not part of my family.'

'That's where you're wrong.' Already the rain had soaked Hannah's shirt, she might have been back in her bathroom, standing under the shower jet. 'And you know something? I'd say he's even inherited his share of the Howes' ruthlessness. Perhaps that's why he killed your dad.'

'You'd better go.'

'I'm staying.'

'You'll get hurt.'

'I don't want anyone to get hurt.'

Oliver cried out, 'For Christ's sake, what are you going to do – gore me in cold blood?'

'That's what you did to him, isn't it?

'It wasn't meant to happen!'

'Confessing, now?' Sam showed his teeth. 'Well, well, you heard that, Mrs Policewoman?'

'I heard, Sam. Now, why don't you put that fork down and we can…'

'Forget it.' Water was dripping off him, but he didn't seem aware of it. There was only one thing on his mind. 'They'll never prosecute the bastard. That's what this country has come to. The guilty walk free while decent people live in fear.'

Hannah took a stride towards him, keeping her arm outstretched. 'Give me the fork.'

'Think you're a heroine, do you? Fuck off.'

'Please, Sam.'

With a swift, fluid movement, Sam Howe twisted the fork upside down and swung the metal handle. It smashed against Hannah's body. She keeled over on the wet stones, slumping heavily to the ground.

Sam was within two paces of Oliver. The chef had fallen to his knees. His eyes were closed, hands put together as if in prayer.

Sam hissed, 'What's that you're saying? *Our father?*

Hannah cried out:

'*No!*'

Sam gave a roar like a wild creature and, as Oliver looked up, thrust the steel prongs into his neck.

Chapter Twenty

Daniel stood by the window, listening to the drumbeat of rain on the roof of the cottage. Puddles had formed on the stone slabs, flowers leaned under the weight of water, clouds merged into a vast grey tarpaulin. Hard to believe that the sodden cipher garden had ever possessed a secret meaning. A foul-tempered wind was howling through the valley, making the trees dance to its angry tune. The tarn looked swollen, the summit of the fell was wrapped in mist. He thought about Alice Quiller and John, about Oliver Cox and Bel Jenner. Some passions defied all wisdom, sometimes devotion justified any sin.

'I should have kept my nose out.'

'You said it, darling.' Miranda ran her fingertips down his cheek. 'Never mind. It'll make a marvellous story.'

He flinched, as if at a wasp sting. 'You're not going to write about what happened?'

'Why not? I may have changed my mind about tracing my birth mother, but everything is copy. Grist to the mill.'

'You can't, it's too close. Too personal.'

'Like telling our bedroom secrets?' She laughed. 'If you could only see your face! Come on, darling, lighten up.'

'Sam got his just deserts,' Marc said.

Rain had streaked Sam Howe's face as he stared down at his half-brother's body. Impossible for Hannah to imagine what was running through his mind. No need to make sure Oliver was dead, the fork buried in his windpipe left no room for doubt. She huddled on the ground, breath knocked out of her, body throbbing with pain. Not making a sound, not daring to move. Would she be next?

Sam spat on the ground and turned on his heel. Hannah closed her eyes, heard Sam pounding down the path. The van door banged, the engine growled, tyres screeched.

Scarcely the perfect getaway. Sam always drove too fast, it turned out that he was famous for it. Half a mile down a lane greasy from the downpour, he'd skidded round a bend at sixty and crashed into an oncoming tractor. The farmhand escaped with shock and whiplash, but Sam hadn't bothered with his seatbelt. He was hurled through the windshield, smack into the oncoming cab. Dead on arrival at A&E.

'Saved the need for a trial, I guess.'

'And a lot of embarrassing questions.'

Hannah rubbed her side. It still ached, but the yellow bruise from Sam's fork was fading. Banishing the nightmare vision of Oliver's lifeblood spilling on to the ground, would take longer.

'Embarrassing questions are the last thing on my mind.'

Interviewing Bel had been a nightmare of embarrassment. And heart-rending pity. In the face of disaster, the woman had acquired a weird dignity. She still dressed as if for a fashion show, the make-up was applied with the old finesse. She'd closed the restaurant – *until further notice* – but it remained spick and span. She spoke distantly, yet readily, like an emotional soulmate of Miss Havisham. Perhaps she'd persuaded herself she was going to wake up soon to find Oliver cooking dinner next door in the kitchen.

'As soon as I told Warren I was expecting a baby, he dumped me. He'd kept pestering me to go out with him, but no way could you ever get him to shoulder responsibility. He wasn't a savage man, Mr Kind, not a wife beater or a fighting drunk. But I never met anyone more selfish. Or more ruthless when it came to taking pleasure.'

'And then he started going out with your best friend.'

'Rubbing salt in the wound, yes.'

'Did she know you were pregnant?'

'God, no. I truly believe she was tormented by guilt simply because he'd dumped me for her. For a while, she and I kept our distance. Even when Warren gave her the push, and the two of us made up, I didn't tell her about the baby for a long time. To tell you the truth, I felt so alone.'

'You kept the pregnancy secret?'

'Until I was so far gone that I had no choice but to tell my mother. I wanted to have an abortion, I hated the very thought of giving birth to Warren's child. But Mum wouldn't hear of it. She gave out that I'd been taken ill and whisked me away to an aunt in Hexham. That's where I had the baby.'

'And you gave him up for adoption.'

'I told Warren our baby was born dead.' She flinched, but did not lose her spooky calm. One day reality would hit her. Hannah didn't want to be around when it happened.

'It was the only solution. Mum said she wouldn't allow me to ruin my life because of one mistake.'

'When did you tell Roz?'

'After I came back from Hexham. One night when we were listening to music in my bedroom, I broke down in floods of tears and it all came out. I made her swear that she'd never tell a soul. I wanted to airbrush the whole horrid episode out of my mind. Make believe it never happened.'

Hannah nodded. There was nothing she could say.

'I swore to myself I'd never think about the child again.' Bel lifted her chin. 'And you know what, Chief Inspector? I never did.'

Roz hadn't wanted to talk. She blamed herself for spilling the beans to Kirsty, kept saying that if she'd held her tongue, the girl would be alive to this day. She only agreed to an interview when she found Bel was willing for her to tell the story.

'When did you realise Oliver was Bel's son?' Hannah asked.

'It didn't click at first, but one night, I was eating on my own in the restaurant. Chris had gone missing, I didn't care to cook for one. The Howes were celebrating their wedding anniversary. Oliver came out from the kitchen to serve and for an instant I saw him framed in between Warren and Sam and saw a resemblance. It was subtle, I'd never noticed it before, but seeing them together set off like a lightning bolt in my mind. I wondered if the similarities might be coincidence. Oliver didn't look much like Bel – but then, there's something about the shape of the nose. And he had her gentleness, too, poor man.'

'He was the right age to be the lost boy.'

'And he'd turned up in Old Sawrey out of the blue. The Lakes attracts more than its fair share of drifters, and I didn't want to let my imagination carry me away. So I made it my business to talk to him the next day while Bel was out visiting the wholesaler. It didn't take me long to wheedle out that he was adopted. I asked outright if he was Bel's son. At first he lied, but his shock was a dead giveaway. In the end he admitted that he'd become obsessed with finding his parents. He believed it would give a meaning to his life. It hadn't been difficult to trace Bel. What he hadn't reckoned for was that the two of them would become besotted with each other.'

'He admitted that?'

'You only had to see them together to know. I warned him he was playing with fire, that it would be a kindness to tell her the truth. She might lose a boyfriend, but she'd gain a son.'

'And he refused?'

'He begged me to let them be. And he can be very persuasive.' Roz tipped her head to one side, a faraway look in her eyes. '*Right now, she needs me as a lover. Not as a reminder of the worst time in her life.*'

'So you promised to keep quiet?'

'Whatever my other faults,' she said drily, 'I have at least proved I'm good at keeping confidences. Whether that's been for the best in the long run – different story.'

'You knew she was his mother and yet…'

'Listen, Bel had been wretched for a long time. Yes, she was fond of Tom and she nursed him selflessly during his illness. But no way was it a grand passion, she settled for comfort and security when she married him. I'd never seen her so happy, not since her first date with that bastard Warren Howe. Meanwhile Warren was sniffing round her again. He'd tired of Gail and was looking out for fresh fields to conquer. I doubt if he ever fancied anyone more than Bel, not even Tina. She knows how to satisfy a man, I think. My nightmare was that if she lost Oliver, in desperation she'd turn to Warren, despite what he'd done to her all those years ago.'

'You really didn't care for Warren, did you?'

'I hated him, is that blunt enough for you?' Her smile was icy.

'You were explaining why you didn't tell Bel that she was sleeping with her own son.'

'I'm no guardian of morals, Detective Chief Inspector. Pragmatism is the best most of us can hope for. Oliver was very different from Warren. Sensitive and passionate. He would look after Bel, I was confident of that. I'd stolen one lover from her and that was one too many. If I'd said something to her, warned her off – I'd have ruined two lives. What would you have done?'

Hannah didn't speak.

'As the years passed, it all worked out to perfection. Warren was dead and gone, he'd never bother Bel again. She and Oliver were blissfully happy.'

'But he was a murderer.'

'I'll believe to my dying day that he didn't come to our cottage intending to kill his own father.'

'Even so.'

Roz glared. 'Frankly, your colleagues on the original investigation didn't have a clue, so I hope you don't blame me for not working out the truth. As far as I was concerned, Chris was back where he belonged and our marriage was stronger than before. Everything in the garden was lovely.'

'Even the prettiest gardens turn bleak in time.'

Roz closed her eyes. 'If only Kirsty hadn't fallen for Oliver. Her half-brother. I did my utmost to discourage her, but she took no notice.'

'Because you were Bel's buddy.'

'Too old to understand about young love.' A single tear trickled down her cheek. 'It was madness. How could she have thought me capable of destroying the happiness of my dearest friend? But there was no convincing her. She was a Howe, and nobody is more determined than the Howes, once they set their mind to something. She refused to give Oliver up. The more he tried to keep her at arm's length, the more she wanted him. Worse, much worse, she told me how she hated Bel, how she fantasised about killing her. A woman who had shown her nothing but kindness. I always believed Kirsty would never hurt a fly, but she was losing the plot. I was terrified of what she might do.'

'So you told her the truth?'

'It was a mistake, I panicked, but I couldn't imagine how else to stop her in her tracks. Their affair could never be.'

She blew her nose loudly. A string of reassuring platitudes trailed through Hannah's head. Stuff you might read in the magazine that Miranda wrote for. It wasn't your doing, she was responsible for her own actions. You did your best, it was an impossible situation.

Empty, empty, empty words.

'I suppose you're going to tell me I shouldn't have interfered,' Daniel said.

'I'm not that ungracious,' Hannah said.

For a minute, neither of them spoke. They'd arranged to meet in a tea shop on the Bowness road and were surrounded by end of season trippers sheltering from the cloudburst. The windows were steamed up, the air had a tang of China tea and carrot cake. A plump and chatty waitress scurried from table to table, getting orders wrong and explaining it was her first day in a new job. She looked the same age as Kirsty Howe.

'I know. Sorry.'

A sip of Darjeeling seemed to revive her. 'Better look on the bright side, huh? The ACC's a happy bunny this week. Suddenly my team's clear-up statistics look wonderful. She practically put her tongue in my mouth yesterday. She's been invited to a garden party at Buckingham Palace and some Home Office apparatchik is quoting her management methods as a model for efficient police leadership. The powers that be are thrilled because we've avoided the hassle and expense of two prosecutions. I suppose I ought to be thanking you on behalf of the hard-pressed taxpayer.'

'Miranda tells me that Bel Jenner has put the restaurant on the market. What about Tina Howe?'

'I did her an injustice. I thought she killed her husband.'

'It's the usual solution.'

'Not this time. She's a strong woman, but she'll need to be made of titanium to survive losing both her kids. Time for her to lean on Peter Flint, rather than the other way round.'

'At least Roz has Chris. Did you find out why he left home before the murder?'

'Long story. Let's not go there.'

'Was it Chris who tipped you off about Tina in the first place?'

'God, no. That was Peter Flint's ex-wife. A sad alcoholic with a grudge against the Howes. She sent them hate mail, but we don't have the evidence to prosecute. Until her liver packs up, she can keep downing the gin and gloating over her enemies' fate.'

'You look shattered.'

'You're so good for my morale,' she said, with a glimmer of a smile. 'Don't let it trouble your conscience, it isn't your fault. Things have been tough lately. The moon's in the wrong quarter or something.'

He savoured the smoky flavour of Lapsang Souchong. 'Want to talk about it?'

'Not really.'

'Up to you.'

She breathed out, as if arriving at a decision. 'Since you ask, I had a miscarriage. I'd only just found out I was pregnant.'

'Oh God, Hannah, I'm so sorry.' Instinctively, he reached across the table and put his hand on hers.

'I feel like a roulette ball. Spinning around randomly, not in control of my own destiny.'

'I guess that goes for all of us.'

'Yes, compared to Tina or Bel Jenner, I should count my blessings. We weren't planning a baby and I wasn't sure I was ready for motherhood. There's no escape from it, ask Bel. You should have seen Marc's face when I told him he was going to become a father. He'd sooner swallow tin tacks than admit it, but I'm sure he sees – what's happened – as a narrow escape.'

'You're too hard on him.'

'You think so?' She removed her hand. 'I mustn't be disloyal. Yesterday he booked us a fortnight in Paphos. Sam didn't do me any permanent damage and I don't like taking sick leave. The idea is, I catch up on my annual leave and get my head sorted out sitting by the pool. As if we hadn't had enough of the sun. I've decided I rather like drizzle after all. Not that I'm complaining,

Marc's doing his best. So why I'm loading all this on you when we hardly know each other, Christ knows. I'm not sure I can even believe I'm doing it.'

'Any time.'

'No, you've had plenty to contend with yourself. You don't deserve any more grief.'

'We all need somebody to load things on to.'

'And you have Miranda.'

'Well.' He considered. 'Louise.'

Her eyebrows rose. 'Both of them, surely? While I have Marc.'

'I suppose I ought to leave you in peace.'

'For a while, perhaps. I hope that doesn't sound rude. I need to do some thinking.'

'Of course.'

She hesitated. 'You know…'

'What?'

'Oh, when your father was alive, once or twice we talked about the things going on in our heads. He never came out with the corny old line that Cheryl didn't understand him, even though it would have been true. He wasn't trying to seduce me.'

He grinned. 'Certain of that?'

'Frankly, Daniel, if he was trying to get me into bed, he was far too oblique to have any chance of success. Ben was a great guy, but as a smooth-talking charmer, he wouldn't know where to start.'

'Runs in the family.'

She contemplated him. 'Not sure about that. Incidentally, your chin is smeared with chocolate.'

She bent forward and wiped his skin clean with her forefinger. A tremor ran through Daniel's body at her touch. The moment of intimacy was an electric shock.

The waitress stopped at their table. 'Would you like anything else?'

Daniel and Hannah exchanged glances. He dared to wonder if she might be thinking what he was thinking.

'Another slice of gateau,' Hannah said. 'Sod the diet, I've decided to spoil myself.'

The waitress scribbled on her notepad. 'It's good for morale to sin a little!'

As she moved away, Daniel said, 'Tell you what, it frightens me sometimes, how little I remember about him.'

'You haven't forgotten his favourite adage? Life is short.'

'He was right.'

On impulse, he seized her hand again and squeezed it hard. She looked down at the lace tablecloth, then closed her eyes. The clatter of the crockery and conversation faded. Her soft breathing was all he wanted to hear. This time she left it longer before easing her hand away from his.

Author's Note

This is a work of fiction, and the village of Old Sawrey and the characters, incidents and businesses which play a part in the story are imaginary. Whether the Crier of Claife does, or ever did, exist, is something I leave to others to figure out. I have made a few adjustments to the topography of those parts of the Lake District in which the book is set to emphasise the gap between real life and the crime writer's imagination. Any similarities between people and events in those respective worlds are wholly unintended and coincidental.

In writing this book, I have again been helped by a large number of people, too many to list individually. I would, though, like to pay express particular thanks to those who have offered special support: my agent Mandy Little; my publishers and editors David Shelley, Susie Dunlop, Rob Rosenwald and Barbara Peters and their teams; Roger Forsdyke; Andrew Shanks, Dian Leppington, Ivan de Beer (who did not manage to persuade me to go skydiving but offered much insight into an unfamiliar experience); Ann Cleeves and my other friends and colleagues in Murder Squad; and my family, Helena, Jonathan and Catherine Edwards, not least for their company on research trips around Cumbria. There could be nowhere better to 'have' to visit.

Martin Edwards